PRAISE FOR TAMMY L. GRACE

"I had planned on an early night but couldn't put this book down until I finished it around 3am. Like her other books, this one features fascinating characters with a plot that mimics real life in the best way. My recommendation: it's time to read every book Tammy L Grace has written."
— *Carolyn, review of Beach Haven*

"This book is a clean, simple romance with a background story very similar to the works of Debbie Macomber. If you like Macomber's books you will like this one. A holiday tale filled with dogs, holiday fun, and the joy of giving will warm your heart.
— *Avid Mystery Reader, review of A Season for Hope: A Christmas Novella*

"This book was just as enchanting as the others. Hardships with the love of a special group of friends. I recommend the series as a must read. I loved every exciting moment. A new author for me. She's fabulous."
—*Maggie!, review of Pieces of Home: A Hometown Harbor Novel (Book 4)*

"Tammy is an amazing author, she reminds me of Debbie Macomber... Delightful, heartwarming...just down to earth."
— *Plee, review of A Promise of Home: A Hometown Harbor Novel (Book 3)*

"This was an entertaining and relaxing novel. Tammy Grace has a simple yet compelling way of drawing the reader into the lives of her characters. It was a pleasure to read a story that didn't rely on theatrical tricks, unrealistic events or steamy sex scenes to fill up the pages. Her characters and plot were strong enough to hold the reader's interest."
—*MrsQ125, review of Finding Home: A Hometown Harbor Novel (Book 1)*

"This is a beautifully written story of loss, grief, forgiveness and healing. I believe anyone could relate to the situations and feelings represented here. This is a read that will stay with you long after you've completed the book."
—*Cassidy Hop, review of Finally Home: A Hometown Harbor Novel (Book 5)*

"Killer Music is a clever and well-crafted whodunit. The vivid and colorful characters shine as the author gradually reveals their hidden secrets—an absorbing page-turning read."

REUNION IN LAVENDER VALLEY

REUNION IN LAVENDER VALLEY

SISTERS OF THE HEART BOOK 6

TAMMY L. GRACE

LONE MOUNTAIN PRESS

Reunion in Lavender Valley
Sisters of the Heart
Book 6
Tammy L. Grace

www.tammylgrace.com
Facebook: https://www.facebook.com/tammylgrace.books
Twitter: @TammyLGrace
Instagram: @authortammylgrace
Published in the United States by Lone Mountain Press, Nevada

ISBN (eBook) 978-1-945591-64-8
ISBN (Print) 978-1-945591-65-5
FIRST EDITION
Printed in the United States of America
Cover Design by Elizabeth Mackey Graphic Design

ALSO BY TAMMY L. GRACE

GLASS BEACH COTTAGE SERIES

Beach Haven

Moonlight Beach

Beach Dreams

WRITING AS CASEY WILSON

A Dog's Hope

A Dog's Chance

WISHING TREE SERIES

The Wishing Tree

Wish Again

Overdue Wishes

SISTERS OF THE HEART SERIES

Greetings from Lavender Valley

Pathway to Lavender Valley

Sanctuary at Lavender Valley

Blossoms at Lavender Valley

Comfort in Lavender Valley

Reunion in Lavender Valley

Remember to subscribe to Tammy's exclusive group of readers for your gift, only available to readers on her mailing list. **Sign up at www.tammylgrace.com. Follow this link to subscribe at https:// wp.me/P9umIy-e** and you'll receive the exclusive interview she did with all the canine characters in her Hometown Harbor Series.

Follow Tammy on Facebook by liking her page. You may also follow Tammy on book retailers or at BookBub by clicking on the follow button.

"No amount of time or space can separate you from the people who are meant to be in your life."
—Unknown

CHAPTER ONE

Georgia turned off the highway for Lavender Valley. The late-June sun still hung in the sky, lighting her path. Her eight-hour drive from Boise had turned into almost ten hours, and she was beyond tired. After begging her doctor to release her to make the drive, he finally caved, but he made her promise to stop every two hours to walk and give her shoulder some rest.

He didn't want her stuck in the driving position for hours on end. She promised to follow his advice, and Georgia was always true to her word. She was so excited to get to the farm and meet her new sisters. The video calls were wonderful, but there was nothing like a real hug.

Lydia had told her she was making dinner, and the idea of a good meal and a hot shower sounded heavenly. Georgia drove along the road she remembered from so long ago. The last time she'd been to Lavender Valley had been with Lee, more than twenty years ago. Tears clouded her eyes.

Her thoughts drifted to Jewel. Before her death, she knew

of Lee's passing, but she had no idea of the state he left things and Georgia's predicament. Georgia was still coming to grips with it, and the last thing she wanted to do was worry Jewel, who was struggling with her own health.

Had Harry's letter not arrived, Georgia wasn't sure what she would have done or where she would be. Lavender Valley Farm had saved her once, and now, it would save her again. Thankful for a place to stay while she healed and figured out what she would do, Georgia looked forward to sharing her days with her newfound sisters of the heart. She only wished Jewel would be there to greet her.

Tears blurred her vision, and she willed her mind to focus on the positive. While her shoulder injury was a huge setback, connecting with her sisters of the heart helped her find a purpose. She made good use of her downtime and after video chatting with her sisters, she poured her energy into creating items for the Lavender Festival. Her car was loaded down with aprons, table runners, placemats, wall hangings, and more. Her trusty sewing machine was carefully wrapped and boxed, resting in the backseat.

As she made the final turn into Lavender Valley, her heart filled with both joy and regret. The quaint feel of Main Street, which hadn't changed much since her first visit almost fifty years ago, welcomed her. She only wished she had found time to visit Jewel more often. Now, it was too late.

At the sight of the Sugar Shack, she could almost taste the warm cinnamon rolls she loved, and the windows of Cranberry Cottage, filled with gorgeous offerings nestled among flowers and vintage furniture, made her want to stop. Her smile widened when she spotted the fabric and yarn store. She longed to spend time looking through the bolts and skeins. There was no point though. Her funds were low, and she didn't have the freedom to buy anything but the necessities.

The cost of the movers had been a stretch, but it was behind her and like Lee always used to say, everything would be okay. No matter what, the stars would shine tonight, and the sun would rise tomorrow. He also always said they'd have each other. His words had always comforted her in times of doubt, but now, he was gone and so was his promise.

He'd been a kind and good man. A wonderful husband and partner. He cherished Georgia, and she missed him terribly. He'd always handled everything, and Georgia was content to let him take care of her. He had given her everything she craved. Love, a home, a purpose. The almost forty years they shared had been wonderful. The only real sadness she'd endured was their inability to have children.

That hole in her life led Georgia to admire Jewel and her selfless mothering of foster children even more. Georgia had longed for her own family for years. At one time, she considered becoming a foster parent, but with Lee's job as a teacher, he'd seen too much failure and heartbreak in the broken system and wanted nothing to do with it.

Over time, they'd learned to accept their fate and poured their parental instincts into guiding the students who crossed their paths each day at school. When they retired only a few years ago, they had big plans to travel more and enjoy their golden years.

Everything changed with Lee's illness. He failed so quickly, and the hope they held faded in a matter of weeks. Looking back, she now realized he'd been trying to tell her. He looked at her with such pleading in his eyes, but he was too weak to get the words out. She'd assumed he was worried about leaving her and reassured him she would be okay.

She didn't know what she would learn after his death. Over the last few months, she'd relied on Jewel's words reminding Georgia she was strong and capable. Georgia's early life had taught her there was no point in crying or shriveling into despair. Life wasn't fair or easy. At sixty years old, Georgia knew that more than anyone.

After assessing the facts and reality, Georgia was left with little choice and a very uncertain future. Until Harry's letter arrived. The chance she'd been searching for had arrived in the kind words of that short invitation. Now, she had hope again and at least the rest of the year to figure out a new path forward.

Without the promise of connecting with her new sisters and the possibilities that came with a new adventure in Lavender Valley, Georgia couldn't have gotten through the last hard months.

Saying goodbye to the home she loved broke her heart. It was like tossing all her memories and life with Lee out the window. Prior to Harry's letter, Georgia was lost and looking for solutions. Now, she was driving down the street where she walked countless times, seeing the same buildings and reminders from her youth.

There was such comfort in the familiar surroundings. The planters overflowing with colorful blooms and the slow pace of the cars making their way down the street, stopping for pedestrians, and waiting for others to back out of parking spots, warmed her heart.

She caught a glimpse of a woman with a young girl walking a dog past City Hall. It was like stepping back into a kinder and gentler time. Georgia needed that right now. She longed for a soft place to heal and not only did Lavender Valley offer that, but it held the promise of the family she'd always wanted.

The sisters she never knew were waiting for her just down the road. She pressed the accelerator as she reached the highway. She couldn't wait to meet them and get settled before the Lavender Festival kicked off next week.

It didn't take long to reach the entrance of Lavender Valley Farm. Georgia's heart beat a little faster as she waited for the gate to swing open. This reunion had been a long time coming, and she could hardly wait another minute.

She drove up the driveway, gawking at the lush green of the pastures as she made her way toward the farmhouse. Her eyes filled with tears when she saw Jewel's house. Memories of the first time she'd walked upon the porch, scared and confused, filled her mind.

She parked her car and eased out from behind the wheel. It was only her second day without her sling, and she felt a bit naked without it. Her shoulder felt pretty good, but the rest of her body was sore and tired. As she reached for her handbag, Harry came up to the driver's side of the car. "Georgia, welcome home. Can I help you with anything?"

Georgia slipped her bag on her good shoulder and smiled. "Harry, how wonderful to finally see you." She hugged her with her good arm. "I think we can just leave everything for now. We can unpack after I've had a chance to rest."

"You won't have to lift a finger. Just point us in the right direction, and we'll handle it for you." Harry smiled at her as she kept her arm looped through Georgia's, and they ascended the porch steps.

Georgia stopped and admired the pots overflowing with bright purple, red, and white blooms. She turned and gazed out at the lush lawn and the barn and fields in the distance, bathed in the golden light of early evening. "It's even more beautiful than I remember."

"Come on in. Everyone is anxious to see you, and we've got a houseful of dogs, too. They're well behaved for the most part but will be excited to greet you."

Harry opened the door and held it for Georgia.

She stepped over the threshold and couldn't hold back tears as Micki, Olivia, and Lydia stood to welcome her. The dogs, including little Vera, wiggled their bums and wagged their tails, inching closer to get a proper sniff of their guest.

Georgia stepped over and hugged each one of the ladies, giving them a good squeeze. "I can't tell you what it means to be here and see your lovely faces."

Lydia stepped back into the kitchen. "Our dinner will be on the table in five minutes."

Georgia sniffed at the air. "It smells wonderful. I just need to make a quick stop in the ladies room first."

When Georgia emerged a few minutes later, she noticed Meg's smiling face and hurried to hug her. "Aren't you a gorgeous young woman? You and your mom look so much alike." She glanced over at Micki, who smiled as she gazed at her daughter.

Meg urged Georgia to sit next to her at dinner as Lydia added a drizzle of the lemon and olive oil marinade over the platter of Greek lemon chicken, potatoes, and asparagus before setting it on the table.

Georgia joined Micki and Lydia in a glass of white wine. She admired the chicken dish. "If that tastes half as good as it smells and looks, I'll be a happy camper. I haven't eaten much today, and I'm starving."

With the large platter in front of Meg, she offered to fill plates rather than pass the cumbersome tray. Georgia took her first bite and savored the lemon flavor of the tender chicken. "This is heavenly, Lydia. Thank you."

"My pleasure," said Lydia, reaching for the bread. "Save room for dessert. I made a lemon raspberry cake."

All the ladies moaned at the announcement of cake. As they ate, Georgia asked to see Lydia's ring. "Ooh, that's a beauty. I can't wait to meet Heath, along with Clay and the others."

Micki took a healthy sip from her wine glass. "We thought we'd let you settle in tomorrow, but on Friday, Harry's got us booked at Wine & Words for a little sisterly celebration of Lydia's engagement. Tomorrow, we can get the linens you made priced for the festival."

Olivia chuckled. "I'm dying to see the goat pajamas you brought. I will say it's tough to keep them clean. They have no concept of staying out of the dirt and mud. I think we'll have to reserve pajamas for the weekend crowd."

Harry refilled her iced tea. "Clay and Heath invited all of us over on Saturday for a welcome barbecue, Georgia. They're excited to meet you, too, and we can watch the fireworks from their place."

"That sounds wonderful. It sounds like we'll be busy right up to the start of the festival."

Micki's eyes widened. "Tyler, who stays in the bunkhouse and helps out around here, has been working on our retail space. Jewel had a tent stored in the barn. We'll set up and designate one side to our food and drink sales with Lydia in charge of that section, and the other will be for Georgia's linens and handiwork, and she can run that side of things."

Georgia was tired from her drive, and the wonderful meal made her sleepy. She was content to soak in the conversation. She loved hearing the excitement in Meg's voice as she talked about helping a very sick cat at the veterinary clinic and learning from Duke. Micki was so enthusiastic for the coming festival and chattered nonstop about the activities and her wish that all her new ideas work to bring more visitors to the farm, along with more revenue.

As Lydia brought out her beautiful cake, the weariness of the day caught up with Georgia. "Would you all mind if I took a little slice to go? I'm afraid I need to get myself situated and get to bed. It's been a tiring day."

"Of course not," said Lydia. "I'll wrap up a slice for you to take with you."

Harry and Micki slid from their chairs, and Micki motioned Meg to accompany them. "We'll unload your car for you."

Georgia smiled. "That would be wonderful. I've just got a suitcase and smaller bag in the trunk, plus boxes of the things I made for the festival. I'll need to figure out where to set up my sewing machine."

Micki held the door as Harry and Meg stepped through it. "I'll put the festival things in the other cottage, and we can get them priced and labeled tomorrow. I think there's room to set up a sewing table in there for you, too. You can check it out tomorrow and see what you think."

Olivia brewed a mug of tea for Georgia to take with her and offered to carry her plate. "You ladies are wonderful to me." Georgia rose and sought out Lydia, who was slicing up leftover chicken. "I must hug our illustrious chef. That meal was top notch."

Lydia beamed and embraced Georgia. "I'm so happy you

liked it. I'll be quiet when Vera and I get in the motorhome tonight. I don't want to disturb you."

"I doubt I'll hear a thing. I expect to sleep like a rock. See you in the morning."

She followed Olivia out the mudroom door and across the pathway to the cottages. By the time they got there, her suitcase and bag were waiting for her in the cottage, and Micki and Meg assured her the linens and sewing machine were safe in the cottage next door.

Harry waved her hand around the space. "Clay and Heath said they'd be happy to help if you decide to store anything. It's a bit tight in here with so much furniture. You can take a look tomorrow and decide."

"I'll do that. Thanks again for all your help."

Olivia pointed at the mug of tea on the counter. "Drink it while it's warm. Sweet dreams, Georgia."

Georgia hugged each one of them as they made their way back to the main house.

She took a sip of tea and studied the stack of boxes, which held some of her favorite books. She was too tired to think about what to do with them and hauled her suitcase to the bedroom.

She changed into her pajamas and washed her face. The mirror displayed her tired eyes and the gray roots that had expanded through her auburn-brown hair. With her shoulder in a sling, she hadn't been able to keep them at bay with her usual home-color job. Her shoulder-length hair could also use a bit of shaping.

Since losing Lee and all that came with it, she'd aged. This last year, more new lines and wrinkles appeared on her face, and her brown eyes looked dull, no matter how much sleep she got. Now that she was here, she vowed to concentrate on herself and finding happiness again.

Georgia worked moisturizer into her face, set on finding a hairdresser tomorrow. She retrieved her mug of tea and slipped under the crisp sheets on her bed, which her sisters had thoughtfully made for her.

She was safe.

She was home.

CHAPTER TWO

Georgia's eyes fluttered awake on Thursday morning, thrilled to have slept in her own familiar bed. Out of habit, she reached out for Lee and felt nothing but the cool, empty sheet next to her. The hole his loss left in her heart wasn't getting any smaller, but she hoped being back on the farm might ease the sharpness of the wound.

The morning sunlight greeted her as did the soft chirping of birds. She breathed in the lovely scent wafting from her bedside table. The lavender bouquets Micki had placed in her bedroom and on the small dining table made her feel so welcome and filled the air with a scent that she always associated with Jewel.

She eased out of bed, careful not to stress her shoulder. Along with her vow of taking breaks on the drive, she promised her doctor she would continue to do the exercises he showed her to strengthen her shoulder. She'd been faithful with her physical therapy and as much as she groused about it, it did help her shoulder.

After a shower, where she tried the sugar scrub Micki left

for her, she made her way to the living area. She left her hair to air dry and despite it needed shaping and color, she was glad she elected to keep the length. When she injured her shoulder, her good friends suggested she get it cut short, so she wouldn't have to worry about it. It was tempting to have one less challenge, but as silly as it sounded, Georgia had already lost everything, and she wasn't about to give up her hair. It had taken her years to embrace the color, which was now sought after, and Lee had always liked her hair longer.

Despite her desire to conserve money, Georgia needed her hair done and with what she'd been through these last few months, she justified it as a necessity. One of the ladies was sure to know a good salon.

In the light of day, she realized Harry was right when she suggested Georgia might want to make some more room in her cottage. Part of her knew she kept too much of her furniture and other items, but she couldn't bear to part with all of it. Selling the house on top of losing Lee was a blow that imploded her world. Her entire life was gone in what seemed like the blink of an eye.

She ran her hands over the large bookcase that took up way too much of the small living space. It needed to go but guilt washed over her as she contemplated asking Clay and Heath to move it for her. She hated being a burden, yet she'd become one. Lee always took such good care of her. Spoiled her. It left her unprepared to deal with all the everyday issues he handled.

She took a deep breath. It's a new page in a new book. She had her sisters, and her heart was full of gratitude for that. She shuddered when she thought of where she'd be right now if not for them.

The living area had a large window that provided a peaceful view of the green pastures and the hills in the distance. She gazed at it, letting her worries float away as she exhaled. She had the rest of the year to figure out what she would do. Right now, staying at the farm was her best and only option.

After one more grateful look at the serene vista out her window, Georgia retrieved the mug she used from last night and turned to inspect the kitchen. As she opened cupboards, she smiled. The girls had done a good job of organizing things for her and making good use of the space. She kept things to a minimum when it came to the kitchen, having sold her beloved china hutch and matching dining room table with six chairs.

She ran a hand over the warm wood of the small dining table wedged into the corner of the kitchen. She and Lee had used it in their breakfast nook. It would be perfect for her, since she imagined most of her meals would be eaten with the others in the main house.

After a few minutes of contemplation, she opened her front door and admired the pot of flowers on the tiny porch. No doubt, courtesy of Micki. She made her way down the steps and studied Lydia's old motorhome parked next to the cottage, its power cord snaked over to the outlet on the side of her new home.

Last night, Micki mentioned that Meg would be returning to college after the festival, and she hoped Lydia would move into the house with them. Georgia wasn't sure if Lydia's independent streak would acquiesce to the idea. She studied the faded metal exterior and had a newfound respect for Lydia's bravery.

As she came through the door, Lydia greeted her with a warm smile, and the aroma of cinnamon hung in the air. "Good morning. Coffee's ready, and the kettle is still warm. Harry's at work, and Olivia is out in the shelter with the dogs. Micki should be in shortly. We're having cinnamon toast this morning."

"Aww, that brings back memories of Jewel. I think she passed along her love of that to all of us." Georgia held up her mug. "I'll just brew a cup of tea. I've sworn off coffee these last months. I was having anxiety issues and trouble sleeping, so I thought it best to limit my caffeine, but I love coffee."

As she brought her tea and toast to the granite counter, she gasped. "In all the excitement of your engagement, I forgot to tell you how glad I was to hear that horrible man who made your life miserable was captured. Harry gave me the highlights. To think he was involved in murdering young women." She shivered and added, "I know it's in bad taste, but I say good riddance."

Lydia brought her coffee to the counter and slid into the chair next to Georgia. "I feel the same way. I'm still kicking myself for being so naïve or stupid in the first place, but I'm glad it's over."

Georgia patted her hand. "I don't know anybody alive who doesn't have a regret or two. In spite of him, you survived, made a career for yourself, and now you've found the man you want to spend the rest of your life with. That's not too shabby."

Lydia smiled and took a long sip from her cup. "I've never been happier."

Micki came through the door, her wide-brimmed sun hat still on top of her head. "Morning, Georgia. If you're up to it, I'd love to give you a quick tour of the fields and garden."

"Oh, that sounds lovely." She touched her damp hair. "I need to get my hair done, so hopefully someone can point me to a good salon that doesn't cost an arm and a leg."

Micki nodded. "Anita at Sassafras is everybody's favorite."

"Wonderful. I'll call her this morning." She finished her tea and rinsed her mug in the sink.

They left Lydia to continue prepping and planning for her festival food and wandered out to the backyard garden first. Micki pointed at her healthy-looking crop of veggies. "Lydia is itching for my tomatoes to ripen. They're getting close."

"It all looks marvelous to me. By the way, thank you for the flowers on my porch. I love them."

"Oh, you're welcome. They're bright and cheerful."

They set out, and Georgia turned to her. "I meant to inquire about your sister, Jade. When we talked last, you were going to confront her about the amnesia you suspected she was exaggerating."

Micki rolled her eyes. "Yes, Olivia and I went to see her and once we confronted her, she admitted she had started remembering weeks ago but was scared and didn't want to face what she'd done."

"Oh, my, that's more drama you don't need."

"Exactly. She's so tiring. Olivia was such a help and without getting emotional like I do, she spelled out how Jade's choices to lie and steal had gotten her into the mess she's in. The rehab center had her seeing a therapist already, but they increased her visits, and Jade agreed to face everything she'd done. I even met with the therapist and Jade a few times, and she apologized for using Meg to get to me and coercing me out of money. We talked a little about the past when we were growing up. She seems sorry, but I think she's blocked out or erased much of the past with her drug use."

She sighed. "All that to say, I think she's making progress, and they're working with her physically to get her in the best shape she can be in before they release her."

Georgia shook her head. "I'm so sorry, Micki. You've got so much on your plate with the festival and worrying about Jade."

"I'm mostly just worried what will happen once she's released. My feelings for her are complicated. I don't wish her any harm, but I think I liked it better when I didn't know where she was or what she was doing."

Georgia changed the subject to the beauty of the farm. They wandered the rows, and Micki pointed out the bees they had on the property, who were doing an excellent job of pollenating the garden and the lavender fields. "We'll have our own honey next year."

Georgia gazed across the property, taking in the lavender sage along the fence line that was in full bloom. The breeze carried the fresh scent of it to her. It smelled like summer. "Sounds like you plan to be here next year. I'm trying hard not to think too far ahead."

Micki shrugged. "I'm not sure, either. I get wrapped up in the planning and forget we have some decisions to make after the season. I do admit, I love living here. More so than I ever expected. And it doesn't hurt that Buck lives here. Like you, I'm trying not to get too far ahead, but I could see myself living out my days in Lavender Valley."

"It's a special place and holds some of my dearest memories. It's hard to believe Jewel's gone. Everything I see reminds me of her. There's a little part of me that hasn't come to grips with her passing yet. I think I was too deep in my grief for Lee to fully process her loss. Now that I'm here though, it's fresh in my mind."

They trudged down the pathway toward the lavender fields. Georgia gasped when she took in the gorgeous purple blooms with the golden rays of light shining through them. A wave of lavender, lifted by the slight breeze, fluttered before the green pastures.

"What a beautiful sight to behold," said Georgia, staring at the fields. "And that aroma is heavenly."

As Micki reached out to touch a stem, her smile radiated happiness. "I think Jewel would be proud of all our work. She'd also be so happy that the five of us are together."

They wandered the lengths of the fields and then back toward the house. Olivia, along with the three goldens, were coming out of the shelter. "Morning," she said with a wave.

Micki pointed toward the barn. "I'll let you do the honors while I run in and get a bit of work done. I'll catch up with you when you're done, and we'll get to work pricing your things."

First, Georgia bent down and gave each of the dogs attention. "You are all lovely and so gentle." She took the time to hold each of their paws and spoke to them in a soft voice. As she rose, she glanced at Olivia. "We lost our dog several years ago and never got another. It broke my heart, and I wasn't sure I could handle that loss again."

"I know what you mean. It can bring such deep despair. Coming here, though, surrounded by Hope, meeting Chief, who Harry adopted after his owner died, and finding Willow, I'm reminded of how much fuller they make our lives. Their lives are always too short, but they cram the most into every moment."

"That's a good lesson for all of us." Georgia followed her and the dogs to the barn. "Oh, that mural is fantastic. I love those sunflowers. So cheerful and inviting."

"Micki painted that when she got here. She also planted sunflowers. They're growing and will be blooming soon." Olivia took her around to the other side of the barn visible from the driveway. "A local painter just finished this logo for us this week."

"Oh, it's perfect. I love those sprigs of lavender, and the purple and yellow looks fantastic. So fresh and welcoming."

"Micki reworked Jewel's original logo and updated the website with it, plus all our retail goods. She's got a great sense for business."

"She's done a great job. All of you have."

"You're no slacker. Those things you sewed are beautiful. I don't have a creative bone in my body, so I marvel watching Micki and Lydia, and you're no doubt the same."

"I'd say what you do with the dogs and animals is a gift. Like Jewel, you have that passion for caring for them." She nodded at the three goldens by her side. "You've got a loyal following."

She laughed and led the way to the fenced pasture by the barn. "These two sweet donkeys always make me happy. That's Olive and Nutmeg. Next door in the pen, you'll see our two alpacas. Agatha, who is very friendly and inquisitive, and Arnold, who tends to travel in her shadow."

"Aww, they're sweethearts. I'd kill for those eyelashes," said Georgia, gazing at the two donkeys at the fence.

Agatha let Georgia pet her, while Arnold observed. Olivia led her and the dogs down the pathway and around the corner to the goat pasture. They were romping around with each other, climbing on their spools and jumping from them. Olivia chuckled. "They're always full of it."

A black and white lamb hurried to the fence line. "This is my little Paisley. Duke rescued her when her mother died, and I helped bottle feed her and then brought her here. She thought she was a dog and now, she thinks she's a goat."

"Oh, she's precious." Georgia laughed, watching one of

the goats try to climb on top of another to reach the branch of a tree. "They're adorable."

"We'll see how you feel after a wrestling match getting them into those cute pajamas you made for them." She chuckled. "We'll have to do that early on Friday and take showers when we're done. Last time, we were covered in dirt and mud."

"Oh, that reminds me. Lydia said you could get me in touch with Anita to get my hair done. It's probably too much to ask, but I'd love to get it done before the festival."

Olivia pulled her phone from her jeans. She tapped in a message and glanced over at Georgia. "We'll see what she says."

She pointed at the bunkhouse. "Tyler lives there. He's actually on sort of a permanent loan to us from Clay and Heath. They had an arrangement with Jewel and left it in place. He's been a lifesaver for us."

"The farm looks better than ever. You all have done so much work. Speaking of, I need to get back and help Micki price my things."

Olivia's phone chimed. She read the message and smiled. "Anita says she can do you tomorrow. She's got an opening at noon."

"Perfect. I'll be there." Georgia's eyes sparkled with excitement.

Olivia tapped in a quick reply and slid the phone into her pocket. The two of them and the dogs wandered back, and Olivia left her at the steps of the second cottage.

Georgia and Micki worked through the afternoon and got all of her items marked and packaged in plastic sleeves to protect them and keep them clean. They found some baskets stashed in the cupboards that were perfect for holding the linens, and Micki made signage for each of the items, advertising the prices.

As they walked back to the house, Georgia felt a sense of accomplishment. After some online research, Micki urged Georgia to up the price on her wares. She also encouraged her to enter the quilt show the town was hosting during the festival.

As they came through the mudroom door, Georgia did the math in her head and if she only sold half of what she made, she'd make a nice profit. Micki offered to talk to Buck about getting the farm to buy everything upfront, but Georgia didn't want to do that. If she ended up having to make more items, she'd consider it and talk to Buck about it.

Harry and Lydia were both in the kitchen, where Lydia was putting together chicken salad for their dinner, and Harry was sipping iced tea. She looked up from her glass. "You two look beat. Did you get it all done?"

Georgia nodded. "Yes, everything is priced and ready to go, and Olivia got me in to get my hair done tomorrow. I can't wait."

"Don't forget our little celebration at Wine & Words to welcome you to Lavender Valley and commemorate Lydia's engagement. We haven't been yet and are looking forward to it. It's new to town."

Georgia smiled as she took the offer of an iced tea Harry poured for her. "Well, I love both wine and words. I can't wait." For the first time since Lee's illness, Georgia had a sense of hope.

CHAPTER THREE

F riday morning, Georgia came to terms with her excess furniture situation. She tagged the large bookcases and a dresser she could do without for storage. She also tagged one of her recliners. The room was too small for two of them. Clay and Heath were due to collect her things for storage this afternoon.

After a late shower and a quick bite for lunch, Georgia selected a maxi-dress she liked but usually only wore to church. It was a pretty coral print with flutter sleeves and a bit of a flouncing hem with a slight slit.

She let the others know she'd meet them at Wine & Words, after her appointment at the salon. She wanted to check out some local stores while she was there.

It had been months since she bothered putting on makeup, but tonight was a special occasion, and Georgia put forth extra effort as she swiped blush across her cheeks, ran mascara over her lashes, and finished it off with a pop of color on her lips.

After one more look in the mirror, she was thankful her

hair was getting done. The ugly gray at her scalp made her look even more tired than she felt.

She slipped into a pair of sandals and drove to town, finding the salon without any trouble. As she drove by the Grasshopper, fond memories of eating there with Chuck and Jewel came to mind. She'd never been to an actual restaurant until she came to Lavender Valley.

Georgia parked and climbed the steps of the bright-yellow house. She admired the flowers planted under the wooden sign lettered with Sassafras Salon. Olivia said the locals often referred to it as Sassy's. Georgia smiled and walked through the door.

A woman with a kind smile and gorgeous green eyes greeted her. "I bet you're Georgia?" She extended her hand. "I'm Anita. Come on over and have a seat."

"Wonderful to meet you and thank you for getting me in today." Georgia took a seat in front of the mirror.

Anita ran her fingers through her hair, studying it. "So, tell me what you're thinking," she said, fluffing both sides of it.

Georgia sighed. "Well, I've been coloring my own hair for several years. I was already overdue when I injured my shoulder two months ago and haven't been able to keep up with it. It also needs some shaping."

Anita nodded. "Would you consider going a little lighter on the color? You're using a dark auburn, and it makes the gray much more visible. I think we should go lighter and add a few highlights; the gray won't stand out as much."

Georgia panicked at the idea of another change, but as Anita kept talking and showed her a few photos from a hair design book, she relaxed. Georgia pointed at a photo. "I like those soft waves along the side of her face, and that color is nice."

Anita nodded. "Yes, that's more of a medium auburn with some lighter highlights. Totally doable for you."

Georgia sighed. "Let's do it." She did her best to relax as Anita mixed up the colors and brushed it onto sections of her hair. Anita offered Georgia a magazine, but she declined, content to shut her eyes and listen to the soft country music that played in the background, letting her mind wander.

It had been years since she had someone do her hair. She got by with the occasional trim in one of those walk-in shops that dotted strip malls in her neighborhood outside of Boise. That's the thing she liked about longer hair. It didn't need the constant upkeep of shorter styles.

As Anita worked, they chatted about the Lavender Festival and all the events that would be taking place in town. When Anita was done applying the color, she removed her gloves. "Can I get you something to drink? I'm going to have a cup of tea, but have water, lemonade, and iced tea."

"A cup of tea sounds wonderful, thank you."

A few minutes later, Anita put a saucer with a floral tea cup on the counter in front of Georgia. "I've got a few calls to make, but if you need anything, just holler."

Georgia sipped her tea and glanced in the mirror. She looked ready for Halloween with her hair plastered to her head and foil sticking out of it here and there. She tried not to fret about the expense and took comfort in the fact that her things should sell next week, and she'd recoup the costs quickly.

A year ago, she would never have guessed she'd be in Lavender Valley, back on Jewel's beloved farm. In some ways, it felt like ages since she lost Lee. At other times, it was like a fresh wound. One thing for sure, Lee would be glad she was with her newfound sisters. He wouldn't want her to be alone and worried.

Lavender Valley was familiar and safe. She could imagine living out the rest of her days in the small town. She wasn't sure how things would work out. An uncertain future had never been part of her plan, but here she was. There was no way Georgia could take care of the farm on her own, but Micki sounded like she might stay on, already talking about next year. Maybe Olivia and Harry would stay, too. Regardless, she'd at least have either a home or a bit of money, which would go further in Lavender Valley than her other options.

As she set her empty cup on the saucer, Anita came behind her and studied her hair. She unwrapped a few pieces of foil and nodded. "It looks great. We'll get it shampooed now."

She swung Georgia around and placed her head in the bowl. Georgia relaxed as the warm water ran over her head and breathed in the faint aroma of coconut as Anita massaged her scalp. She let the conditioner sit for a few minutes and then rinsed her hair and wrapped a towel over it.

With her hair wet, Georgia couldn't distinguish much about the color. Anita combed it out, parted it on the side, and then picked up her scissors and went about trimming it and shaping it, adding in dimensions along the sides of Georgia's face.

She snipped away and within twenty minutes, put her scissors down and stood behind Georgia, checking the length in the mirror. "I didn't cut any bangs, even though some of those photos you showed me had them. I think you've got enough layers along your face that it will give you the look you want. If you decide you want bangs, just pop in, and I can do them. Most people who haven't worn bangs for a long time aren't happy with them, so I want you to play with this and see what you think."

Georgia nodded and closed her eyes as Anita employed her blow dryer. Despite Anita only taking the ugly ends from her hair, it felt much lighter as the brush traveled through it, from the top of her head to the ends. Her hair had a bit of a natural wave, so even without the use of a curling iron, Georgia liked the style. Although worried about the color change, Georgia smiled at her reflection and loved the lighter auburn look.

Anita used the iron and gave her soft waves along the side of her face. She finished the back and turned Georgia to face the mirror, brushing the shortest layer from her forehead. "There you go," Anita said with a smile. "What do you think?"

Georgia turned her head each way and grinned. "I love it. You were so right about the color. I think I might even look younger."

As she unsnapped the cape from Georgia's neck, Anita laughed. "I think so, too. Those highlights add some dimension along the crown, too. We'll see how you do with the gray. I'll put you down for six weeks and if you need to change it to earlier or later, just call me."

Georgia stood, admiring her new color and style. It looked fabulous with the corals and greens in her dress. She tried not to think about the ongoing expense, knowing she could never master the complicated color and highlights on her own. She followed Anita to the counter, took her appointment card, and pulled out her credit card.

She signed the receipt, shocked at the reasonable price. Small-town living had its advantages. "Thank you again, and I hope to see you at the festival."

"I wouldn't miss it," said Anita, leaving her with a warm embrace. "You look fabulous. Enjoy the rest of your day."

With a new spring in her step, Georgia slid into the driver's seat, drove the few blocks downtown, and parked in front of Winding River Coffee. Happy that her trip to the salon was less than expected, she stopped in and splurged on a lavender honey iced tea. The shop was bustling with people, and Georgia opted to take her lavender-hued drink and wander the shops.

As she walked along the sidewalk, she stopped and gazed at the window of the yarn and fabric store. She longed to study the bolts grouped by color and touch the skeins she noticed in baskets. As soon as she finished her drink, she could circle back and spend the rest of the afternoon there.

With one more look at a gorgeous quilt hanging on the wall, she turned and caught her reflection in the window. She did a double take. She didn't recognize the woman she saw. Anita was a genius.

She turned and wandered down Fir Street, making note of Wine & Words, where she was due in a couple of hours. She did a bit more window shopping at the cute boutique, gazed at the beautiful window display at the florist's shop, and noted the lavender-themed window at the pharmacy. Seeing it reminded her she needed to transfer her prescriptions.

The bad thing about moving from a place she'd called home for decades was the chore of finding a new doctor, dentist, and hairdresser. At least she had one of them checked off her list. She opened the door to the pharmacy, determined to get one more chore done.

The helpful woman behind the counter took down Georgia's information and promised to get in touch with her old pharmacy and get her prescriptions transferred. She confirmed they were on her insurance and within fifteen minutes, Georgia was on her way down the street.

She couldn't resist stopping in Cranberry Cottage, where two women were in the large display window, putting the finishing touches on the most gorgeous display of lavender-themed items Georgia had ever seen. She marveled at the beautiful scarves, bags, pillows, and lotions set among the unique furniture items. She fell in love with the hammered-copper firewood bucket that held sprigs of purple flowers.

She sipped the last of her tea and tossed the cup in a trash bin before pushing on the door of the shop. The petite woman, with dark hair, stood on the floor in front of the window, where another taller woman rearranged some towels.

"Welcome in," said the woman with the short hair. "I'm May and if you need any help, just let us know. We're just finishing up our window display."

"It's lovely," said Georgia. "Perfect for the upcoming festival."

May smiled. "Is that what brings you to town? I don't remember seeing you before."

Georgia laughed. "Well, yes and no. I'm actually here because my foster mother from long ago, Jewel Austin, asked five of us to come back to her farm."

May's eyes sparkled as they widened, and she hurried toward Georgia. Before she knew it, May engulfed her in a hug. "You're Georgia. I'm so happy to meet you. I know all the others, and I'm Duke's sister."

Georgia soaked in the warm embrace. "I've heard such wonderful things about Duke, and he hit the gold mine with Olivia. She's a wonderful and caring person."

May motioned to the other woman. "Janet, come and meet Georgia. She's the last of the sisters of the heart to arrive in Lavender Valley."

The woman with long, dark hair, wearing a felt cowboy

hat, climbed from the window and greeted Georgia. "We've heard so much about you and are so glad to finally meet you."

"Great to meet you," said Georgia. "All the ladies have nothing but wonderful things to say about both of you." She glanced around the space. "Your store is lovely."

"Take your time and look around. We've got some iced tea and wine in the back if you'd like a glass."

Georgia held up her hand. "Oh, no. I just finished a tea from the coffee shop, and I'm due to meet everyone at Wine & Words soon."

Janet carried a small box of supplies. "We've always got a bottle on hand, so stop by anytime and visit."

May nodded. "Oh, yes, we're always up for a break and a reason to open a bottle. In fact, Harry and Olivia told us to stop by after we close the store and join the engagement and welcome party."

"Oh, that will be fun. I'll just snoop around a bit, then I'm going to wander down to the fabric store."

The phone rang, and Janet hurried to answer it. May strolled the aisle with Georgia. "Olivia told me you're quite the seamstress."

Georgia's cheeks blossomed. "I've always loved to sew. In fact, Jewel got me started and bought me my first sewing machine. I worked in a school library, but sewing is my hobby. I just love it."

"Well, I happen to know Edith, the owner at In Stitches, is looking for some part-time help. I'm not sure if you're interested in working, but I bet she'd hire you in a New York minute."

"Hmm, that's good to know. I'd probably spend every dime I made on product." She laughed but feared it was true.

May rolled her eyes. "You're preaching to the choir, sister. Janet and I have a hard time restraining ourselves here."

A customer came through the door, and May left Georgia with the promise to see her soon and the offer to help her find anything she needed. Georgia wandered through the store, stopping to inhale the fragrant candles and run her hands over some of the textiles. She couldn't resist sniffing the homemade soaps and checked the price tag on a scarf that looked like a Monet watercolor painting.

She made her way back toward the front of the store, thanked May and Janet and vowed to see them at Wine & Words soon.

It didn't take Georgia long to backtrack and step through the door of In Stitches. As soon as she saw the bolts of colorful fabrics arranged along the walls and aisles, she felt right at home.

A woman with beautiful white hair that immediately reminded Georgia of Helen Mirren, greeted her. "Can I help you find anything in particular today?"

"Just browsing. I'm a bit of a fabric addict."

The woman laughed. "I can relate. That's part of what made me open this store. I'm Edith, by the way. That's a beautiful dress. Did you make it?"

Georgia shook her hand and nodded. "Yes, I make most of my clothes. I'm Georgia and happy to meet you."

"Feel free to browse and let me know if you need help with anything."

Georgia set off in the direction of the quilt she'd seen from the window. It was a gorgeous dragonfly in the midst of what looked like a stained-glass window. It was done in blues, purples, with black and gold. After Georgia studied the striking quilt, she turned and said, "This is a stunning piece."

Edith grinned. "Thank you. It's one of mine. I hope you're

in town long enough to enjoy the quilt show we have coming up during the festival."

"Oh, yes, I'm here until at least the end of the year. I grew up here on Jewel's farm."

Edith brought her hand to her chest. "Oh, my, you're *that* Georgia. Jewel's Georgia. One of the sisters of the heart. That's just wonderful that you're back. Jewel loved to tell me how talented you were with a needle."

Georgia's heart swelled at the mention of Jewel and her kind words. "She helped me discover sewing. It's been a lifelong hobby of mine, along with reading."

Edith retrieved a few pieces of paper from a box at the end of one of the aisles of fabric. "By all means, you need to enter something in the quilt contest. We've got several themes, and it's free to enter." She handed Georgia the entry forms.

"Oh, wow, I just might do that. I've made a few wall hangings for the festival."

Edith pointed at the form. "We have several categories that are just squares, so you don't have to make a whole quilt. That seems to encourage more entries."

As she perused the categories, Georgia nodded. "That sounds great. I'll see what I've got in my fabric stash that might work." The lavender category was at the top of her list, but there was also a floral category, a tea pot and cup theme, farming, birds, black and white, trees, hometown, and food also piqued her interest.

Edith hurried back to the counter and returned with a business card. "I don't want to be too forward, but I'm looking for some part-time help and would love it if you would consider it. My longtime friend worked with me, but she moved away to take care of her mother, so I've been trying to find the right fit. My clients are used to a certain caliber of service and knowledge. You'd be perfect."

"That's kind of you. May mentioned to me that you were looking for someone. I need to get my footing and figure out what I'm doing. I'm committed to helping at the farm for the festival."

Edith waved her hand in the air. "Of course, and just know I'm happy to work around your schedule. I just need a break, and it doesn't really matter when. Working so much and trying to keep up with classes in the evenings is wearing me out."

"Now, evenings are probably way more flexible for me. Weekends, I think will be the worst during the festival, but once it's over, I'd have much more time. I just need to figure out how to retain most of my paycheck and not spend it all in here."

Edith laughed and then lowered her voice. "You'd get a fifty percent discount on everything, so that would help. You can sew while you're here. Use any of the machines and supplies you need. For any classes you can teach, I give you one hundred percent of the course fees. I don't really do it to make money, but as a service, and the students buy their supplies here." She went back to the counter and plucked a yellow sheet from behind it. "Here's the class list for this year. Take a look to see what you think and if you have an idea for something, we can talk about it."

"Thanks, I'll take a look, and I'll be in touch next week when I know more." Georgia put the papers in her handbag before studying the bins filled with color-coordinated precut fat quarters for quilting. She was drawn to so many of them but resisted buying anything, resolute in using her stacks of fabric before she invested in more.

She'd been in the store for almost two hours, and it was time to get to the party. She wished Edith a good evening and hurried down the street. A tingle of exhilaration filled her heart as she turned the corner. The woman had no idea how much she'd boosted Georgia's ego by asking her to help in her shop. Now, she had to figure out how she could make it work.

CHAPTER FOUR

Still excited about the prospect of a part-time job and being surrounded by all those fabrics and threads, plus the use of the shop's sewing machines and supplies while she worked, and a little extra spending money, Georgia stepped through the door of the wine and book shop.

The stamped-tin ceiling drew her eye, as did the gleaming wooden floor and the original brick walls. Bookshelves lined the perimeter, and additional displays were on wooden tables positioned throughout the floorspace. Colorful pillows scattered in the window seat made for an inviting reading nook.

The wooden bar took up a small space, only allowing enough room to order and take delivery of drinks. Various-sized tables with chairs were scattered about the space, and the rear of the store had two rows of built-in booths. Stairs in the back corner, with a lighted arrow pointed up, advertised rooftop seating.

Not seeing anyone she recognized, Georgia made her

way to the bar. The young man behind it smiled at her. "What can I get you?"

"I'm here for a party. Harry McKenzie had a reservation."

He pointed up with his finger and then extended his hand to her. "I'm Brandon. My wife and I are the owners. We've got you set up on the rooftop. Just take the stairs, and you can't miss it."

She noticed a sign for Book Happy Hour, letting customers know if they bought a book during the week from three o'clock to five o'clock, they got a free drink. That was one way to encourage reading. She wasn't above bribing the students who came to the library and had been known to reward them with cookies or fancy bookmarks. This was just the adult version.

"Great to meet you. You've done a great job with the place." She thanked him and wandered to the back of the store.

A few people were at the tables, some with laptops, others with a book, all with drinks. A woman with curly, dark hair came from behind a door marked storage and smiled at Georgia. "Hello," she said. "You must be here for the party. Several ladies are already upstairs. I'm Marissa and if we can do anything to make your evening better, don't hesitate to let us know."

"I'm sure it will be fabulous. I met your husband at the bar and told him the shop looks terrific. You're so smart to open now and take advantage of the tourist traffic." Georgia left her with her thanks, climbed the stairs, and went through another door that led out to the roof. Harry, Lydia, and Micki were seated at a large table under the shade of a green umbrella.

"Wow, this is a gorgeous view." Georgia gazed out over the downtown area and recognized the pale-pink steeple of the historic Presbyterian Church and the white cupola on City Hall with the flag flying above it. Trees in shades of green ranging from dark evergreens to vibrant spring hues dotted the landscape as far as her eye could see. Beyond the town, the tree line gave way to fields and rolling hills.

Harry's wave encouraged her to quit gawking and head to the table. She took a chair next to Lydia. "Your hair looks wonderful," said Micki. "I love the color." She held up a bottle of white and a bottle of red and raised her brows.

"Thank you. Anita is a true genius. I'll take the white, please."

Micki dispensed a healthy pour and handed Georgia the glass. "Olivia is on her way."

"How's our newly engaged sister?" asked Georgia, smiling at Lydia and reaching for her hand to admire her ring.

"It's been a productive day. I was able to bake a few things and put them in the freezer for the festival."

Olivia appeared at the end of the table and took a chair next to Micki. "Sorry, I'm a little late. Duke got tied up. He volunteered to come to the house and watch over the dogs."

Harry chuckled. "Clay and Heath are joining him. I think it might be more about beer and poker than watching dogs."

Micki set her glass on the table. "Buck told me he's picking up pizzas after work and he and Stubbs are joining them."

Lydia grinned. "It sounds like they're having their own engagement party. Heath asked me to make them some of my bourbon brownies."

Georgia's mouth watered at the mention of them. "Oh, those sound delish."

Lydia glanced down at her tote bag and winked. "I made us some, too."

Harry poured herself more iced tea from the pitcher on

the table. "May and Janet are bringing one of their charcuterie boards, and I've got tacos coming from Roosters."

Micki refilled wine glasses and smiled. "That sounds perfect."

Olivia glanced around the rooftop. "This is such a unique idea for a business. I hope they do well."

Harry nodded. "I think they're opening at the right time. They can capitalize on the tourist crowd and create lots of buzz. They don't have a kitchen, but that probably eliminates some headaches for them."

Lydia took a sip from her glass. "Liquor doesn't go bad, and you can make quite a bit on alcohol. I saw they have a few items from the bakery for snacks, along with packaged chips and pretzels, but the overhead of a kitchen is huge, so I think they're smart to forgo it."

"They allow you to bring in food for parties on the rooftop and if you want to have a gathering off hours, you can rent the space downstairs. They told me they plan to have author and music events eventually."

"I hope they do well," said Micki. "It's tough to make it in a small town."

Janet and May came through the door, with Janet toting a large wooden board she placed in the center of the table. May sat next to Olivia, and Janet took the empty chair at the end of the table.

The ladies unwrapped the board and gushed over the beautiful arrangement of meats, cheese, fruits, and veggies. Moments later, Rooster arrived with two long trays of his famous taco flights. "Ladies," he said, placing one at each end of the table. "Congratulations to Lydia and a warm welcome to Georgia." He looked down the table and caught her eye.

"These ladies are so excited to have you here. I hope you'll stop by and have a burger soon."

They offered their thanks, and Rooster disappeared as quickly as he'd arrived. As Georgia filled her plate with a taco and several nibbles from the charcuterie board, she sighed. "This is such a lovely welcome. I can't tell you how much this means to me. To be here with all of you. To be in Lavender Valley. I've been lost since losing Lee, and this makes me so happy."

Everyone raised a glass and toasted Georgia and then did the same for Lydia. Harry reached for a taco. "I'm just so glad you're all here. When I got Jewel's letter and read her last wish, I wasn't sure any of you would come."

Olivia was the first to speak. "Coming here was the answer to my prayers. I'm not sure I would have survived had I not received your letter, Harry. It came at the right time and offered me a lifeline. In the past few months, my life that I thought was over is filled with hope and happiness. The loss and grief were all I had before. Now, it will always be a part of me, but I've found a new purpose. A new life."

Georgia dabbed at her eyes with her napkin. "I can relate to the letter from Harry feeling like a life raft in a very stormy sea. Losing my husband and being alone was a horrific experience." She took another sip from her glass. "You all know I had to sell my house, but what you don't know is that Lee left me in a very bad position. He handled all the finances and bill paying. He earned the bulk of our money and had always taken care of everything. What I didn't know was he'd been gambling and ended up mortgaging our home. When he died, we were already behind on the payments and without his income, there was no way I could ever catch up."

Tears clouded her eyes. "I was truly at a loss, and I still

have a hard time believing Lee could do what he did. Granted, I didn't pay any attention to things he asked me to sign. I trusted him completely. And he was a wonderful man and husband. He made a huge mistake. A costly one. I wallowed and cried in the months after his death. Losing him was enough, but then to have to face the huge nightmare he left behind almost did me in. Had it not been for Jewel's request and Harry reaching out to me, I shudder to think where I'd be. Now, at least I have some time to figure out what to do."

Lydia placed her hand over Georgia's. "I'm so sorry. I know the fear and angst that comes from having to leave your home and start over. It's scary and intimidating."

Georgia smiled through her tears. "Well, you've all made it so easy, and I love being back in Lavender Valley. It's wonderful to have an unexpected family. Not having children, I knew one day I'd most likely be alone, or Lee would, but those thoughts were fleeting. You always think you'll have more time." Her voice caught. "Until you don't."

Micki nodded. "I understand your dread of being alone. I got a taste of that last year with Chad off in England and Meg in Colorado. Of course, Meg wasn't just gone, she'd cut off all contact and communication. Outside of Steve's death, it was the worst period of my life. Coming here, finding all my sisters of the heart, was exactly what I needed."

Harry finished her taco and wiped her hands with a napkin. "I think Jewel would be so pleased that we're all here and working together on the festival she started so long ago. I know there's no way I could have done it alone, so having all of you here means the world to me. I didn't know what to expect when I came. I just knew I trusted Jewel and had to come to honor her. I wasn't sure what the next chapter in my life would bring, but being here feels like home now."

Olivia glanced over at Harry. "It's hard to imagine leaving, but I'm trying not to think too far ahead and do as Jewel asked. I'm not sure what the future holds and for the first time in my life, I'm not worried about it. That's because of all of you and what I've found here."

Georgia swiped at another tear on her cheek. "I vote we change the topic. Lydia, have you and Heath set a date or planned your wedding?"

Her blue eyes shimmered as Lydia blushed. "Not yet. We just want something small, and we're thinking of having it at the ranch. Nothing too fancy or elaborate."

As the ladies chattered on about ideas for the wedding, they ate more tacos and emptied more wine bottles. As the conversation continued under the soft glow of the lights strung overhead, the summer sky darkened. Georgia sighed as she took in the happy babbling of her new sisters. They and this little valley had renewed her spirit.

She accepted another refill on her wine and sat back to enjoy the gorgeous summer evening.

Early Saturday morning, Georgia squinted at the bright sunshine coming through her bedroom window. Last night at Wine & Words, she'd indulged in far too many glasses of the wonderful wines and was too tipsy to drive. After moving her car over to Buck's office for the night, Harry drove her home.

Despite her embarrassment at overdoing the wine, Georgia smiled as she remembered the fun and never-ending conversation. They might not be related, but her sisters sure could talk. May and Janet only added to the fun. They were both so funny, and the snacks they brought were out of this world.

They were all so excited for her when Georgia shared the news that Edith offered her a job at In Stitches. They all assured her they could make it work and for her to take the job if she wanted it.

The more she thought about it, the more she wanted to do it. She stretched and rolled out of bed, noticing the extra space she had with her large dresser gone. It looked so much better. She wandered out to the living area and felt a weight lifted from her shoulders. Without so much furniture, the space was welcoming and looked perfect.

The option of storing the furniture was the perfect solution. She realized she'd been reluctant to part with it. It felt like all she'd done these last months without Lee was lose bits of her life. It was the death of a thousand cuts, with not only losing her house and yard, but having to downsize and give up more and more of the things she treasured. They were just things, but they were a comfort to her.

Feeling lighter and more at ease, she found her purse she had left on the kitchen counter and dug out Edith's card. After talking to her for a few minutes and letting her know how happy she was for the chance to work at her shop, Georgia knew she'd found a friend. Edith was overjoyed at the news and invited Georgia to stop by whenever she had time to learn the ropes.

"I looked at the classes you're offering and since I'm not an experienced instructor, I'd feel better tackling the beginning courses. I'm comfortable with crochet, knitting, quilting, or the sewing classes where they make an apron or table runner. Those are all in my wheelhouse."

"That's wonderful. Let's go ahead and slot you in for the

first-time quilt class since that's coming up, and we'll make sure you like it before we do anything with the fall classes."

"Sounds great. Talking with everyone here at the farm, they think Tuesday and Wednesday would be the best days for me to work at the shop for you, but they're flexible and can make anything work."

"Those days work for me. Like I said, I'm not picky, and we can change things as we go. Just knowing I'll have a break is a godsend. You stop by when you have time, and we'll get you comfortable and then start you on your own."

"I'll make a point of coming in this week before the festival begins. Thanks again, Edith. It means so much to me that you're trusting me with your shop."

"You're the one who deserves thanks. I was considering just closing down for a couple of days a week, so you're a true lifesaver. I'll see you soon."

Georgia disconnected and smiled. Things were coming together, and she was finding her footing. She'd been noodling an idea she had since last night and eyed her sewing machine she chose to place on the small dining table. She located a plastic bin of fabric and went about cutting from a piece of black fabric. In no time, she sewed the edges of her project and pronounced them ready for personalization.

She found the box where she kept her cutting machine and all the accessories. Lee had gifted it to her two Christmases ago, and she loved creating all sorts of fun items with it. She went through her designs and collections and found a sheet of white glitter iron-on material. She chuckled as she used the small ironing device to iron the lettering onto the fabric.

She let the material cool and then removed the backing and revealed her creation. They weren't much, but they were a gift from her heart, and she hoped Heath and Lydia would like them. She set them aside, checking the time. She was committed to getting more exercise and surrounded by the beautiful acreage outside her door, she had no excuse. She slipped into some exercise pants and a t-shirt and headed outside.

Sunshine filled the blue sky and elevated Georgia's already high spirits. She wandered to the edge of the property line along the fence that separated Jewel's farm from the Nolan ranch. The worn pathway was perfect for a jaunt. She walked past the thriving purple sage, and the loud hum of bees made her stop.

They reminded her of Jewel and how she'd reassured Georgia when she'd been afraid and swatting at them while they buzzed among Jewel's flowers. Jewel explained that the hum was from the bees working; they weren't concerned with Georgia but focused on their work. They beat their tiny wings and communicated through the soft humming noises they made. She didn't remember all the information Jewel shared but couldn't believe how many miles each flew and the number of flowers each visited to make less than a teaspoon of honey over a lifetime.

She did remember having a new respect for bees and instead of fearing them she thought of them as Jewel described them—magical and essential to human life. Jewel took the time to explain how they worked to pollenate plants and provide food for humans. She also reminded Georgia to watch them and simply leave them alone; they'd ignore her and move on to their next flower.

They all worked together for a common purpose. Jewel thought humans could learn from them. The memory made Georgia chuckle. Jewel was right, of course.

She made a loop around one of the lavender fields, thick

with purple blooms, where the bees were active, and she stopped to take in the beauty and watch the bees work. She circled back to her cottage, focused on the hum of the bees. It was a delightful sound. Georgia loved walking in the morning and soaking in the beauty around her.

Since Lee's death, Georgia had gotten out of the habit of her morning walks. Without him, the world suddenly seemed scary to her, and she'd taken refuge in the home she loved. When she found out she had to give that up, her world shrank even more. Then, the move and her shoulder injury had taken all her energy.

It felt wonderful to be out in nature, the morning sun shining upon her while the birds tweeted a greeting. Her fears of being alone and scared lessened with each passing day spent at the farm with her newfound sisters.

After her shower, she made her way to the house, anxious for her morning elixir. The scent of brewed coffee guided her to the counter. She filled a cup and took a long sip, hoping with her stress level lower, she could handle coffee again.

Micki came through the mudroom door and poured herself a glass of iced tea. "Harry hosted a Fourth of July breakfast on the lawn at City Hall this morning and when she got home, she and Lydia went over to the ranch. Olivia is at Duke's but will be heading to the ranch soon. Meg's working and will join us as soon as she gets off." She took a long swallow and smiled. "I think Lydia wants to supervise Heath's meal prep, and he's so set on doing it all himself."

Georgia laughed. "It sounds like he's quite the cook, too. That will be interesting to see how they juggle the kitchen. I just went for a walk and stopped to take in the beauty of the lavender. It's quite stunning."

Micki's eyes sparkled. "Everything is looking great for the

festival. Tyler's been working hard to get the field by the driveway ready for parking, and we've got the tents organized so we'll have spots for selling our products. He's got tables and chairs in the barn ready for our paint and sip parties. I think we're on schedule."

She emptied her glass. "I'm going to take a shower and then, if you're up to it, we can head over to the ranch."

"Sounds perfect. I can't wait to see it. From what you've all described, it's sure to be magnificent. I'll finish my coffee and be ready when you are."

Micki made for the stairs, and Georgia took her cup and wandered back to her cottage to find a gift bag and tissue for her gift. She couldn't wait to present it to Lydia and Heath.

CHAPTER FIVE

On Sunday, Georgia missed the sunrise. Two late nights and too much wine caught up with her, and she dozed until eight o'clock. Not wanting to break her one-day exercise streak, she opted for a walk around the fields before taking her shower.

Olivia and Duke invited her to church with them, and she selected a long skirt and blouse from her closet. Many of her closest friends in Boise were from her church family, and she welcomed Olivia's kind invitation. She walked over to the house and found Lydia in the kitchen, with Vera sporting the black bandana Georgia gifted Lydia last night. The three golden retrievers were huddled together on the area rug with little Vera between them.

Georgia made a matching bandana for Ace, Heath's dog, too. The glitter letters spelled out *My Humans Are Getting Married* and included a cute glitter paw print. Heath and Lydia had gushed over them and put them on their dogs as soon as they opened her gift.

It made Georgia smile to see Vera wearing hers this

morning. Never one to spend money on extravagant gifts, Georgia always tried to create something special that came from her heart.

Lydia was busy slicing colorful cabbage, and Georgia detected the aroma of something delicious coming from the slow cooker. "You're a busy bee," she said, reaching for a cup from the cupboard.

"Well, I have to top Heath's wonderful meal from last night. He really is a talented cook." She chuckled and added, "Not that it's a competition or anything."

"Between the two of you, you're an unstoppable team. And that kitchen is to die for. What a gorgeous house, not to mention the barn and the rest of the property. It's like something from a magazine." Georgia flicked on the tea kettle and retrieved a bag of Earl Grey. "Do you want a cup of tea? I think we have time before we leave for church."

Lydia glanced over her shoulder. "That sounds lovely, thank you."

Georgia grabbed a second cup and teabag. "What smells so yummy?"

"Oh, I decided to use the slow cooker instead of heating up the house with the oven today. It's pulled pork. I'm working on a cabbage salad, plus I thought I'd make a bruschetta salad and an onion flatbread for an appetizer. I was able to snag some fresh peaches at the farmer's market, so we'll have peach pie for dessert."

"My mouth is already watering," said Georgia, pouring the water into the cups. "I'm going to have to up my exercise if you two keep cooking up a storm. Those twice-baked potatoes Heath did last night were the best, and I ate way too much."

Lydia nodded as she slid the purple cabbage into a bowl.

"Thank you again for the cute bandanas for the dogs. They're so clever."

"My pleasure, and Vera looks so smart in hers." She delivered Lydia's cup of tea and took a seat at the large granite counter, watching her work. "So, where is everybody this morning?"

"Olivia is upstairs getting ready, Harry went to the office to work on her speech for the opening ceremony for the festival and a few other special events, and Micki and Meg went to visit Jade in Medford."

Georgia shook her head. "That's a tough situation Micki is in with her sister. I understand how hard it is for Micki to be around her. I hope they're able to find a way to forge a new relationship." She sighed. "I had a younger sister, Amelia, who was adopted before I came to live with Jewel. She's about ten years younger than me. Years ago, I tried to find her but didn't get far. She probably wouldn't even remember me. She was so young when we were separated."

Lydia frowned. "That's so sad. I wonder if Harry and Buck could help."

She shrugged. "We have enough to do right now, and I don't want to bother them."

The dogs raised their heads and moments later, Olivia came from around the corner. Georgia swallowed the rest of her tea and rose from her chair. "I love that blouse, Olivia. That green is gorgeous on you."

She smiled. "Thank you. I don't have very many nice clothes, so the folks at church will have to get used to seeing me in the same few things each week."

Georgia's eyes twinkled. "If you stop by In Stitches, you could pick out some fabric, and I'd be happy to make you some new blouses."

"That's so thoughtful of you. I would hate to have you go to that much trouble." Olivia reached for her purse.

"It's no trouble at all. I love to sew and would like nothing more than to make something for you. I'm going in this week to get trained. I suspect I'll be working Tuesday and Wednesday. I could help you pick something out. It would be fun."

The two of them said goodbye to Lydia and the dogs and were still chatting about fabrics when they stepped onto the porch. Olivia drove them to Lavender Valley Community Church, where she assured Georgia that Duke would save them seats in their row.

Georgia climbed the steps of the charming building, set in a residential neighborhood, a few blocks from the main downtown area. She noticed the pretty lavender wreaths on the doors of the church, as they stepped into the entryway. Olivia led them down the aisle and to the row where Duke and his dad waited.

Georgia sat next to Leland, who greeted her with a smile. She enjoyed talking to him last night at the ranch. His sincere love for animals and his kindness were evident in the way he spoke and interacted.

Duke leaned across his dad and said, "May and Wyatt aren't coming to church this morning, but she wanted me to be sure to invite you to come out to the house for lunch after the service."

Georgia smiled as her heart filled with happiness. "I'd love to; that's so kind of her to include me." He winked and then squeezed his dad's hand. Olivia had found a true gem in Duke, who was cut from the same cloth as his dad. Both kind and genuine.

After some scripture readings, singing, and a special soloist, the pastor took to the podium and delivered his message. Olivia sang his praises as she drove into town, and she was right. He was a gifted speaker and held Georgia's attention. She was surprised when it ended and realized ninety minutes had passed.

The pastor stood at the door and shook hands with each of the congregants. He paid special attention to Georgia and thanked her for coming, welcoming her to Lavender Valley. Olivia was right again. He was younger than most of the pastors Georgia had met, but he was engaging and sincere, especially with his more mature congregation.

She promised she'd be back and followed Olivia down the steps to her car.

Olivia pulled away from the church and headed out of town. "I'm so glad you're coming to lunch. Duke's family means the world to me. They've welcomed me with open arms and have been so kind to me." Her voice wobbled. "I came here lost and without a family and now, I have all of you and so much more."

Georgia reached across the console and put her hand on Olivia's arm. "You're pretty special, so I can see why they adopted you like one of their own. I'm so happy you've found what you needed here. I already feel the same. I wasn't sure what I would do, but coming here, I already feel like I've come home."

Olivia smiled and nodded. "Jewel definitely knew what she was doing."

Tuesday, Georgia woke with a renewed sense of purpose. As she made her morning loop through the property, she reflected on the lovely day she'd had on Sunday. May's lunch and visiting with the entire family had been a wonderful way to spend the afternoon.

She and Olivia left early to return to the farm and help Lydia with anything she needed. She'd invited Duke's family and Buck to join them all for dinner. Georgia enjoyed cooking but couldn't hold a candle to Lydia. Her pulled pork was out of this world, and the crunchy cabbage salad, plus the bruschetta pasta salad, were refreshing and perfect side dishes. The onion flatbread she made for an appetizer was scrumptious. She didn't need any help but let the others set the table for her, and Micki and Georgia insisted on doing the dishes while she relaxed and visited with everyone.

Yesterday, Georgia spent the entire day at In Stitches with Edith. She loved the shop and couldn't wait to get to work later this morning. Last night, she'd stayed up, sipping tea and working on a surprise for all her sisters.

Micki showed up at her door around nine o'clock. Over more tea, she divulged that Jade was scheduled to be released no later than early August. From the slump of her shoulders, Georgia could tell it would bring a new set of problems for Micki. She was shouldering the weight of the festival, and Georgia hoped once it started, she'd be less stressed and worried about it. Along with that, she suspected her worries about Jade were causing the most stress.

After she was ready for the day, Georgia added her secret project to a large tote bag and collected her purse. The first day of her new job was a day worth celebrating and after saying goodbye to everyone at the house, she parked downtown and strolled to Winding River Coffee to treat herself to a latte before her day started at the fabric shop.

Laurie greeted her with a warm smile. "Hey, Georgia, how are you?"

"I'm great, Laurie. I'm starting my first day over at In Stitches and wanted to celebrate with a latte."

She plucked a cup from the stack next to her and wrote Georgia's name on it. "Congratulations to you. I know Edith has been hoping to find someone to help out." She went about preparing the latte and set it on the counter. "No charge today in honor of your new job."

Tears threatened to spill from her eyes as she took the warm cup. "Thank you, Laurie. That's so kind of you." She moved out of the way of the next customer and sat near the window. As Georgia looked out on Main Street, it wasn't lost on her that this was the very place she'd first experienced unconditional love and kindness. Here she was all these years later, being welcomed with the same warmth as Jewel provided fifty years ago.

So many things had changed in the past five decades, but Lavender Valley hadn't and as Georgia let the warm drink soothe her throat, the little town she remembered did the same for her heart.

Georgia finished her latte, wished Laurie a good day, and walked down the sidewalk to In Stitches. She was early but was anxious to work on the black and white quilt square she had in mind for the upcoming show, but she needed to finish her surprise for the others first. Once she had everything ready, she settled into her happy place and started stitching.

Even with customers trickling in throughout the day, Georgia was able to finish her project and laid out two quilt squares she planned to finish before the end of the week. She had ten days before the show but wanted to get them done and off her plate.

At the end of the day, she balanced the cash in the drawer and filled out the deposit sheet before dropping it at the bank. With a sense of accomplishment, she drove to the farm.

Lydia had dinner ready and as they all lingered, Georgia rose and retrieved her tote bag. She unearthed the tissue-wrapped gifts and handed one to each of them. Olivia was the first to untie the purple ribbon around the tissue. She grinned as she held up a gorgeous lavender-colored apron. All the aprons were similar, but Georgia had used slightly different accent fabrics on the handy pockets. Along with Micki's new logo embroidered in the center of the apron, Georgia used Edith's fancy machine to add each of their names in a dark-purple thread.

They all loved the gifts, but Micki's face lit up the most when she tried hers on. "Oh, I need to get a photo of this. Let's all get together and stand outside by the field. It would be great for the website."

As luck would have it, Buck and Stubbs pulled up to the house as they were stepping off the porch. He'd come to check on Micki but was happy to serve as their official photographer. The sisters didn't make it easy on him. They laughed and goofed around, posing with their legs in the air, like the Rockettes.

Buck, with his usual patience, captured lots of photos of their antics and all of the more serious poses Micki wanted for the website. When they finished, and she was happy with the photos, he slipped his arm around her and suggested they take a walk.

It warmed Georgia's heart to see them together. Like Micki, he was busy with work but took time to drive out and make sure she was coping with the stress of everything. Micki would need to lean on him when Jade got out of the rehab center.

The rest of them walked back to the house and while

Georgia did the dishes, Olivia brewed some tea, and Lydia got a plate of cookies ready. They put Harry in charge of picking something to watch and settled in for a series set in France, focused on a divorced mother of four, who is a police commander in a gorgeous coastal town.

As Georgia nibbled on one of Lydia's chocolate chip cookies and sipped her tea, she glanced over at her four sisters of the heart. Jewel had been so wise to bring them all back to the farm.

CHAPTER SIX

Thursday, Georgia and the others spent the day setting up for the festival. Heath and Clay arrived mid-morning and together with Tyler, they got all the heavy lifting done and the easy-up tents erected for the retail spaces. They also placed all the props in the fields, so both the professional and amateur photographers could use them for inspiration.

Georgia loved the old bicycle with the basket filled with lavender and the bench resting among the purple blooms. A few painted chairs, weathered and peeling, were also scattered among the fields. Olivia found a cream-colored velvet sofa at the thrift shop, and they placed it in the midst of one of the fields.

Micki and Harry concentrated on setting up the tables for the paint and sip event. The tables faced the barn, with a view of Micki's gorgeous mural of sunflowers. Some of the ones she had planted were also blooming with the promise of many more on the way. Together, with the haze of purple from the lavender fields, it made for a pristine setting.

Lydia, Olivia, and Georgia focused on the retail space and organized the sales and display area. They took the simplest approach and kept all their products, including Georgia's fabric creations, in plastic totes, organized by each type of product. Clay hooked up a small trailer to the UTV in the barn that would allow them to transport all the totes back and forth each day and not leave them out and exposed.

When Georgia was in the barn with Clay, she spied the old yellow Chevy truck she remembered Chuck driving. She touched the faded paint along the fender. "Too bad this old girl isn't all shined up. That would make a great prop in the lavender field."

Clay nodded. "It would. I think Harry mentioned it once, but they've all been so busy, I'm sure they didn't have time to investigate. Plus, it would be expensive. It does still run, so it might just need body work and paint."

Georgia walked around it, noting the faded lettering on the doors. "Maybe someday. I can picture Micki's new logo on the door."

"We could talk to Jim down at the garage and see what he thinks."

Georgia waved her hand in the air. "Aw, it's something we can tackle once we're done with the festival. Like you said, there's already enough to do, and the farm looks terrific. I'm excited to see how many people we get."

He showed her where they kept the key to the UTV in case she needed it, and they wandered back out to the retail space. Storing the totes in the barn meant the only things they'd have to worry about putting up and taking down each day, were the display items they selected to showcase. They used the same approach with Lydia's area, where all of her goodies were bagged or boxed and stored in totes, with trays set out to display things and a tray set out for small samples of treats. They used a tablet to keep track of sales with Meg stationed in the middle between Lydia and Georgia to take care of the sales.

After they took a lunch break, Clay and Heath went home, and Olivia took all the dogs to the shelter to check on her guests. Georgia stood back to admire the table set up for her creations and smiled at Lydia standing under her canopy. "I saw all those stacks of goodies in the freezer this morning. I hope you can make it through this first weekend without being stuck baking each night."

Lydia nodded as she set the lemonade dispensers on a table. "Yeah, this first weekend will be a good gauge for how much we'll sell. None of us really know what to expect, so it's a bit of a shot in the dark. I just put two cakes in the oven. We can have one with our painting party tonight, then I can package up some cake slices or squares, but everything else is ready."

Georgia raised her brows. "I'm looking forward to our paint and sip dry run. I used to see those advertised all the time in Boise and thought they sounded like fun."

Lydia rested her hand on the glass dispensers. "It should be fun, and May and Janet are bringing one of their epic charcuterie boards, so we'll have plenty of snacks." She glanced at her watch. "I better get inside and keep an eye on the cakes."

Georgia wandered over near the barn, where Harry and Micki were adding the final touches to the table where the easels were awaiting painters. They had a refreshment table set up for the party and a metal trough full of ice for bottles of water and soda, along with some beer and bottles of white wine. Harry had the bottles of red stored in the house.

Georgia joined Harry and Micki at the edge of the barn.

"This looks wonderful. What a fun way to celebrate the eve of the festival."

Harry tipped the cowboy hat she wore back from her face and smiled. "Micki assures me anyone can paint, even me."

Micki laughed. "It'll be loads of fun. Meg promised to take photos for us. I'd like to post them on the website and use them to entice people to book more events after the festival. Our sunflowers and dahlias will make for a lovely setting too."

Harry glanced down at her dirt-covered jeans. "I'm going to take a quick shower and get ready for tonight."

Micki checked her watch. "I should do the same. I told the ladies coming from the San Juan Islands to be here between five and six o'clock."

As they discussed logistics, Olivia walked up to join them, the goldens and little Vera following her. She looked down at a smudge of something on her shirt. "I'm going to get these pups an early dinner, then I'll hop in the shower after you, Micki."

At the mention of one of their favorite words—dinner— the dogs' ears perked, and they focused on Olivia.

"I'll be quick," Micki said, as she took a few quick steps toward the house. Olivia followed, with her gang of furry buddies.

Harry gazed over at the canopies. "Everything looks great." She wiped the sweat from her forehead. "It'll be nice to relax tonight, pretend to be a customer, and enjoy all that we've created."

Georgia nodded. "You've all done a terrific job. I only wish I'd been able to come earlier and help more."

As they walked toward the house, Harry shook her head. "You've done a ton of work. Look at all those totes filled with your beautiful creations. I couldn't do all that in five years."

She stopped and met Georgia's eyes. "Each of us has a talent or gift, as Jewel would say. Together, we make the perfect team to run the farm and the festival. You're a huge part of that. Not to mention, you'll be putting in lots of hours under the canopy over the next month."

Georgia chuckled and linked her arm through Harry's. For years, she'd longed for her sister who'd been adopted. She wanted more than anything to have a relationship and feel that special connection. Now, she had that, with four women whose warmth and kindness were exactly what she needed.

***

A few minutes before five o'clock, May pulled up to the house. Georgia and Lydia, who only had to change clothes to get ready for the party, hurried out to help her. Lydia toted a pretty glass cake stand with her layered cake atop it, decorated with a few sprigs of lavender.

May greeted them with her usual cheerful smile. "I'm so excited to relax and paint with you tonight. We've been swamped all day at the store." She raised her brows at Lydia's cake. "That looks beyond delicious and so pretty."

"Thanks; hopefully, everyone will like it." She went over to place it on the refreshment table.

Georgia waited for May to open the back of her SUV. "We were saying the same thing. I think we're ready for a little mini-celebration after all the hard work. It will be nice to have a little break before what we hope is a busy month."

May swept her eyes over the barn and the canopies. "Everything looks perfect here. I think you're going to be swamped." She handed Lydia a wooden board tightly wrapped in plastic. "I decided to make two smaller boards instead of a big one." She handed Georgia the other one.

Lydia's eyebrows rose. "These look terrific. I can't wait to dig into them."

As they were setting them up and organizing plates and napkins, the other three arrived, and Micki opened two bottles of wine. May's phone chimed, and she excused herself, walking toward the house.

While the ladies selected beverages, a large SUV pulled into the yard and parked. Moments later, four women came from it and walked toward them.

Micki handed Olivia the bottle of wine she was pouring and took a few steps in their direction. "Hey, one of you must be Kate. I'm Micki and spoke with you on the phone."

A woman with dark hair, streaked with silver strands that glistened in the early evening sun, smiled and extended her hand. "I'm Kate. So nice to meet you, Micki." She turned to the others. "These are my friends."

A woman with chestnut hair laced with copper highlights smiled and waved. "I'm Sam and have to say this is a gorgeous farm. I can smell the fresh lavender already."

Micki turned to the others behind her. "Well, we've all worked really hard to get it ready for the festival. We all grew up here at different times and were foster children who lived here during our teens."

"Wow," said a woman with a head full of blond highlights, who smiled at all of them. "I'm Jess and can't wait to hear more about your experiences and how you all came to be here now."

Micki grinned. "It's quite the story."

The fourth woman with gorgeous silver and gray hair mixed with a few strands of darker brown took a few steps forward in the direction of the refreshments. "I'm Izzy and can't wait to try whatever wine you're pouring." She pointed back at the SUV. "In fact, we brought you some wine to thank you for squeezing us in tonight. My family owns a winery in Washington."

Olivia held out a glass of white and one of red. "Wow, that's so nice of you. It's wonderful to meet all of you. I'm Olivia, and we've partnered with a local winery, Whispering Vine. They've provided a cabernet sauvignon and a chardonnay for our events."

Izzy smiled and took the glass of red. "I've never met a wine I don't like, but I'm partial to the reds."

Harry took two more glasses and offered them to the others. "I'm Harry, well Harriet, but everybody calls me Harry."

Sam held up her hand. "I'm our designated driver tonight, so I'll let one of the others take those off your hands."

Harry chuckled. "I'm not much of a drinker, too many years as a cop and never partaking, so all I'm allowed to do is hand these out." She approached Kate, who took the glass of red.

Izzy took a sip from her glass. "Along with growing up on a winery, too many years as a lawyer has driven me to drink even more than when I was younger. So, I'm intrigued, Harry. How long were you in law enforcement?"

She helped herself to a bottle of iced tea. "My whole life. I just retired this year with thirty years working for the Salem Police Department."

Georgia put a hand on Harry's shoulder. "She's quite humble. She was the deputy chief of investigations there, and she was elected mayor of Lavender Valley in March of this year. She's the one who spearheaded getting all of us back here to the farm."

"Wow, that's impressive. Kate's significant other is retired from Seattle. Same type of job you had. And you're the mayor?" Jess eyed the chardonnay and added, "That's my favorite, so I can't resist."

Harry shrugged. "It's a bit of a story. I got involved in helping solve what everyone thought was some petty crime and mischief when I arrived, but it turned out to be a bit bigger. Long story short, they had an election and wrote me in. I was shocked to say the least. I'm not very skilled when it comes to farming and animals, but Olivia here..." She turned toward her. "She's taken over the dog rescue program that was close to our foster mom's heart."

Olivia poured herself a glass of chardonnay. "If any of you are looking for a new furry friend, I've got a few guests in our shelter. I can show you."

Sam held up her hand. "I've got a sweet golden retriever, and my husband has a chocolate Lab." She glanced over at her friends. "We're all dog lovers, and we all have golden retrievers, but I don't think I have time for any more."

Olivia smiled. "We've got goldens, too. You'll have to meet Hope, Willow, and Chief before you go. Lydia's little Yorkie is named Vera, and she's a total sweetheart, too."

Izzy laughed. "I adopted a dog on the last vacation I took. Sunny's a golden, too."

As they continued sharing about their love of dogs, Lydia and Georgia waved them over to the charcuterie boards. Lydia handed Jess a plate. "I'm Lydia and so glad you're all here to help us with our soft opening and paint party. We're all excited to hang out and relax before the event kicks off tomorrow."

Georgia presented Sam with a plate. "I'm Georgia, and we've got some soft drinks and water in that trough." She pointed at the end of the table.

Sam smiled at her. "Wonderful, and that cake is gorgeous."

Georgia gestured toward Lydia. "That's all Lydia's genius. She's a famous chef and blesses us daily with her yummy creations."

Sam's mouth hung open. "Wow, a real chef. I love to bake and when I moved to Friday Harbor, I bought a little coffee shop and make pies and brownies, but nothing like that. I can't wait to try a piece of that."

Lydia blushed. "I think Georgia's being generous. I'm a chef, but not really famous."

Georgia shook her head. "She won that bakeoff show they televised from Portland about ten years ago."

Sam's eyes widened. "That's impressive." She pointed at the cake and looked behind her. "Kate, we need to send a photo of this to Ellie and tell her about Lydia."

Kate hurried over and snapped a photo with her phone. "Ellie is a friend of ours who is married to Izzy's brother. They run the family winery on the island, and this is the height of their season, so she couldn't come. She's a wonderful baker who ran the local bakery until a few years ago."

Georgia moaned. "A bakery, a winery, and an island. I'm sold. That sounds like a wonderful place to live."

Sam chuckled. "It's the best. I grew up in Seattle but moved to the island after a tough divorce."

Izzy put her arm around Sam's shoulders. "And she ended up falling in love and remarried to the nicest hometown guy around."

Micki walked over to the table with Jess. "Help yourself to the snacks. Our instructor, Ashleigh, won't be here until close to seven, so we have plenty of time. I can take anyone who wants to go on a quick tour of the lavender fields."

May came from the house and stepped over to the group, taking a drink from her bottle of water. "Hey, everyone! Sorry, I got hung up on the phone." She turned toward Micki. "Janet sends her apologies, but she's too tired and is going to make an early night of it."

Georgia reached out and touched May's shoulder. "This is May, who owns a beautiful shop downtown called Cranberry Cottage. She's also the one who made these yummy charcuterie boards for us tonight. Now, let's see if I can remember everyone, and I'll introduce you."

Georgia went around the table where the guests stood and recited their names for May. When she was done, Kate stepped forward to fill her plate. "We saw your shop when we were wandering downtown this morning. We arrived last night and then did a little exploring today. I own an art and antique store, so I'm itching to check out your place."

May beamed and told her all about how she and Janet like to restore old furniture.

Olivia noticed Izzy's glass needed a refill and took a bottle of the cabernet over to her. "Care for some more?"

Izzy threw her head back and laughed. "You'll find that to be a question you need never ask." She held her glass out for Olivia, and she filled it with the deep-red wine.

As Micki organized the others for a quick trip to the lavender fields, Izzy's phone chimed. She waved them on. "It's the guy from the house. You go ahead, and I'll talk to him."

Georgia stayed with her and filled a plate for herself to give Izzy some privacy while she took the call.

A few minutes later, Izzy joined her. "We've got a huge problem."

CHAPTER SEVEN

As Izzy talked with Georgia, Harry walked up, spoke into her phone for a few moments, and disconnected the call. Georgia and Izzy looked up from where they sat at the paint table. Harry slipped the phone in her pocket and sighed. "Small electrical emergency on Main Street. They're getting set for the street dance tomorrow."

Georgia tilted her head toward Izzy. "Izzy's got a bigger emergency."

Izzy shook her head. "Kate found this great house online, and we all chipped in on it. We got there last night, and it's great, just like it was advertised. It's downtown, so easy walking distance to everything. Everything was fine until early this afternoon when we discovered we had no water."

Harry frowned. "Oh, no."

Izzy took a long swallow from her glass. "That was the owner. He's had a plumber over there, and it's not simple. The pipes rotted, and it's a big job. They can't get it fixed quickly. They had to turn the water off and can't rent it without water. So, he's refunding all our money, even last night's stay, but that leaves us in a pickle."

"One of the worst times to try to find a vacancy anywhere near Lavender Valley is this weekend," said Harry.

"Right. We've been calling around today, just in case, to try to find anything, and there's nothing within a hundred miles."

Harry's eyes widened. "Give me a minute. I have an idea." She pulled the phone out of her pocket and hurried toward the house.

Georgia smiled. "If anyone can solve your problem, it's Harry. She's a master when it comes to getting things done and finding solutions."

As they sipped wine together, Georgia told Izzy more about their foster mother Jewel. "I was the first foster child she took in almost fifty years ago." She explained how each of the girls lived with Jewel, but at different times and that Micki was the last child Jewel fostered and the youngest of the five.

"Jewel put Harry in charge of her estate and tasked her with convincing the rest of us to return to the farm and work together for one season. She called us sisters of the heart and thought we needed each other." Georgia ran her finger along the stem of her glass. "She was right. We needed each other and this place. It's where I first felt unconditional love and where Jewel nurtured me in sewing and making things with yarn. She was a special person, and we all loved her very much."

Izzy leaned against the back of her chair. "What a touching tribute to her that you all came back to the farm."

Georgia gazed at the barn and the brightly colored sunflowers. "We all feel like she's still watching over us. Bringing us together was the best thing for each of us. I had lost my husband and found out I had to sell our home, so I needed a place to stay. Coming here and having the love and support of my new sisters has been such a blessing. Harry, as you know, was newly retired and looking for a challenge and something to do. Olivia, Micki, and Lydia all have their own stories. We all need one another."

Harry hurried back to where they were seated. A smile filled her face. "So, I've got good news." She took a few swallows of iced tea. "Clay and Heath Nolan are brothers who run the ranch next door. They've got a huge house, and I just spoke with Clay, and he and Heath are more than happy to have the four of you stay with them, as their guests."

Izzy put up her hand. "Oh, no. We'd hate to intrude."

Harry grinned. "I figured you'd say that. If we had spare rooms here, we'd have you stay with us, but honestly, their house is huge. They've got spacious empty guest rooms, and they're the best guys. Totally trustworthy."

Georgia smiled at Harry. "Harry and Clay, the eldest brother, are an item, and Heath and Lydia are engaged. Their parents were great friends of Jewel's and like Harry said, you won't find two nicer guys."

"Well, maybe Duke and Buck. You haven't met them yet, but Duke is our resident veterinarian, and he and Olivia are a couple. Buck was Jewel's attorney, and he and Micki spend quite a bit of time together," said Harry.

Georgia laughed as she swallowed another sip. "Yes, that's right. We have four of the nicest men in Lavender Valley on our doorstep. All that to say, all of you will love Clay and Heath, and it's worth staying just to see the house. It could be in a magazine."

Izzy laughed and shook her head. "Okay, you two. I'm convinced. Now, we'll have to work on the other three. We've been worried all day that this might happen. We even loaded up our stuff in the back of the SUV because we thought we might have to drive up the interstate toward Eugene to find a place."

Harry clapped her hands together. "Perfect, then you're all set to go. When we're done painting, we'll take you over and introduce you."

"Kate feels horrible, like it's all her fault for picking the house. She's been beside herself worrying about it all day." Izzy sighed. "She might be a tough sell."

As Harry reassured Izzy she could handle it, Kate and Lydia returned and refilled their plates and beverages before taking their seats at the paint table. Kate raved about the fields and showed Izzy some of the photos she took of the ladies posed on the bicycle and the sofa. "You'll have to pose for a few tomorrow."

Harry met Kate's eyes. "Izzy told us about the water problem at the house, and we have great news."

Kate sighed. "Oh, he got it fixed? That's a relief. I was just telling the others about our rental woes."

Harry wrinkled her nose. "Not exactly, but I found you guys a place to stay." She turned toward Lydia. "Clay and Heath said to bring them over, and they could stay at the ranch." She turned back to Kate. "They'll be ready for you when we're done painting, and you can stay until Monday, like you planned."

Lydia smiled at Harry. "That's a great idea."

Kate frowned and looked over at Izzy. .

Izzy reached for a bite of cheese from her plate. "They own the ranch next door. Heath is Lydia's fiancé, and Clay is Harry's beau. I think they're totally trustworthy." She winked at Kate.

As her eyes widened, Kate smiled. "I'm sure they're

trustworthy, and that's so kind of them, but we really hate to be a burden."

Harry gestured toward Izzy. "Like I told Izzy, their place is huge, so much so that they may not notice you there. The guest bedrooms are like suites in a fancy hotel. They have two dogs, Ace and Maverick, who will be thrilled to have some new people in the house. If we had more room, we'd just have you stay here, but the ranch has plenty of space."

Sam and Jess, along with Micki and Olivia, joined them at the table, and Izzy explained they couldn't return to the rental, but Harry had found a solution for them next door. They both let out a sigh at the news. Sam reached over and put her hand on Kate's arm. "See, it all worked out. We'll have a place here, and we won't have to add hours to our day driving each way."

Kate nodded. "I just feel horrible that I got us in this mess."

Izzy shook her head. "You didn't do anything. We all liked the house and agreed to it. You just found it. Anybody can have a plumbing problem, and we got our money back, so all is well."

Kate met Harry's eyes. "Thank you for going the extra mile to help us."

"I have a feeling all of you would do the same for us, so don't give it a second thought. The guys are happy to have you."

Another car pulled up to the house, and Micki said, "That's Ashleigh, our instructor. Everybody, fill your plates and glasses, and we'll get going."

The young woman lugged a huge tote and joined the group. Micki introduced everyone, and they took their seats. Ashleigh added blobs of acrylic paint to paper plates and passed them around the table. She gave a quick introduction to the four brushes at each easel and made sure everyone had a disposable cup full of water to rinse their brushes.

She took a sip from her wine glass and smiled at all of them. "Tonight, it's all about fun. Nobody needs to stress about being perfect or matching what I'm painting exactly. You can add in anything you want or put your own twist on this beauty. I'm keeping it simple and instead of having you mix your purple paint from blue and red, I'm giving you some purple, and we'll use the white to lighten as much as you need to for the lavender blooms. Also, no need to rush; just relax and enjoy the event."

She reminded everyone to put on a paint apron and started with the large brush and yellow paint to create a horizon. May was an expert with all her artistic skills, and Kate and Georgia had both dabbled with painting before and had no trouble following Ashleigh's strokes.

Micki loved graphic design on the computer but had never painted on canvas. She laughed as she mixed in some white in the blue she was trying to get just right. "This is so much easier on a computer screen."

Olivia and Lydia laughed as they worked on the mountains at the top of the painting, trying to get the shades of blue and purple to look realistic.

While the others took a break to let the paint dry for a few minutes, Harry and Izzy were still working on the colors of the horizon and sunset. Ashleigh offered them a few pointers to catch them up with the others.

Harry laughed as Ashleigh helped her blend the colors. "I knew I wouldn't be good at this."

Izzy refilled her wine glass. "I have a theory I want to test. I think if I drink more wine, I'll do a better job." She laughed as she sat. "Or at least I'll be more relaxed about it."

With them caught up, Ashleigh had everyone add in a

row of green trees at the base of the mountains and then work with a smaller brush to create the lavender blooms, which were thin dashes of blue, purple, lavender, and an even lighter color that almost looked pink.

At the next break, Lydia served everyone a slice of her lavender lemon cake to go with their savory items, and Micki made sure everyone's glass was filled. As Ashleigh ate her cake, praising Lydia, she gazed over at the barn. "This really is a perfect setting for this." She tilted her head toward Micki. "Normally, we don't take so many breaks, so we'll be wrapped up by seven-thirty or so for your evening dates."

Micki nodded. "That's perfect. We're on the verge of it getting too dark right now."

Ashleigh looked up at the sky. "We'll be done in a jiffy. We just need to finish painting the edges and have everyone sign their painting. Then, we can clean up and call it a night."

With everyone pitching in to help clean up, it didn't take long, and Ashleigh left with her supplies and a slice of cake to take home. After saying good night, May followed and left all the goodies but took her wooden boards with her.

The others gazed at the paintings on the table. Georgia loved the shades of purple and lavender used not only in the flowers, but the mountains. They gave way to a striking sunset that resembled the one that filled the sky as they painted. Thinking it best to let them dry overnight, they toted them to the sunroom.

With everything buttoned up for the evening, Harry and Lydia suggested they lead the way to the ranch and let their guests get settled. Micki, Olivia, and Georgia squeezed in with them, and Sam followed as the nine women made the short journey next door.

As the four visitors piled out of Sam's SUV, they gazed at the entrance, their mouths agape. "Wow, that's some statue," said Kate, pointing to the bronze horse.

Izzy smiled at Harry. "You weren't exaggerating when you said it was huge. This is something else."

Clay and Heath opened the door, and Harry made the introductions. The brothers welcomed everyone inside, while they insisted on carrying the women's luggage. Clay held up two bags and said, "I'll take the two owners of these to the first guest room."

Izzy and Jess raised their hands and followed him down the hallway. Heath gestured toward Kate and Sam. "And you ladies can follow me this way." He led them to his wing of the house.

Once the four ladies were settled, they returned to the kitchen, where everyone was gathered. Heath made coffee and tea and offered wine, but they all held up their hands and requested coffee and tea.

It was a gorgeous summer night, and they opted to sit on the patio, where Clay and Heath introduced Maverick and Ace to their new guests. The ladies slathered them in attention and by the time Georgia followed Lydia and Heath from the empty kitchen, the dogs had calmed and were lounging on the cool stone surface.

After Heath took his seat, Kate raised her cup. "I speak for the four of us when I say how very grateful we are that you opened your magnificent home to us. If not for you, we'd be driving a few hours back and forth, so thank you."

After their coffee cup toast, Sam took a quick sip from hers. "Your home is lovely. Harry told us we'd have first-class accommodations, and she wasn't kidding."

Clay laughed. "Our parents built this place and while it's easy to get used to it and take it for granted, we love it and are happy to have your company."

Izzy looked between the two brothers. "We'd love to repay you somehow and thought perhaps we could treat everyone to dinner on Sunday, our last night here in Lavender Valley."

Heath shook his head. "Oh, that's not necessary. Our guest rooms are empty, and it's no trouble at all. I'm afraid we'd be hard-pressed to get into a restaurant on Sunday. Everything is booked for the festival, especially for a party of eleven."

Clay's forehead wrinkled. "As our lovely neighbors will confirm, we like nothing more than hosting a gathering. If you're set on doing something, we could have a barbecue here. We've got a freezer or two full of beef and can grill something, and you ladies could probably get some takeout side dishes from one of the restaurants downtown, or you might be able to talk Heath into letting you use the kitchen." He raised his brows at his brother.

Heath grinned. "They look responsible to me."

Jess looked around the table. "I love the idea of getting some takeout side dishes. Let's investigate that tomorrow before we commit to making anything."

Kate nodded. "Sounds great to me and will keep things simple. We're taking in downtown tomorrow and will make some inquiries."

Lydia glanced over at Heath. "I could handle a simple slab pie for dessert. They'll have lots of fruit at the farmer's market on Saturday."

Heath reached for her hand. "I'll be there anyway, and I'll pick up some berries. Consider it done."

With sleeping arrangements made and plans for a

celebration on Sunday, Georgia took delight in listening to the four women tell them more about San Juan Island. They made it sound lovely, highlighting not only the beauty of the area, but the warm community they loved.

As Sam described the view of the coast from her property, Georgia could picture it. She let her mind wander with the fanciful idea of planning a trip to visit. She and Lee never had much money for travel, and she longed to do a bit of wandering. She vowed to save her pennies while she was living at the farm and tuck some of the money she made at the fabric store away for travel.

Sam offered to let any of them stay if they came to visit. All Georgia would have to do is make the drive and with all that had happened these last months, she knew she could handle it.

CHAPTER EIGHT

F riday, Harry was gone by the time Georgia wandered over to the house for a cup of coffee. She found Lydia icing some fresh cupcakes. Georgia pulled out a chair at the granite counter. "I should have gotten up earlier to wish Harry luck on her speech."

Lydia added a dusting of lavender sugar to the frosted cakes. "I know I feel bad that we can't watch her big moment. Clay and Heath are there and promised to record it for us."

Georgia brought her cup to her lips. "She'll do a fantastic job. I'm going to check with Olivia. We've got goats to dress."

She left with a chuckle and found Olivia and Meg coming from the shelter with the three goldens and Vera following them. As they walked toward the goat pen, Micki came from the fields and joined them. "Once we get the goats handled, I think we're ready. I moved all your totes under the tent, Georgia. We'll just have to help Lydia with hers."

Olivia settled the dogs in the house before they tackled the goats. Georgia unearthed the pajamas, and Lydia stayed behind to finish getting things set up in her area. Georgia and the three others stood at the edge of the pen and surveyed their opponents. They all took a deep breath, and Olivia raised her brows at them. "Ready?"

They nodded and set about wrestling the goats into their pajamas. The goats thought it was a game and took great delight in running from the women and wriggling out of their grasp.

Paisley, who was close to seventy pounds, was more cooperative, and Olivia coaxed her into the special matching fabric outfit that was more of a vest or jacket that covered her back. Georgia equipped it with straps and buckles similar to a dog harness to make it easy to get on and off.

After almost an hour, the four of them got the job done. Glancing down at the mud and straw stuck to her clothes, Georgia was glad she made the decision to shower after that task.

After a quick shower and a change of clothes, she joined the others at the tent, where they were sampling one of Lydia's lavender scones. They'd just filled the dispensers with iced tea and lemonade when the farm officially opened at ten o'clock. Harry left the gate open for easy access, and the four of them stood at the ready, clad in their fresh aprons. In no time, several cars pulled into the field designated for parking, and visitors walked along the driveway to the big tent.

Parents with children, young couples, older couples, and several people on their own filtered by the tent. Laughter filled the air when visitors wandered over to the goat pen and watched them romp around their field.

Georgia stayed busy all day, helping customers select gifts from her selection of handmade items. Between her sales and Lydia's constant stream of customers, Meg only had time for a few short breaks from her duties as the cashier.

Micki and Olivia, with their large-brimmed hats and gardening gloves, spent most of their time helping customers in the fields, and Harry did the same when she returned from town.

Kate, Sam, Izzy, and Jess stopped by to say hello on their way back to the ranch. As Sam looked over Lydia's treats and took a sample cookie, she grinned and wandered over to Georgia's side of the tent. "Her cookies are not only gorgeous, but they're also delicious. What a talent."

Georgia nodded. "I know. She spoils us with her wonderful food."

"Speaking of food, we ordered all the side dishes for Sunday from the Back Door Bistro. We had lunch there, and it was terrific."

"Hopefully, we'll all still be standing by Sunday. We've been steady all day, with barely a minute to run to the ladies room. Thank goodness Lydia was smart enough to make us sandwiches this morning, or we wouldn't have had time to eat."

Sam shook her head. "I'm sorry it's been crazy, but what a testament to all your hard work. We're planning to go back to town tonight for the street dance and were hoping you'd all be there."

Georgia laughed. "I might go for a bit, but I think my dancing days are long over, and I'm beyond tired. The others are younger, so they might be more apt to make a night of it."

Jess hurried up to Sam and tapped her on the shoulder. "We're taking some more photos in the field. Come and join us."

As they rushed off, Georgia promised to see them downtown later and turned to help a couple who were interested in a table runner. A steady stream of visitors and customers strolled through the farm all afternoon. She sold dozens of her creations and lavender soaps and lotions.

It was five o'clock before Georgia had a chance to sit and sip a glass of lemonade. She eyed the totes behind her, happy to see lots of empty space in them. At this rate, she might have to make a few more things to get through the whole festival.

The farm was open until six o'clock on the weekends and with the street dance and barbecue due to start in town, the visitors made their way to their cars and by five thirty, the farm was quiet.

Meg was itching to count the cash in her drawer, and Micki helped her take it and the tablet with all the sales information to the house, while Olivia went to feed the dogs and let them out for some exercise. Harry pitched in and helped Georgia load her product totes on the UTV trailer. Lydia had sold everything, and she and Harry transported the empty totes back to the kitchen.

As Georgia pulled the last of her display items from the table to store in the one remaining tote, a red Mini Cooper came hurrying up the driveway. She frowned as the driver parked near the house instead of the designated field.

A man, wearing a baseball cap, who looked much too tall to fit in the little car came from the passenger door, and a young man climbed from behind the wheel. As Georgia snapped the lid on the tote, she noticed the man pointing at the house and barn as he talked to the younger man, who looked to be a teenager.

After admiring Micki's sunflower mural, they wandered out into the lavender fields. She noticed the man gazing out toward the mountains in the distance. He put his arm around the boy and continued to talk and point around the property.

After a few minutes, the two of them sauntered over to

the tent and stopped in front of Georgia's table. The man smiled at her. "The farm is stunning." He pointed at the young man next to him. "My grandson and I are on a bit of a road trip, and I spent some time in Lavender Valley when I was a kid, so we decided to make a stop here for the festival."

Georgia returned his warm smile, fascinated by the gray stubble along his cheeks and chin. It wasn't often she saw men of that age embrace their graying beard. She turned her attention to the young man. "I saw that snazzy little car of yours. I bet you're having a blast driving it."

His eyes, a vivid blue, twinkled. "It was Grandma Sarah's car, but Grandpa thought we should take it."

The tall man with sturdy shoulders looked at his grandson. "My wife passed away about six months ago, so taking her little Mini makes me feel like she's with us. I know it sounds silly."

"Grandpa says it's not good for cars to sit."

He ruffled the young man's mop of blond hair. "That's right, Chet. We can't let her pride and joy rot away."

The man turned back to Georgia and removed his cap. "Pardon my manners, I should have introduced myself."

Without the cap, Georgia noticed his darker hair, sprinkled with lots of silver and the blue eyes that matched his grandson's. While the silver temples and scruff along his cheeks hinted at his age, his piercing blue eyes reflected a youthful resilience. As she studied him, she gasped. Those eyes. Could it be?

CHAPTER NINE

"Dale?" she asked, her voice unsteady. "Is that you?"

He tilted his head, and the crease in his forehead deepened. "That's right, I'm Dale. Dale Campbell, and this is my grandson Chet." He stared at Georgia. "Have we met?"

Her heart fluttered as she extended her hand to him. "Almost fifty years ago, right here on Jewel's farm." She laughed and said, "I'm—"

"Georgia," he said, shaking his head and reaching for her hand. "Oh, my gosh. I can't believe you're here." He reached across the table and embraced her in a hug. "I was just telling Chet about being a foster kid and how kind Jewel and Chuck were to me."

Georgia blinked back tears. The shy and serious boy she remembered had grown into a handsome and confident gentleman. "I'm the one who can't believe you're here. It's wonderful to see you. I often wondered what happened to you. We knew you were adopted, but nothing more."

The slow smile she remembered peeked out from his scruffy beard. "Yes, I was fortunate to be adopted by a wonderful couple. They both passed away several years ago, but I have them, along with Jewel and Chuck, to thank for giving me such a wonderful start in life. In fact, working with my dad led me to become an electrician."

"That's terrific to hear. Jewel definitely had an impact on so many children."

"So, how long did you live here at the farm?"

"Until I graduated and went to college, with Jewel's help and prodding."

His blue eyes went wide. "Wow, that's great. I was so hopeful she might still be living, but when I looked into coming here, I saw her obituary. I've never forgotten her kindness." He grinned and added, "Or yours, Georgia."

"I'm sorry to hear about the loss of your wife, Dale. I lost my husband last summer, and I understand that heartbreak. We'd been married for so long, it's hard to know what to do. That's part of the reason I'm back here in Lavender Valley."

Meg poked her head under the tent. "Hey, Georgia, Mom said she's going to lock the gate and wondered if you needed any help before we head downtown?"

Georgia turned to her. "I'm fine, dear. This is an old friend of mine who lived here with Jewel when I did. This is Dale Campbell and his grandson Chet. This lovely young lady is Meg, the daughter of one of my friends."

Meg shook hands with Dale and waved at Chet, whose tongue had a hard time untangling itself in his attempt to greet her. He finally got out a few words, his face blotchy with embarrassment.

"Chet's interested in the street dance and festivities." Dale's eyes met Georgia's. "Are you heading downtown, too?"

She sighed at his hopeful expression. "To be honest, I'm exhausted after the long day we've had, but I could probably handle an hour or so."

Dale nodded. "I understand. I'd love to spend some time and catch up with you. Maybe I can run Chet downtown and then come back here and visit?"

Meg looked between the two of them and glanced over at Chet. "I can give Chet a ride, if you'd rather stay here at the farm."

With a huge smile on his face, Chet nodded with enthusiasm.

Dale shrugged. "That works for me. We're staying at the Lavender Valley Inn downtown. You've got your key, right?"

Chet patted his pocket. "Yep, got it right here."

As they discussed details, the four ladies came from the house, ready to head to town. Georgia introduced Dale to all of them. "He lived here with Jewel and Chuck when I was at the farm but wasn't here long before he was adopted."

They took a few minutes to welcome Dale and explain they'd all been foster kids at the farm. His brows arched as he took in their brief introductions. Micki pointed at Meg, waiting impatiently by her borrowed truck. "We better get a move on."

Harry smiled at Dale. "We'll take good care of Chet and make sure he gets back to the inn."

Dale chuckled. "He's a good kid, but I appreciate the mayor looking after him." He winked at Chet. "I'll see you back at the room."

Olivia let Georgia know the dogs were fed, and Lydia whispered that she'd left some soup in the slow cooker they could have for dinner.

Georgia made her way to the porch, waving as the four left in Harry's SUV.

Dale followed Georgia, carrying her display tote and when she opened the front door, the delicious aroma of Lydia's chicken soup greeted them. The three goldens and little Vera rushed to welcome them. Dale laughed as he bent to pet them. "I see Jewel's love of goldens is still thriving."

She set the display tote on the bench by the front door. "They're wonderful. Olivia's taken over Jewel's rescue program and has her same soft heart and gift for healing animals." She put her hand on top of Hope's head. "This is Hope, and she was Jewel's dog. Chief is Harry's, and the beautiful Willow is Olivia's." She picked up the Yorkie. "And this little diva is Lydia's. Her name is Vera."

"Aww, she's a cutie. Sarah and I had a couple of dogs when the kids were growing up, but I think when Sally was in college, we lost the last one and decided we couldn't go through that again. Then, we started traveling more and time slipped by, but I miss having a dog. Especially now."

"They never fail to make me smile." Georgia wandered over to the granite island and looked in the slow cooker. "I'm starving."

He grinned. "I could eat."

She filled bowls with the steaming soup, while he cut slices from a loaf of bread from the bakery. After she filled two glasses with iced tea, Georgia slipped into her chair at the counter, but not before Dale made sure to hold it for her. He took his seat next to her.

With his first taste of the soup, Dale groaned. "Oh, that's good."

"Lydia is a professional chef. She's so talented and spoils us rotten." Georgia went on to explain more about each of her sisters of the heart.

As she continued, he tilted his head, engrossed in the story of Jewel's last wish and her instructions to Harry to find the other four women and convince them to return to the farm. "Before we can elect to sell the property or make any decisions like that, we have to stay here and work the festival and through the fall harvest season in October. We all think she knew we needed to be here. Each of us was facing a difficult change, and this was a place of healing for all of us."

"There's nobody like Jewel. She was a true angel." He finished his soup. "So, you mentioned you lost your husband. Tell me more about where you lived. Did you have children?"

Her smile melted away, and she shook her head. "No children, sadly. Lee, my husband, was a teacher, and I worked at the school library. We lived outside of Boise and enjoyed a quiet life, but we were happy. He became seriously ill, and it wasn't until after he passed away, I discovered he'd taken out a second mortgage on our house, turned in his life insurance policy, and depleted most of our savings. I had to sell our home, and that's when Harry's letter arrived."

Dale frowned; concern etched on his face. "I'm so sorry, Georgia. That had to be incredibly hard, especially when you're already grieving his loss."

She nodded. "I honestly wasn't sure I'd survive it all. Lee handled all our finances and took care of things." She shook her head as her shoulders slumped. "Well, I thought he was. I never suspected a thing."

She took a swallow from her glass and sighed. "Don't judge him too harshly. He was a good and kind man. He had a gambling problem he hid from me and now that I know what he did, I imagine the stress of trying to keep things going contributed to his illness. I wish he would have told me."

With a gentle touch, Dale placed his hand over hers. "He probably wanted to. He might have even tried to, but I'm sure he feared disappointing you more than anything. It's hard for men, especially those of us of a certain age, to admit weakness or risk those we love thinking less of us. It sounds like he was under extreme pressure."

Overwhelmed by Dale's kind words, tears leaked from her eyes. He reached into the pocket of his jeans and pulled out a soft handkerchief. He touched the white fabric to her cheeks, and Georgia closed her eyes. As he dabbed at her face, a hint of citrus drifted over her nose. Something fluttered in her tummy at his gentle and kind touch.

When her cheeks were dry, he handed her the cotton square. "I've shed so many tears since Sarah's illness. You can sympathize with others when they're dealing with a huge loss, but until it happens to you, it's hard to fully understand. It's like a piece of my heart actually broke off the day I lost her."

This time, she reached out and held his hand. "I know exactly what you mean. Tell me about her," she said, with a soft smile.

His eyes lit up as he talked about the woman who'd been by his side since he met her at a business conference. "My old boss was retiring and wanted me to take over his electrical business. I was only twenty, totally inexperienced but so excited at the chance. I went to this conference at a hotel by SeaTac that was designed to help first-time business owners. Sarah was there. She was an accountant and looking for new clients."

Georgia laughed. "A match made in heaven."

His grin widened. "Exactly. I was clueless when it came to bookkeeping. I knew she was the one from the moment we met, and it didn't take long for us to decide to marry and together, we started DS Electrical and a family soon after. We were a great team."

Georgia refilled their glasses, content to let Dale reminisce. Along with telling her about their son and daughter, Mark and Sally, he told Georgia how they worked together to expand their one location into ten more, across the Pacific Northwest. He and Sarah had been transitioning to retirement when she became ill.

Georgia noticed the glint in Dale's eyes as he spoke about the woman he clearly adored. "She was a wonderful wife, mother, and partner. We have a gorgeous home on Lake Stevens, but without her, it's just a house. That's partly why Chet and I are on this trip. He planned to spend the summer with us, and Sally thought I needed the company."

Georgia nodded. "I'm sure he's been great for you. It's wonderful to be around young people. I do miss that since I retired."

"Much like your dogs, Chet always brings a smile to my face. It's been a breath of fresh air to have him at the house. We took a trip over to the San Juan Islands in June. That's a long-time tradition and a yearly treat for the grandkids, but Chet is the last one and so this year, it was just the two of us. Bittersweet."

"Oh, I can only imagine. We had some women here last night visiting from the San Juan Islands. Four of them, and they're lovely. In fact, we're having a barbecue with them over at the Nolan Ranch next door on Sunday. Will you and Chet be around? I'd love to have you come."

His grin widened. "We'd love to. We're here through the weekend. Heading out Monday. Sally lives in Sherman Oaks, California. It's almost seven hundred miles, so a long day, but Chet's young, and he can drive most of the way."

"That little car looks pretty zippy to me."

He laughed. "Yeah, Sarah had a bit of a heavy foot, too. Don't say anything, but I'm going to give Chet the car. He'll be going to college next year, and I'm sure Sarah would love him to have it. She always had a soft spot for him. I never drive it, so I'd rather see him enjoying it."

"Oh, that's a fun surprise. I'm sure he'll be over the moon."

"Sally might not be as enthused. She's in the film industry in Hollywood, makes plenty of money, but she's old school. Made Chet get a job to buy his first car, which is an old Toyota. It's been great for high school, but I think he deserves an upgrade."

"Where is he going to school?"

"Cal Poly. It's over two hours away from where they live. He's interested in engineering and architecture. Smart kid."

"You mentioned your son Mark. Where does he live?"

He waved his hand across the counter. "All the way in Vermont. We only see each other once a year, sometimes twice. He's just a year older than Sally. He's a surgeon and works at the University of Vermont Medical Center. He's a great guy, just busy."

Dale went on to explain Mark was married to a physician and had no children, but Sally had two other children, twin girls in their last year of college in Santa Barbara. The more they talked, Georgia's exhaustion disappeared. She found her second wind and relished the chance to catch up with Dale.

As the hours drifted by, Georgia brewed coffee, stored the leftover soup, and plated up two slices of the leftover cake from last night's paint party. The two of them retired to the couch in the living area. The dogs followed and, to Georgia's embarrassment, piled onto the couch with them. She tried to shoo them off, but Dale laughed. "I'm fine with them. Let them stay."

Hope and Willow nestled close to him, while Vera made camp on Georgia's lap, and Chief sprawled at her feet. Dale took a bite of cake and looked over at Georgia. "Wow, you weren't kidding when you said Lydia could bake."

"Jewel helped her find her passion in the kitchen, like she helped me find my love of sewing and books."

"She and Chuck both encouraged my fascination with horses. Chuck, more so. He always involved me in caring for them and let me ride a few times. He also let me help him tinker and fix things. I had a knack for mechanics and building things, and he helped me discover that. I have only happy memories of the farm."

"Speaking of Chuck, we were just admiring his old Chevy truck. It's in the barn and in need of a little TLC."

Dale's eyes went wide. "I'd love to take a look. Maybe tomorrow or Sunday. I've restored and bought several classics over the years and am partial to Chevrolet." He pointed at his baseball cap that had the iconic bowtie emblem stitched on the front of it.

"That would be wonderful. We'll be here both days, so whenever it works for you. Sunday will probably be less hectic though, and then you can join us for the barbecue."

He reached out and held her hand in his. "I can't believe how lucky I am to reconnect with you after all this time. I had my hopes set on seeing Jewel, but finding you here is the best surprise."

Even with her stomach full from dinner and cake, it quivered at Dale's touch. Georgia's heart warmed at his words, and she found herself captivated by his stunning eyes. It felt wonderful to laugh and remember the good times.

CHAPTER TEN

Saturday, Georgia forced herself out of bed in time to get in a walk. Last night, she and Dale talked until almost midnight, and he left only minutes before the others returned home from the street dance.

After her walk, she helped outfit the goats and Paisley into clean clothes. They'd been a hit with everyone yesterday, especially the children. Micki's eyes lit up when she showed all of them the tags on social media where people had posted photos of the farm and goats, along with the fields and other animals. She used the word viral a few times and although Georgia wasn't a whiz when it came to social media, she understood it was a good thing.

After a shower, coffee, and a fresh muffin, courtesy of Lydia, Georgia was ready to face another day under the tent. As soon as Harry opened the gate, guests poured in, and they didn't stop until they closed at six o'clock.

Georgia looked up from her table to help the last customer and grinned when Dale stood before her. "Looks like you ladies have been busy today."

"Nonstop. It's been wonderful, and people love the farm. Lots of sales and happy customers."

"I was hoping you might join me for dinner. I snagged a reservation at the Riverside Grill."

Despite her tired feet, Georgia couldn't resist. "Give me a few minutes to help with the totes and freshen up, and I'll be ready to go."

He insisted on taking care of loading the totes and while she hurried to her cottage to change clothes, he pitched in and helped the others. With a fresh blouse and a bit of lip gloss, Georgia walked from her cottage and met up with Dale as he came from the barn.

"Olivia let me drive the UTV back to the barn, and I looked at the old truck. She's a beauty."

"It would look fabulous with a fresh coat of shiny yellow paint and our new logo, sitting in the midst of the lavender. We ran out of time to tackle it, and Clay suspects it would cost quite a bit."

Dale offered her his arm. "Yeah, restorations aren't cheap. Not if you want quality. I've got a couple of guys I work with for my cars. I could make a few calls and see what they think."

"Oh, that would be great, thanks."

He led her to the little red car and opened the passenger door for her. She stepped in and gasped. "Oh, my, that is a low seat, isn't it?"

He chuckled and made sure she was settled before he closed the door. He folded himself behind the wheel. "Sarah was petite, and the car fit her, but it takes some getting used to. It's better suited to Chet."

She laughed. "That's for sure. We take bending and climbing for granted in our youth."

They zipped along the quiet country road. She glanced

over at Dale. "What's Chet doing tonight?"

"He's meeting Meg and a couple of her friends from work. There's a concert. Some group I've never heard of, but it seems to appeal to the younger crowd."

"I read about it on the festival flyer, but I don't know them either. I'm still appalled that music from the 70s and 80s is considered oldies. I usually listen to it or country stuff, but I'm not a music aficionado."

He chuckled and took the turn for downtown. He pulled onto the side of Buck's office. He turned and winked at Georgia. "I know people."

She laughed. "Micki is a sweetheart, isn't she? She told all of us if we needed to find parking, Buck's was the place."

He was still laughing when he came around to open her door and give her a hand. "While I was helping with the totes, she told me I could sneak over here and park, since spots are at a premium downtown."

They walked down the sidewalk to Main Street, which was full of cars and people. Georgia couldn't believe the transformation of the quiet town. The sidewalks were crowded with tourists, and all the benches along them were full of people waiting for tables at restaurants.

Even Brick's Pizza and Rooster's had people loitering outside, waiting for a spot. They made their way to the restaurant, and the hostess led them to a table outside with a view of the creek.

As she took the menu, Georgia glanced around the space. Every table was full. She raised her brows at Dale. "I don't know how you managed to get us in tonight. I expected places to be busy, but this is crazy."

He slipped on a pair of reading glasses and grinned. "Persistence and a little luck. That's been the story of my life."

They ordered and sipped on strawberry lemonade while they waited for their food. He told her about the ride he and Chet took around the valley, stopping by a few wineries. He shared he missed working and had turned over the company to a long-time employee who managed it well but was worried about how he'd handle life when Chet went home.

Conversation with Dale was effortless. Despite not seeing each other for almost fifty years, it was like having dinner with an old friend. It had been a long time since she'd enjoyed an evening out and part of her hated to think he would be leaving after tomorrow.

Sunday, Georgia was up early and after her walk, she made a point of soaking the goat pajamas to get the grass and dirt stains out of them before tossing them in the machine to wash.

She should have found some darker print fabrics that would hide the dirt better than the light backgrounds she'd chosen for most of them. As she sipped from her cup of coffee, one by one, the ladies strolled into the kitchen and greeted her while they helped themselves to the fresh brew.

Micki leaned over the counter and sighed. "So, everybody with the festival assures me things will slow down during the week. I sure hope so. Meg and I are planning to visit Jade on Monday, but if it's this busy, we can reschedule."

Harry shook her head. "We'll be fine. I've heard the same from everybody at work. The weekends are packed, but weekdays are slower."

Micki took another sip. "We'll leave early and make it a quick trip. We could be back by noon or one o'clock."

Olivia echoed Harry's reassurance. "We can handle it. No

photographers, no paint events, just people who want to buy a few things and some lavender. The four of us will be fine."

Lydia was busy putting together a crust for her slab pie for tonight. "I'm glad we decided to close at three o'clock on Sundays. It'll be nice to have a breather, and most of the out of towners will leave by then."

Micki nodded. "Next weekend will be busy. I've been told the quilt show brings in a ton of people. There's a local group headlining the concert, too."

Georgia nodded. "Yes, Edith said they have a record number of entries for the quilt show. I need to finish mine up this week."

"We expect to see some blue ribbons hanging around your neck," said Harry, with a smile. She glanced at the clock. "We better get moving and set up."

Lydia stayed behind to finish her pie, and the others pitched in and organized the retail tent. When they were ready, Harry offered to handle opening the gate.

In no time, the field was filled with cars, and customers flocked to the tent to make their purchases, while others wandered into the fields, taking photos and gathering lavender.

Before Georgia knew it, three o'clock was looming. Dale's little red car pulled up to the house, and he emerged toting a white bag. His smile widened when he saw Georgia. Chet walked with him and when they reached the tent, he took charge of the bag.

Meg finished with her customer and looked over at him. "Whatcha got there?"

"Grandpa and I thought you all could use a treat, so we stopped by the ice cream shop."

Meg took a container and spoon and smiled at Chet.

"Thank you." Dale grabbed two containers and two spoons before Chet took off to find the others.

Dale smiled as he handed Georgia hers. "I remember how much you liked those lemon cookies Jewel used to make, so I got you a lemon custard ice cream." He held up his. "I've got rocky road if you'd rather have it. I'm not picky and will eat almost any flavor."

Georgia took the container from him. "Lemon sounds delightful." He joined her behind the table and took the spare chair. Georgia took off the lid and dug her spoon into the pale-yellow ice cream.

"Yum, that is so good. It hits the spot."

Dale nodded. "Just as delicious as I remember it being. We didn't want to spoil dinner but couldn't resist stopping in to the old shop. The lines were so long yesterday, we skipped it, but this afternoon, the crowd has thinned out downtown."

Georgia took another bite. "That's good news. We were hoping the weekdays would be slower. It's been beyond busy here." She eyed the totes behind her. "I think I need to sew a few more things."

"You mentioned you're working at the fabric store, and you have a class this week, right?"

She nodded. "Yes, Tuesday and Wednesday I work and teach a class Tuesday evening. I probably should have held off committing to it. I feel guilty not being here to help at the farm."

Dale gestured to Lydia, who was boxing up some baked goods. "I think the others are very capable and will manage on their own. It's great that you're doing something you enjoy. I have too much time on my hands and need to find something to do."

"You mentioned your cars. Do they keep you busy?"

He shrugged. "Not really, they're all done. I have a bit of

maintenance but not enough to stay busy." He rested his spoon in the empty container and gasped. "That reminds me, I heard back from a guy who has done lots of work for me. He said he can get Chuck's truck in and painted this month. I'd love to handle that and gift it to the farm, in memory of Chuck and Jewel."

"Oh, that's so kind of you. We need to ask the others what they think, but I'm sure they'll love the idea. That's very generous of you. Are you sure?"

He reached over and put his hand on hers. "Georgia, I have the money, and I'd like nothing more than to do some small thing to contribute to this wonderful place. It would be my pleasure."

She smiled and then worry furrowed her brow. "How would we get the truck to him?"

He winked. "I think I have a solution."

CHAPTER ELEVEN

Monday, Georgia woke with a heavy heart. She gazed at the clock and wondered where Chet and Dale were. They'd been on the road for two hours already. Somewhere in northern California, no doubt.

As she walked the property, she breathed in the fresh air and the lovely scent from the fields that calmed her angst. Last night had been such a wonderful evening at the ranch. Not only was the food delicious but sitting around the table, visiting the four ladies from Friday Harbor was such fun.

As it turned out, the resort where Dale and his family went on vacation every year was the same one Sam's husband's family owned. Dale's mood brightened as he visited Sam and the others, who were familiar with the exact cabin they reserved and the gorgeous views it provided. He even remembered going to Sam's coffee shop on their last visit.

Heath and Clay welcomed the case of wine Izzy gifted them from her family's winery, and the group enjoyed sampling it with dinner and lingered over Lydia's berry slab pie and coffee until almost midnight.

As she recalled Dale explaining his idea about Chuck's old truck, her heart lightened. Everyone thought it was a wonderful tribute, and the best part was Dale would be back on Wednesday to pick it up and drive it to his painter in Everett. Georgia offered to pick him up from the airport in Medford.

That meant one more day to visit with him before he left on Thursday. On the last weekend of July, when the festival closed, there was a car show and barn dance. Dale promised his guy would have the truck ready in time, and he'd drive it back to Lavender Valley.

Jewel's Celebration of Life was scheduled to take place the following weekend, in August. Micki and Harry were already working on invitations to invite everyone in Lavender Valley to help them celebrate Jewel's life and legacy with a huge feast at the farm.

Clay and Heath volunteered to man the grills, Lydia was tinkering with a menu, and Harry was assured the special headstone would be installed in time for the event. Dale promised to stay in Lavender Valley the week after the festival so he could be there for the celebration.

Although sad that Dale couldn't stay longer on this visit, Georgia focused on the end of July when he'd be back to stay for a whole week. She'd be done with her classes at the fabric store by then, and she was already looking forward to spending time with her old friend. She'd often wondered what happened to Dale but never dreamed she'd see him again.

During the week, the farm closed at three o'clock and on Monday, they soon discovered they didn't need everyone working and could get by with two people at the retail tent and one other to watch over the fields. With Tyler on hand to help people in the fields, Harry worked out a schedule to give everyone a day off during the week.

At noon, Georgia's phone chimed with a text from Micki. She and Meg were running later than they thought. As Georgia sat in the chair by the cash register, with no customers and only a few people roaming the fields, Georgia assured her they were fine and not to rush.

Most of the people who visited on Monday were considered more local to the area, from neighboring towns only a short distance from Lavender Valley. They sold a few products and some fresh cut lavender, with Lydia's homemade treats attracting most of the business, but the pace was much more laid back than it had been over the weekend.

When three o'clock rolled around, the parking field was already empty and in no time, they had the cash sheet balanced and everything stored in the barn for the next day. Georgia and Harry were helping Lydia with her totes, and Olivia was tending to the dogs, when Micki and Meg drove up to the house.

Meg was beaming as she stepped from Micki's SUV. Micki, on the other hand, looked wrung out and stressed, her shoulders hunched. Meg skipped up the porch steps and took the totes from Georgia, offering to help Lydia put things away in the kitchen.

Georgia and Harry hung back and met Micki at the bottom of the steps. "What's wrong?" asked Harry.

Micki sighed and shut her eyes for a few seconds. "They're releasing Jade early. They wanted to do it Friday, but I put them off until Monday. She's progressed as much as they think she can, and they've arranged for outpatient therapy. She's got some permanent damage to her leg and arm. The social worker is helping her with applying for disability benefits."

She pointed at the house. "Meg is so happy and excited. Of course, she thinks we can just have her stay here." Tears pooled in her eyes. "I'm not so coldhearted that I don't want to help her, it's just the worst possible timing. I'm also not looking forward to being around her. I've been trying to research group homes for her, but there isn't much available. Waiting lists are a mile long."

Georgia put her arm around Micki's shoulders. "Between the five of us, we'll figure something out. Let's get you inside and have a cup of tea."

Meg came out the door, dressed in her uniform for the veterinary clinic. "I need to run. I promised I'd go to the clinic when I got home and help for a few hours." She hurried off with a wave.

Olivia came in from feeding the dogs, and the five of them gathered around the dining room table, comforted with a pot of tea and a plate of cookies courtesy of Lydia's stash. Harry asked about Jade's court date, which had been postponed until her medical release, and Micki confirmed it was set for the week she would be released.

After Micki explained, Harry sighed. "Most likely, with her ongoing therapy and disability, the court will take her license for a year or more and give her some sort of probation or house arrest. From what I know, the county will want to steer clear of incurring a huge medical liability by incarcerating her, when she's essentially housebound anyway."

Micki took a bite of her cookie. "Yep. No car, no license,

no assets, no skills, no belongings. She is in a sorry state for a fifty-year-old woman. They don't know how much she'll get in disability benefits, but it won't be much."

Lydia took a sip from her cup. "I might have an idea. Heath and I have been talking about dates for the wedding. Neither of us are inclined to wait and drag out a long engagement. We want a simple ceremony with family and maybe a few close friends. We were looking at doing it in early August, after the festival. I could move into the house at the ranch a little early and let Jade use my motorhome."

Georgia smiled and nodded. "That would keep her from being underfoot but close enough if she needed help, we'd be nearby. That sounds like a good solution. What do you think, Micki?"

Micki's tired eyes looked across the table at Lydia. "That's so kind of you. I know how much you love Gypsy, and it sounds like it might work, but I'd hate for Jade to damage it or worse."

Lydia's blue eyes sparkled. "I think my motorhome days are over. So, as much as I love Gypsy, I have no intention of living in it again. I'm sure Jade will be fine in it. Plus, it's not overwhelming when it comes to taking care of it."

Olivia reached over and put her hand on Micki's arm. "You mentioned she was working with a social worker. Does she see a counselor or go to therapy sessions?"

Micki nodded. "Yes, she's been doing group sessions with a therapist who comes to the rehab center, and they can set her up with a local therapist to help her transition to her new normal. As much as I don't trust her, she has apologized and expressed remorse at what she's done. I've just been on this ride before. She's very manipulative."

Harry put her mug on the table. "I wonder if we could frame this as a temporary measure. Let her stay in the motorhome until a group home opens up and place some conditions on her being here. She has to contribute and help in some way. I'm not sure what her medical restrictions are, but I bet between the animals, garden, and housework, we could find something she could do."

Micki nodded. "She's got Meg wrapped around her finger, but Meg is going to fly back to Colorado in two weeks. She wants to get settled and see her friends before school starts. It will be easier to keep Jade accountable without Meg in the midst. I thought about seeing if I could find somewhere for Meg to stay and move Jade into her room, but the stairs would be a problem."

Harry's eyes widened. "I could move upstairs and let her have my room."

Micki shook her head. "This is just what I didn't want to happen. I don't want everyone's life disrupted because of her. She's my problem."

Georgia caught Micki's tear-filled eyes. "We're all family now. You don't have to face everything on your own. We can help. Between all of us, we ought to be able to keep an eye on one middle-aged woman, who by all accounts can't move too quickly." She smiled at Micki. "We can manage. Look at all we've been through. I don't think Jade will break us."

Lydia nodded. "Gypsy is the perfect solution. I'd much rather stay in the guest room at the ranch where Heath and I can spend more time together and get the wedding planned, plus work on another venture we're considering."

Olivia raised her brows. "Do tell."

"I've been trying to figure out what I'm going to do once we're married. With my love of cooking, it's not something I want to give up, and I'm not sure I want to work in a restaurant. Heath talked about helping me open a new place in Lavender Valley, but owning a restaurant is so much work. I suggested we have a food truck. He and I could both work in it but do it seasonally or for special events. It would give us more flexibility, and the overhead costs are low."

Micki's eyes brightened. "That sounds perfect for you. Having a food truck at the farm during the festival next year would be a wonderful addition." She looked around the table and sighed. "I appreciate all of you so much. As much as I'm not excited about having Jade here, I think Lydia's idea of letting her stay in the motorhome makes the most sense. I hope she'll behave while she's here, and I'll do everything I can to find her a group home or a place she can afford. Thank you for your willingness to help me."

Harry nodded. "Like Georgia said, that's what families do. We'll just make a pact not to leave her here on her own until we know she's capable and responsible. With you working from home, that shouldn't be a problem and if you have to be gone, one of us will make sure we're here."

Lydia took another sip from her cup. "Yes, and even after I'm married, you can count on me. I'm not disappearing, I'll just be next door."

Tears spilled onto Micki's cheeks. "I'm not sure what I'd do without all of you."

Lydia stood and gestured toward the kitchen. "I think we deserve a celebration after all that. I've got some leftover pie that needs eaten."

Wednesday afternoon, Georgia must have checked the time on her watch over a dozen times. Edith had given her permission to close the shop an hour early so she could make the drive to Medford and meet Dale at the airport.

Neither Tuesday or Wednesday was busy, so in addition

to finishing her quilt projects for the upcoming show, Georgia was able to get several more aprons and table runners made for the farm.

Last night, after a quick bite for dinner at the Grasshopper, she was back at the shop to greet her beginning quilting class. There were only five students, which made things easy. Two mothers and daughters, plus a young pregnant woman were her pupils. Georgia chose to teach them an easy quilt that she could make in a day. It was a small size, perfect for a crib. She showed them the sample of hers, a red, white, and blue themed piece.

All five of her students had returned to the shop on Wednesday to work on their projects. Edith had several sewing machines set up in the store, which made the sewing portion go quickly. Last night, they'd succeeded in using the cutting wheel and straight edge to cut all their squares and rectangles and had time to sew a few of them together, where Georgia stressed the importance of keeping the seams even and straight and using the iron to flatten them as they went along.

By the time she was ready to close the shop, all five of them had made good progress and were more comfortable with the process. Georgia took great delight in their increased confidence and couldn't wait to see their finished projects.

At four o'clock, she locked the door and hurried to her car. It didn't take long to get to Medford, and she found Dale waiting for her outside the small airport. He stowed his suitcase and slid into the passenger seat, greeting her with a huge smile.

"How was your trip?" she asked, merging back onto the highway.

"Sally put up a bit of a fuss about the car, but it didn't take long for her to bend, and Chet is thrilled about it. Sally got divorced last year and sometimes gets prickly when I try to help out. She's determined to do it all on her own."

She glanced over at Dale. "I'm sure she understands the significance of her mom's car. It's not a handout; it's a treasured memory. Something special for Chet."

He reached across the console and took her hand in his. "Exactly, and that's how I phrased it to make her accept it."

As they approached the outskirts of Lavender Valley, Georgia said, "Clay and Heath insist you stay at the ranch tonight. They took the truck down and got new tires put on it, so you're set for the drive. Harry verified it's licensed and insured. I thought we could stop in town and have dinner."

"That sounds terrific and as much as I don't like to impose on them, staying at the ranch would be wonderful. I enjoy talking with them. They're both such great guys. When I come back at the end of the month, I'd love a tour of their property."

She nodded as she turned onto Main Street. "I'm sure they'd love to show you around, and I agree. Harry and Lydia hit the jackpot with those two." She pulled into a parking spot. "Does Rooster's work? I'm craving a burger."

He smiled and hurried around to open her door for her. "I'd be happy sharing a peanut butter and honey sandwich as long as I was with you, but Rooster's sounds great."

"Oh, now you've reminded me of Jewel's famous peanut butter and honey sandwiches. They were so yummy." She slipped her arm through his, and they made their way down the block. Downtown was busier than before the festival, but the hordes of people from the weekend had disappeared. It was easy to get a booth by the window.

While they waited for their meal, Dale flipped through his phone and showed her photos of some of his cars. "Chip, he's the guy I'm taking the truck to, has done some great work for me. I can't wait to see what he does with Chuck's pride and joy."

His enthusiasm for building cars and restoring them made Georgia smile. Not only was Chuck's truck a wonderful gift and tribute, but she loved to see the spark of excitement it created for Dale. It would make his trip home alone have a purpose and much less sad.

As she listened and took in the photos of his beloved 1969 Camaro, a classic Chevelle, and a 1957 Chevy, the decades melted away. The blue eyes she remembered from her youth twinkled as Dale smiled and explained how he'd taken each of them from junk to gems.

Their server brought their platters and as Georgia bit into her juicy burger, and they both reached for some fries from the plate they were sharing, her hand brushed against Dale's, and a spark of electricity buzzed through it. She wished this night could last forever.

CHAPTER TWELVE

When Georgia woke on Friday, she checked her phone and smiled. Dale had already messaged her to wish her a happy day. Last night, when she got home from delivering her entries for the quilt show and sticking around to help Edith set up the quilt displays in the community center, Dale called.

After his long day on the road and delivering the truck to Chip's shop, he was tired but glad to be home, relaxing on his patio with a rare, but well-deserved, cold beer. He sent her a photo of his view of the water in the distance. It was breathtaking as the last of the swath of pink light touched the horizon. The wistfulness in his voice was evident as he talked about how much he loved the house he and Sarah built over fifteen years ago. He'd found the seven-acre property with a view and couldn't resist it. Their grandchildren had enjoyed it with them, especially the game room and huge yard, until they moved away a few years ago.

She recognized the hint of loneliness in his voice.

Her mind drifted to Wednesday, when after visiting over their burgers, they wandered around downtown, and he treated her to an ice cream cone while they sat on a bench. They talked about their earlier lives with Dale opting for trade school, setting him up for a successful career and Georgia's time at college where she met her dear husband Lee.

One of the many things she admired about Dale was his quiet dignity and deep love he had for his wife. He spoke of her with such tenderness. Despite his business success and all that it brought, Dale was still the kind and humble boy she remembered, just a few decades older.

After their ice cream, they held hands as they walked back to the car. His hands, roughened by years of hard work, were a testament to his dedication and work ethic. Georgia touched the palm of her hand and remembered how wonderful it felt to rest it against Dale's hand.

It had been a perfect evening, but with Dale getting up early to hit the road and get back to Washington, they'd made it an early night. She dropped him at the ranch, and he left her with a long and heartfelt hug, along with a promise to see her at the end of the month.

She would miss his hearty laugh and the sparkle of his eyes, but at least she knew he would be back, and he'd already made good on his promise to keep in touch via texts and phone calls.

She hurried outside for her morning walk and took a photo of the lavender fields with the mountains that looked almost purple in the morning light behind them. It reminded her of the painting she'd done with the others. She tapped her phone a few times and sent Dale the photo and a quick message letting him know she was thinking of him.

After a hot shower, she collected the additional items she'd made at the fabric store and met up with Lydia in the kitchen. As soon as she stepped into the kitchen, the scent of something that reminded Georgia of pumpkin pie made her stomach growl. The aroma of fresh coffee led her to the pot where she poured a large mug for herself.

"What smells so yummy?" she asked, taking her first sip of the warm brew.

Lydia smiled. "I was in the mood for pumpkin scones." She was busy getting a cooling rack set up on the counter. "Did you hear from Dale? I was a little worried about him driving that old truck so far."

Georgia settled into a chair at the counter and held the warm mug in her hands. "He called last night. He made it home fine. Just a long day."

Lydia added cinnamon to the glaze she was stirring. "We were all talking last night about how cute it is that you and Dale reconnected after all these years. He's such a sweetheart of a guy."

Georgia's heart did a little flip. "Yes, so unexpected, but it's been wonderful to see him again. He was so shy and a bit unsure of himself when he was here at the farm. Chuck was so good to him, along with Jewel, of course. He wasn't here long, and I often wondered what became of him. I'm so glad to know he was adopted by loving parents."

Lydia readied an oven mitt. "Chet's a cute kid, too."

Georgia chuckled. "Yes, Dale said it took some convincing to get his daughter to agree to the gift of the Mini Cooper, but Chet is on cloud nine."

Taking one of the baking sheets from the oven, Lydia laughed. "He'd get my vote for favorite grandpa of all time."

As Georgia watched her set the scones on the rack to

cool, her mouth watered. She lowered her voice. "Micki seemed a little better yesterday. I feel so bad for her having to deal with Jade, and I hope her sister behaves. It was so kind of you to offer her the use of your motorhome. At least that will give Micki a little space from her."

With the scones cooling, Lydia dipped a finger into the glaze to test it. "I know what it's like to need a second or third chance, and I understand how hard this is for Micki. Usually, I'm the one who usually needs help, so it feels nice to be able to help someone else for a change."

Georgia finished her last swallow of coffee and rinsed her mug. She put a hand on Lydia's shoulder. "I don't think you realize how strong you are, Lydia."

She shrugged and smiled at Georgia. "I've got to glaze these, and then they'll be ready. It might be the only chance we'll have to eat today." She laughed as she drizzled the cinnamon glaze across the scones.

"They look delicious." Georgia pointed at the new items she left on the dining table. "I'm going to run out and get my totes moved so I can add in these new items. I'll be back in a few. Save me a scone."

Georgia made quick work of hauling the totes and returned the UTV to the barn. By the time she got back to the house, Micki and Harry were gathered in the kitchen, sipping coffee, brewing tea, and adding scones to their plates. Moments later, Olivia, her furry brood at her heels, came through the mudroom and into the kitchen.

The goldens and Vera wandered over to the area rug by the dining table and stretched across it, waiting for belly rubs. Georgia obliged them, bending over each one to pet them and scratch under their chins. Olivia set her plate on the table and glanced over at them. "I took them on an extra-long walk, so they should be ready for a nap." She laughed and added, "I carried Vera most of the way home, but the others got in some good exercise."

Georgia gave Hope one last pet and then stood and took a few steps toward the kitchen. "They're such good dogs." She washed her hands in the sink and collected a scone and a cup of tea before settling in next to Olivia.

As Micki sat, she slipped her phone in her pocket and smiled. "I emailed Chip the logo for the truck. He's going to paint it on the doors."

Harry joined the group. "I heard from the stone mason this morning, and he's got the headstone done. He's going to install it later this week, so we'll be set for the celebration."

Lydia took the chair next to Micki. "I think I've got the menu finalized for it. Heath and Clay are going to barbecue brisket and ribs, plus a few kabobs. I'm doing baked beans, potato salad, that bruschetta salad everybody loves, a fruit salad, a cake, and maybe some brownies or cookies. With it being outdoors, I'm trying to keep it simple."

Harry's eyes widened. "If that's your idea of simple, I'd hate to see complicated. Seriously, that sounds fabulous. Jewel would love it all."

Micki laughed. "And now I'm already thinking about dinner." She turned her attention to Olivia. "I have the flyer done for the pet parade next weekend. Meg is so excited she'll be here for that."

"Oh, that's great," she said. "We'll just have to decorate the trailer Clay and Heath have for us. It'll be sort of like a float but not that extravagant. They'll pull it in the parade, and we're going to have a little pen set up for a few of the goats and Paisley. Then, we'll have all the dogs, of course."

Harry finished the last bite of her scone. "As long as you don't have those pesky chickens on the float, I'll be there. They really don't like me."

They all giggled, and Olivia promised no chickens. They finished off their scones and then pitched in to help Lydia clean up the kitchen and get her goodies hauled outside. By ten o'clock, they stood ready to greet their visitors and kick off the weekend.

By Sunday afternoon, Georgia was exhausted. Three o'clock couldn't arrive soon enough to suit her. The last three days had been even busier than the opening weekend. She surveyed her totes and shook her head. The table runners and aprons were almost gone. She would have to find some time to sew a few more.

All the ladies were anxious to close for the day and go into town to check out the quilt show. Clay even made a reservation at the Riverside Grill early in the week and wanted to treat everyone to dinner.

Once they had the retail space buttoned up, Georgia fed the dogs in the house, while Olivia tended to the dogs in the shelter. After they all changed clothes, four of them piled into Harry's SUV with Micki and Meg following them in hers and headed to town.

Harry parked in her spot at City Hall, and Micki left her car at Buck's office. She and Meg met up with them as they arrived at the community center. Edith sat at the main information table and when she saw Georgia, her face filled with a wide grin. She rose and hurried over to greet her.

"Georgia, you're the belle of the ball. You won every category you entered, and your lavender quilt honoring the festival was awarded Best in Show. I have your five-hundred-dollar prize for that."

Georgia gasped. "I had no idea there was prize money involved."

Edith laughed and took her by the arm. "Only for Best in Show. The other prizes are ribbons and gift certificates, but Benson's Food and Hardware, along with Ranchland, sponsored the prize money. I'm so thrilled you won. That quilt is a beauty."

Curt from the newspaper was on hand to take a photo of Georgia next to her winning quilt. He positioned the other squares she'd made with their blue ribbons attached around her, so she was surrounded by all her work.

After shaking hands with spectators and other quilters, Georgia extracted herself from the spotlight and found her sisters waiting for her by Edith's table. They all engulfed her with hugs and congratulatory wishes.

Harry pointed at the display. "Do we need to help you take those down?"

She shook her head. "No, Edith said she'll take them back to the shop. She wants to display them there for the rest of the festival."

"Shall we head over to meet the guys for dinner? Clay texted and said he and Heath have the table."

Olivia slipped her phone into her pocket. "Duke is on his way."

Micki chuckled and said, "Buck texted and said he just walked through the door."

Georgia waved goodbye to Edith and let Harry lead her down the block. "I feel like a superstar with her entourage."

Micki smiled at her. "That's exactly what you are, and you deserve all those awards. Your work is fantastic."

The heat of embarrassment crept up from Georgia's neck and colored her cheeks. Never one to seek out attention, Georgia was overwhelmed. She couldn't help but wonder how much richer her life would have been had she met these four women decades ago.

Over the years, she always wished she could have found her sister. She longed for a bond, a family she could count on no matter what. This, this warmth and love, was what she wanted and now, she had not just one, but four sisters.

CHAPTER THIRTEEN

Monday morning, the five of them gathered for their last breakfast with Lydia living on the property. It was bittersweet but with her being next door, it wasn't like she was leaving town. Still, they all told her how much they would miss her.

With tears in her eyes, Lydia promised when the festival was over and the wedding was behind her, she was committed to hosting Sunday dinners. "I already talked to Heath about it, and he loves the idea. So, you've all got a standing invite to come to the ranch for dinner. If you can't make it, not a big deal, but you're all welcome."

Harry nodded. "I like that idea. I just have one concern." She gave them all what could only be described as her cop face.

Lydia arched her brows. "Yeeess."

"How do you feel about delivering scones and muffins for breakfast?"

The others burst out laughing. Olivia nodded. "Yes,

you've spoiled us for far too long. It's going to be hard to let you go."

Lydia smiled and reached out for Olivia's hand. "I'm sure I could stock the freezer with a few things each week."

Micki sighed. "Thank goodness. Oh, and your panzanella. Maybe you can show us how to make that. Or I could just bring you the fresh tomatoes and herbs from my garden, and you could make it for us."

"I think I've created four monsters," said Lydia, reaching for her cup.

Georgia met Lydia's eyes. "It's wonderful to be so loved, isn't it? I was thinking of that last night at dinner. All of you fawning over me and celebrating my quilts. It was just lovely. I'm truly blessed to have found all of you."

Micki slipped her arm around Georgia's shoulders. "We feel the same way. I can't imagine my life without the four of you."

Georgia took a sip of tea. "I also figured out what I want to do with my winnings." She turned to Micki. "I'd like to use it to buy Jade some clothes, shoes, a few things. You said she has nothing, and I think we all know what that feels like."

Tears fell from Micki's eyes as she leaned against Georgia. "You're the best."

Olivia glanced across the table at Micki. "I know Jade has always let you down and each time you've trusted her, or she's promised to change, she failed. Believe me, I understand that sense of betrayal. This time, I hope, with all of us here to help her and you, it might be different. She's had months away from the life she led and if we give her a good start and a little support, it could help."

Micki sat up and shrugged. "I do hope it works and things are better for her. Like you said, I've been let down so many times, it's hard to believe in her."

Georgia gave Micki's hand a squeeze. "The difference is this time, you're not alone, and neither is Jade. She'll have to be accountable to more than just you. Like Jewel did with each of us, we have to help her find her gift and nurture it."

Harry stood to take her dishes to the sink. "I'm cynical a bit, like you, Micki. I've seen the worst of people over and over, and I understand you're tired of the games Jade plays. We can give her boundaries and rules. She's going to have five people watching out for her and watching over her to make sure she doesn't falter. She's not going to have any freedom without a car and license and being out here so far from town. Like Olivia and Georgia, I think this time might be different."

Micki sighed. "I hope you're right. Thank you all so much. It means the world to me. I'm going to head over to Medford and pick her up around two o'clock."

Georgia caught her eye. "I'll come with you, and we can stop to get her some clothes or let her pick some out on the way home."

Micki smiled. "That's a great idea."

Harry stepped back into the dining area. "I'll pick up pizzas tonight. We can celebrate her arrival."

Lydia added, "I'll make a dessert to go with it, and we'll all be here tonight to welcome her. I can show her around Gypsy a little, so she knows how everything works. It's all cleaned up and ready for her."

Micki took the last sip from her cup. "I've been dreading this, more than you know. But you've all made it so much easier."

Georgia and Micki headed outside to take the first part of the day, so they could leave early for their road trip.

A few minutes before two o'clock, Micki parked the car in the parking lot of the rehab center. Georgia followed her to a small conference room, where Micki introduced her to Jade's social worker, Paula. She welcomed them both with a quick smile and offered them bottles of water.

Georgia studied the woman, with graying hair and a no-nonsense blouse and jeans. Her casual appearance put Georgia at ease, but as she discussed Jade's situation, it was clear she was all business and had been around the block a few times.

Micki explained Jade would be staying on the farm, living in a motorhome that a friend offered. She also made it clear she'd have responsibilities on the farm and be expected to pitch in and help with chores.

Paula nodded as she scribbled a few notes. "That's good. She needs structure. Rigid structure is best for her. She's going to continue with counseling, and I found one in Lavender Valley willing to take her." She passed Micki a sheet of paper. "She's set up for twice a week appointments and physical therapy on the same days."

While Micki studied the list, Paula flipped a page in the file. "She has to make a court appearance later this week, on Thursday, in Lavender Valley. Her public defender has already been in discussions with the prosecutor, and they've agreed to a plea deal with probation, loss of her license for a year, counseling, and mandatory drug testing. If she violates, she'll go to jail."

Micki nodded. "Does Jade understand all of that?"

Paula moved her reading glasses down to the tip of her nose. "She does. I've explained it, as well as the public defender. We've made it very clear. This is her last chance to avoid jail. Provided the judge accepts the plea, which we think he will because of Jade's medical condition and ongoing issues."

Georgia met Paula's gaze. "Does she have certain medical restrictions?"

Paula glanced over another sheet of paper in the file. "She's got limited use of her leg and one arm, which is still in a brace. Lifting anything over five pounds with that arm won't be possible until she progresses more with therapy. She has no computer skills or other marketable skills and with her lack of ability to work as a laborer in a physical type of setting, it makes it tough. Now, that doesn't mean she can't do some cleaning, help take care of things around the house, stuff like that. She just doesn't have the physical stamina to work a job. Her disability is in process, and I suspect it will be approved in the next month."

Micki pointed at Georgia. "We're going to stop on the way home. Georgia has kindly offered to treat her to some clothes and shoes, things she'll need to start fresh."

Paula smiled. "That's a lovely gesture, and I'm sure Jade will appreciate it. She's worried about what's going to happen to her. She understands she has nothing and knows staying with you, Micki, is a temporary solution." She sighed and closed the file. "Like I told you before, she's on a waiting list for several group homes, but it could take months, even a year, to get her into one of them or any type of housing."

Micki bit into her bottom lip. "I understand. I honestly don't know what's going to happen in the future. My stay in Lavender Valley might be over at the end of the year, but I have a home in Washington. It really depends on Jade and her behavior and attitude. This is her last chance with me, too."

As she stood and collected the file, Paula nodded. "Jade understands that, too. I think being clean and sober and enduring all the painful therapy has had a huge impact on her. She shows remorse, and I believe she's sincere, especially when it comes to you and Meg. Over the years, I've seen lots of good actors and been tricked by a few. I've watched Jade when she didn't know I was there, and I believe her intention to start again and be better is authentic. She just needs a very short leash right now."

Micki gestured toward Georgia. "You know I was a foster kid. Georgia was also. We and three other women are living at our foster mother's farm. She passed away in December and wanted all of us to come home. None of us had ever met. We all lived with her at different times, but she thought we needed our sisters of the heart."

Georgia smiled and looked at Paula. "She was right. Now, the five of us are there and between all of us, we'll keep a close eye on Jade."

Tears filled Paula's eyes. "That is such a heartwarming story. I've been doing this a long time and worked for a few years in the foster system. We don't get too many happy endings, so hearing your wonderful story makes my heart happy. What a wonderful foster mom you had."

Georgia nodded. "Her name was Jewel and as we like to say, she was a true gem."

With a smile, Paula led them out of the room. "Jade is ready and waiting in the lounge. She's got a cane for a little balance support since her leg has a brace, which may be a permanent situation, but only time will tell. Her right arm is also still in a brace, but the therapist is hopeful she'll regain much of her strength in it."

Georgia noticed the angst in Micki's eyes. She put an arm around her. "It's going to be okay."

Micki introduced Georgia to her sister, and Jade's beautiful eyes lit up when she explained Georgia was treating her to some new clothes. "That's nice of you, thank you."

Micki fetched her SUV, and Georgia waited with Jade under the shade of the portico. Georgia let Jade have the front seat and stood ready to help her should she need it. With slow and deliberate motions, Jade finally settled in and wedged her cane next to her. Georgia shut her door before climbing into the backseat.

Micki drove to the shopping center they'd found with a discount store and a consignment shop with good reviews. Micki led the way to it first, and Jade surveyed the racks and selected several things to try on in the dressing room.

Micki went in with Jade to help her in and out of her clothes, while Georgia took a chair and waited for the fashion show. The shop was having a buy-one get-two free sale and for less than a hundred dollars, they were able to find several pants, tops, sweaters, some slip-on shoes, a cross-body handbag that would be easy for her to use, and even a nice winter coat.

Next, they went across the parking lot to the discount store and found undergarments, sleepwear, and toiletries. Jade couldn't stop smiling and thanked Georgia over and over for her generosity.

With the bags stowed in the back of the SUV, they headed back to Lavender Valley. Micki made one last stop at Ranchland. "I'll be right back," she said, leaving Jade and Georgia to wait in the car.

Jade sighed as she watched her sister hurry to the store. "Thanks for being so nice to me, Georgia. I'm sure Micki told you all the horrible things I've done and how I ended up like this. I'm going to try my best to prove to her that I can be a better person. I've been a lousy sister, and I know it's unfair to expect her to help me now."

Georgia couldn't see Jade's face. Only the top of her head, with her short strawberry-blond hair was visible. Like Paula, Georgia had interacted with thousands of kids over her career working at the school library. She liked to think she had a good BS meter and listening to Jade, Georgia agreed with Paula. Jade sounded sincere and filled with remorse.

Georgia took a deep breath and channeled her librarian voice. "While I think it's admirable that Micki knows you're sincere and sorry about the past and that you take responsibility for what you've done, the most important thing you can do is to show her you've changed. Demonstrate that in all that you do. You can be kind and responsible and let her know how much you appreciate this chance she's giving you. The past is over and done, but you're in charge of your future. Micki is an absolute treasure. You're so blessed to have a sister like her and a lovely niece like Meg. But Micki is our sister, too. The four of us who are linked by the wonderful farm where you'll be staying, we'll protect her and stand by her. We'll be there to help you, too, but if you hurt her, you'll have four of us to contend with."

Jade didn't have time to respond before Micki opened the door, but Georgia was confident her message had been received. Micki tossed a pair of green waterproof boots covered with yellow bumble bees and a pair of gloves on the backseat. She slid behind the wheel and glanced over at her sister. "You can't work on a farm without the proper gear."

Georgia smiled as she glanced in the rearview mirror and noticed Micki wink at her. This would be interesting.

CHAPTER FOURTEEN

Thursday, Georgia was up early, intent on keeping up with her walking schedule. As she made her way to the creek, her cell phone chimed. She smiled at Dale's name on her screen.

"Good morning," she said, her voice light and full of happiness.

"I figured you'd be on your walk, and I'm on mine. I liked chatting with you yesterday while we walked. It made it feel like we were walking together."

She chuckled. "I feel the same way. It's nice to have the company."

"Well, this will be my fourth day of going back to the office. I honestly don't think it's going to work for me. I promised myself I'd give it a full week before I decided, but they don't really need me there. It's really hard to walk by Sarah's old office and see another person there. It's all different. Nothing is the same." He sighed. "Derek, my manager, is more than capable of running things, and everyone is so kind and nice, but I sort of feel like I'm just in the way. It's just a place to go that's familiar."

"I understand that feeling, and it would be hard to see Sarah's chair filled by someone new, no matter how wonderful the new person is. I was just trying to come to terms with Lee's passing when I found out I had to sell the house. I can't tell you how devastated I was. I loved our home, and I didn't even have time to adjust to him being gone, before all my memories of our life together were gone too. Being here, with the others, I feel so much better. I was sinking into a deep despair, especially after falling and messing up my shoulder."

"I don't know how you did it, Georgia. That would break me. I also think when you're grieving, everything else that goes wrong is amplified. So, another problem, like your shoulder, adds a huge weight to an already impossible load. I really admire your strength."

She wished she had brought a bottle of water with her. The dry lump in her throat could use it. She swallowed and said, "Life isn't easy, is it? I'm trying shift my focus from not only cherishing my old memories and life, but to making new memories and finding my new path forward."

Dale chuckled. "I'm a little bit of a slow learner. I think I'm mastering that lesson this week, Georgia. It's clear I need to shift my focus to making some new memories. But, enough of the sad stuff. How's that float coming for the parade?"

"I haven't been over to check it out. I haven't had a spare minute with working these last two days. I might sneak over tonight and take a look. Olivia and Micki are doing most of the planning, so I'm sure it will be fabulous. Now that Jade's here, I know they've tasked her with helping."

"How's it going with her and Micki?"

"Lukewarm. Micki is trying, but Jade isn't the easiest person. She's lacking in social skills and social graces. I think Jade is trying too, but it's like she's in a foreign country and doesn't speak the language. Jade has a tendency for drama, so that gets old. She's never had a job, and Olivia is having her help with the dogs and showing great patience with her. Micki doesn't trust her anywhere near the retail space and the cash drawer, so it's hard to find things for her to do, but we'll get through it. She goes to court today, so that will be more excitement."

"I wouldn't want to be in her shoes. Starting over with nothing at fifty doesn't sound easy to me."

Georgia nodded as she turned back toward the house. "Jade's not going to have an easy time of it. Micki's holding out hope they find her some housing, but I think it's going to be months before that happens. Hopefully, they'll settle into a routine, and I think once Meg goes back to school, it will be easier. She coddles Jade."

"Ugh. That has to make it worse for Micki. Well, give her a hug from me. I'm almost home. I'm going to lunch with Derek today. I think I'll break it to him that tomorrow is my last day in the office."

She burst out laughing. "Something tells me he'll be okay with that."

He chuckled and promised to talk to her tomorrow, if not before.

She tucked her phone into her pocket and quickened her pace. Talking to Dale always made her feel better. It was a lovely way to start her day and made her realize how much she missed the companionship of being part of a couple. She understood what Dale was dealing with at his office. His partner was gone.

Thursday afternoon, when the farm closed, Lydia and Vera left for the ranch to work on wedding details and Olivia and Willow were at Duke's with a new rescue she picked up earlier in the day. Georgia and Harry closed down the retail tent and stored the totes in the barn and carried Lydia's into the mudroom to be refilled tomorrow.

Nobody was in the mood to cook dinner, so Harry took out a pan of Lydia's enchiladas from the freezer. The two of them sat at the island with a well-deserved glass of iced tea topped with a splash of Lydia's lavender lemonade, with Chief and Hope resting at their feet.

As they relaxed, Micki drove into the yard. After several minutes, she and Jade came through the door. From the scowl on Jade's face, Georgia was afraid to ask how her court hearing went.

Micki deposited her bag and smiled at the two of them. "That drink looks good. Do you want something, Jade?"

"No," she snapped. "I'm going to go lie down. I'm exhausted."

Micki continued to the kitchen. "Suit yourself. Looks like we're having enchiladas for dinner."

Jade made her way through the kitchen, and the mudroom door slammed behind her. Micki came around the corner with a tall glass of iced tea and plopped down in a chair next to the couch. "I'm not sure I'm going to survive having Jade here."

Harry raised her brows. "What happened?"

"Well, it started with her physical therapy appointment. Jade didn't like the lady. She was all business and not too sympathetic. Jade likes to be the victim, and the lady was focused on getting through the exercises and didn't have much patience for her whining. Then, she met her new counselor. That seemed to go better than the physical therapist. She goes back to both of them on Monday."

After a healthy drink from her glass, Harry nodded. "Oh, right. I forgot she had those appointments. I meant with court."

Micki blew out a breath. "Judge Hastings, the same one I went before when Buck helped me with the restraining order, was very stern with Jade. He didn't pull any punches. He had her entire criminal record and had studied it. He admonished her for the awful choices she made and basically ripped her a new one."

Micki took a sip from her drink and smiled. "It was magnificent. He said so many things I've wanted to say for so long. He mentioned that she was the subject of a harassment and stalking order that he'd granted and then later withdrew at my request. He went on a long diatribe about her actions and how she wasn't a contributing member of society and that at her age, she should know better. He went with most of the plea deal, as far as no jail time, unless she violates probation, but added on two hundred and forty hours of community service. He didn't mince words and said she deserved to be in jail but understood that would only create a hardship for the jail, so he wanted Jade to understand the seriousness and made sure she understood if she failed to log at least forty hours a month or didn't stay clean, she would be back in his courtroom and on her way to jail."

Harry's eyes widened. "I like this guy."

Micki nodded. "Jade's never been one for accountability. She likes to live in denial, so he shook her up, and she's not happy. Olivia gave me a book to read about addicts, and it seems that's common. They blame others, don't take responsibility, and always have an excuse."

Georgia ran her bare foot over Hope's back. "I think the judge was wise in requiring her to contribute. Helping others is often a key to helping yourself. She's going to be busy with community service. Hopefully, she'll find a good fit."

Micki took a long drink from her glass. "She needs to keep busy and since working is basically impossible, this is the next best thing. He stipulated because of her past drug history and the abuse she inflicted on me and Meg, she's restricted from direct contact with children and needs to be supervised."

Harry rose with her empty glass. "I need a refill. There are lots of non-profit organizations in Lavender Valley. I'm sure Jade will be able to find one that needs some extra help. The food pantry is always looking for volunteers, and Olivia's church does a meal for anyone in need on Tuesdays. The community center and the senior center are two other possibilities."

Georgia smiled at her. "Leave it to our illustrious mayor to come up with four possibilities just like that."

Micki reached out to hand Harry her glass. "I'll take another one, too. Those are all great ideas, but I'm done spoon-feeding Jade. She'll have to show some initiative and do some research, then figure out how she's going to get to and from these places. She's lived her whole life getting handouts and like the judge told her, it's high time she grew up and acted like a responsible adult."

They enjoyed their cold drinks, and Micki shifted the conversation to the pet parade. "I think the float is close to being done. Olivia wanted us all to go over tonight and finish it up since tomorrow will be a busy day." Micki's phone buzzed, and she slipped it from her pocket. "Lydia said she's making tacos and brownies and invited us over to join them before we finish up the float tonight."

Harry nodded and grinned. "I'll put those enchiladas in the fridge, and we can have them tomorrow. Tell her we'll be there."

Olivia came through the door with Willow. Georgia took in her tired eyes. "You look like you've had a long day."

"It's the new rescue. She's dehydrated, and Duke thought it best she stay overnight and get fluids." She glanced over at Micki. "Meg is taking good care of her." She brought up a photo on her phone and showed it to Georgia.

"Oh, what a sweet face."

Olivia nodded. "Her name is Suki. Duke thinks she's around five. A black Labrador, but she's got a pretty white patch on her chest. Super sweet and a little shy."

Georgia's forehead creased. "I hope she'll recover and be okay."

Olivia smiled. "She'll be good as new once she gets hydrated and rested. Duke said I can pick her up tomorrow, and we'll take good care of her."

They brought her up to speed on Jade's hearing and the dinner invitation. Olivia looked at her watch. "I'll go get the dogs fed and taken care of, then we can head over."

Harry jumped up from her seat. "I'll take care of our three, while you do the shelter."

Georgia took her empty glass into the kitchen. "I'll go roust Jade and get her to come to dinner with us." She wandered out the door and took the pathway to her cottage, stopping at the door of the RV.

She knocked on the door, and Jade hollered out to come in.

Georgia found her sprawled across the bed in the back of the motorhome. "Hey, Lydia called and invited us for tacos. We're heading over in a few minutes, then we're going to finish up the float."

Jade sighed, placing her hand on her forehead. It reminded Georgia of something an actress in an old movie would do. "I'm so tired, I don't think I can make it."

The limp woman on the bed brought to mind some of the children Georgia encountered in the library, not a fifty-year-old woman. She needed prodding and attention. Georgia patted the edge of the bed. "Come on. I know it's hard, but if I can suffer through physical therapy and moving at the same time, you can do it. Plus, there are tacos."

Jade's lips lifted into a smile.

"Come on, it'll be fun. You'll see."

After a bit more cajoling, Jade propped herself up and scooted off the bed. With more pieces to sew for the weekend and beyond, Georgia opted to take her own car so she could leave early. She offered to drive Jade and waited as she maneuvered into the passenger seat.

Micki was right about the drama. Every move Jade made was completed with lots of grunts and sighs. As Georgia followed Harry's SUV past the barn, she glanced over at the tall sunflowers that were blooming, arching their heads toward the sun. They were gorgeous and a good reminder to always look for the light.

CHAPTER FIFTEEN

O n Saturday morning, at the last minute, Jade decided she couldn't ride on the float, and Clay's truck was too high for her to climb into, so Lydia volunteered to stay behind and make some treats while she kept an eye on Jade. She vowed to keep Jade busy, helping her with the baking projects.

With an irritated look nobody missed, Micki opted to take a walk in the fields, while they waited for Clay and Heath to arrive with the trailer.

Buck was the first of their extra helpers to arrive and by the time Duke drove into the yard, ready to help load the goats, Buck had Micki smiling again. Georgia stood back and watched, leaving the goat loading to the professionals. Heath's dog, Ace, was anxious for the work.

Georgia watched in awe as the border collie maneuvered the goats to the ramp the men had set up at the back of the trailer leading into the portable pen. They made it look easy. Especially Ace. Heath and Clay filled the troughs they'd positioned for the animals with water, while the rest of them climbed aboard their ride.

Duke gave Georgia a hand up, and she opted to take one of the hay bales in the middle of the trailer between the dogs and the goats. After her shoulder injury, she didn't want to take a chance of losing her balance if the trailer went over a bump. Everyone else sat on the bales stationed along the perimeter of the trailer.

Olivia sat closest to the goat pen, talking to them and Paisley as they jostled their way to town. They were sporting the new dark-purple pajamas Georgia made for them earlier in the week. She'd added some lighter lavender print fabric as accents but hoped the darker color would hide any dirt.

Duke sat next to Olivia, and Meg was across from them on the other side of the pen. Harry and Clay sat nearest the front of the trailer, surrounding the dogs and the small fence corralling them. Buck and Micki were stationed atop the bales at the rear of the trailer.

Everyone was focused on watching over the animals and making sure nothing fell off the trailer, including the banners advertising the farm attached to the sides of it.

The dogs were well-behaved; even little Vera enjoyed the fresh air and the ride. Olivia left Suki behind at the shelter since she was still recovering but brought along two other rescues. All the dogs sported bandanas, and the ladies were decked out in their lavender aprons. Micki even convinced the guys to wear lavender polo shirts.

It was a gorgeous morning, with the sun shining down from a clear blue sky. The scent of lavender from the wreaths Micki made and stuck to the sides of the hay bales drifted through the air. Georgia snapped a few photos on her phone. Everything was perfect.

Until it wasn't.

As Heath made the turn to get to the staging area, one of the sassy goats took the opportunity to jump on top of another one, using her companion as a ladder, and launched herself over the fencing.

She landed next to Georgia and in an effort to keep her from escaping, and without much thought, Georgia bent and tucked herself into a ball and rolled onto the small goat. Duke was quick to react, but Ace was quicker. The dog jumped over the short fence and stood between the fence and Georgia's hay bale, blocking the goat's pathway. Duke hurried to contain her by wrapping his arms around the wiggly goat, while Olivia handed Georgia a rope to slip over the goat's head.

With the rope secured, Olivia took hold of it and extracted her from Duke's arms. He turned his attention to Georgia, who was sprawled across the bottom of the trailer in a very unladylike position. "Please tell me you didn't hurt your shoulder. Are you okay?"

She laughed so hard, tears swelled in her eyes. "No, I'm fine. I basically just bowled over the goat, hoping to block her from breaking free. I was afraid to use my arm for fear of injury."

He did some quick checks of her ability to move her extremities and checked her neck before he helped her sit up. Then, he lifted her onto the hay bale, taking great care not to pull on her arms and keep them next to her sides as he positioned her. He ran his hands over her legs and arms again and around her neck and shoulders. "Does anything hurt?"

She shook her head. "No, really, I'm fine. It was a short trip, and all the hay on the bed of the trailer made for a soft landing. Hopefully, I didn't squish the poor girl."

Olivia shook her head. "She's always the first to start

trouble, and she's fine." Duke lifted the goat over the fence, and Olivia kept hold of the makeshift leash. "I'll just hold onto her for the parade. Not sure we need a repeat of that action."

Clay got Ace back with the other dogs and chuckled. "Georgia, I had no idea you were a goat wrangler. Impressive moves. We might need to enter you in the next rodeo."

She, along with everyone else, laughed as Heath, oblivious to all the action, pulled into the line of vehicles waiting for the parade to start.

Georgia picked a few stray pieces of hay from her clothes, and Olivia plucked a few from her hair for her. Clay made sure everyone had a cold bottle of water and as Georgia tilted the bottle to her mouth, she grinned. She couldn't wait to talk to Dale tonight and tell him about her goat-wrangling escapade.

CHAPTER SIXTEEN

Micki's marketing techniques worked their magic. While parading through town, many people asked about buying the lavender wreaths she made that were attached to the hay bales. By the time they were done, all of them were sold.

Micki had the supplies ready to go and when they returned to the farm, she set up the table next to the barn where visitors could pay to create their own lavender wreath. Georgia was a natural, and she recruited Jade to help her with the customers who came to make wreaths.

Jade's limited use of her arm wouldn't allow her to do much, but Georgia had her fetching supplies and helping the crafters. Georgia and Meg traded off throughout the weekend, with Georgia handling the cash register, and Meg working with Jade to help at the wreath-making station.

By the time they closed on Sunday afternoon, everyone was tired and ready to relax, but they had one more surprise. As soon as everything was put away in the barn, and they were enjoying iced teas and lemonades in the dining room, Lydia tapped her spoon against her glass. "Since this is Meg's last night with us, and she flies back to Colorado tomorrow, Heath has invited all of us to the ranch. He and Clay put together a special send-off dinner for Meg."

Tears shined in the young woman's eyes as she reached for her mom's hand. She turned back to Lydia and smiled. "That's so nice of you. I'm going to miss all of you so much. I'm excited for school, but this has been the best summer ever. Duke told me I could come back and help next summer, too."

Jade took a long drink from her glass of lemonade and cleared her throat. "Meg, I'm going to miss you. You're such a kind young lady, and I want you to know how sorry I am. I tricked you to get to your mom and wasn't very nice. I've made a huge mess, and I'm going to work hard to be a better person. I'm really sorry."

Georgia focused on Micki and noticed her face soften as Jade spoke. It was one step on a very long ladder that Jade had to climb, but Georgia's heart filled with the small progress she witnessed between Micki and Jade.

Meg rose from her chair, stepped over to Jade, and embraced her in a long hug. "It's okay. I'm just glad you're out of the hospital and here now. I won't be back until Christmas, but we can video chat."

Tears spilled onto Jade's cheeks, and she smiled. "I've never done that, but I'm sure Micki knows how."

"Yeah, we can use my computer or tablet. It's easy." For the first time since Jade came to stay, Micki smiled at her. Hardened hearts were softening, and Georgia prayed things would continue in that direction.

Monday morning, Meg hauled her suitcase downstairs and hugged Harry, Georgia, and Olivia goodbye. She'd already said a tearful goodbye to Lydia last night when after dinner, she gave her a container of cookies to take on the plane.

Micki loaded her bag and Jade into her SUV while the ladies showered Meg with hugs and happy tears. They stood on the porch, waving as Micki drove down the driveway to take her beloved daughter to the airport before dropping off Jade for her appointments in town.

Micki returned to the farm before lunch with takeout containers from the Lucky Duck Deli. Things were slow relative to farm visitors, and the five of them gathered around the tables under the tent.

As Micki passed out sandwiches and containers of salads, she smiled at them. "I want to thank you all so much for being patient with Meg and Jade. I know it hasn't been easy to have them here, especially Jade, and Meg can have a bit of an attitude at times. It means the world that you've welcomed and done so much to help them and me."

Midbite, Harry set her sandwich on the table. "We've said it before, but we're family now. There's no need to feel guilty about us helping each other. By that logic, I should be the guiltiest of all. Without you and your expertise with the flowers and marketing, we would have never opened this year. Not to mention what Lydia has done in cooking for us all the time and making these wonderful lavender treats. Georgia and her gorgeous creations. Olivia, oh my, if not for Olivia Jewel's dog rescue and shelter wouldn't be here. Each one of us has a gift and we have used them to make Lavender Valley Farm a success. This, what we have right here, was Jewel's wish."

Georgia nodded. "Harry's right. Jewel thought we'd need

each other, and I think she had a vision of all of us working together, using our talents to enrich not only her beloved farm, but our own hearts. She called us sisters of the heart for a reason. I don't think any of us are keeping track of who we've helped. We just all know we're here for each other and willing to do what it takes."

Micki dabbed at her eyes with a napkin.

After a swallow from her glass of tea, Olivia met Harry's eyes. "Like when I first came to the farm over forty years ago, this place and all of you rescued me. Jewel didn't tell me, she showed me how helping others, especially her sweet dogs who had nobody else in the world, I could help myself. My life is happier because of the time I spend with the animals and all of you. Harry's letter was my last hope and once again, Jewel saved me. Without Harry and all of you who came after me, I don't think I'd be here. I was done trying and ready to give up. So, more than anyone, I'm thankful for all of you. I have a purpose. More than that, I have a family because of each of you."

Tears glinted in Lydia's eyes as she smiled at the women around the table. "I agree with everyone else, Micki. You've worked harder than anyone to make this farm and festival into a huge success. Bigger and better than Jewel's wildest dreams, I'm sure. And, like everyone here, I found a new sense of purpose and in my case, a whole new chance at a life I only dreamed of since coming here. My instinct is always to run, but you all showed me I didn't have to run. You helped me find a way to stay, a path to a real home. A family."

Even Harry, who didn't cry easily, ran a finger under her eyes. Micki used another napkin to blot her face. "I couldn't ask for better sisters and family than all of you. I know these next weeks and months aren't going to be easy with Jade. I'm trying to stay positive and cling to the hope that she's sincere and will make steps in the right direction. I really couldn't handle this without all of you."

Georgia reached over and put her hand on Micki's shoulder. "It will probably be like working with a youngster. They tend to take a few steps forward and inevitably, a step back at times. I watched her this weekend at the wreath table, and it took her some time, but she started to relax and enjoy herself. I think it helps her to be around people and get into some new habits. You've said she's been this way her whole life, so she has to unlearn decades of bad behaviors. It's going to be slower than you like."

Micki laughed. "Yeah, patience is probably not my strong point. I'm going to work on my attitude and try to get into a routine again. When we were in town, I stopped by the senior center with Jade, and she got set up to use their transport bus. It's limited, but something she can use when all of us are unavailable. I left her with the physical therapist, then she's going to search out some community service opportunities before her therapy appointment this afternoon."

Harry finished her sandwich and wiped her hands. "I've got to run into work for a quick meeting later. I can pick her up and bring her home if that helps."

"That would be great. I need to get some work done, and it would be wonderful to have a few uninterrupted hours." She pulled out her cell phone. "I'll leave a message with her therapist to tell her to walk over to City Hall when she's done and wait for you."

"Perfect," said Harry, rising from her chair. "We'll figure this out and like you said, once Jade gets into a routine, things will settle down. The festival ends this coming weekend, and that will take lots of pressure off you, Micki."

As she finished off the last spoonful of potato salad, she

nodded. "Yes, as much as I've enjoyed all of this, it will be nice to get back to a quieter life. The only things we'll have to contend with are a few bookings from photographers who want to use the flowers for some shoots, and I've got two brides interested in having their showers here."

Georgia pointed toward the fields. "Your dahlias are looking gorgeous. Along with your cheerful sunflowers, those will be a spectacular addition."

Micki gasped. "That reminds me, I had a message to call the florist, Suzy. She was here this weekend and noticed the dahlias. It sounds like she's interested in buying cut flowers from us."

Harry raised her brows. "That sounds like a win-win."

Micki nodded. "Yeah, I think so. I mostly planted them because I love them. Sort of the same with the sunflowers, they remind me of the time I was here with Jewel, and they look so pretty against the barn. I thought about trying to get people to visit the dahlia garden, but honestly, after all this work, I'm ready for a break. Selling cut flowers to one shop makes sense."

Georgia took the last bite of her sandwich. "Thanks for lunch, Micki. It was yummy."

Micki's smile widened. "I love you all so very much."

Even though Georgia visited with Dale Thursday morning on her walk, she couldn't resist calling him as she sipped a cup of tea before turning in for bed. He answered on the first ring. "I was just thinking about you," he answered.

The sound of his voice made her heart skip a few beats. "I'm doing the same. Counting the hours until you arrive tomorrow."

"I've got Chuck's truck in my garage. I picked her up after lunch, and she is gorgeous. I can't wait for everyone to see it. I'm leaving early, probably around five in the morning. Did you make a reservation for dinner?"

"We can't wait to see it either. We're set for the Back Door Bistro at seven. One bit of news I found out this afternoon. Heath and Lydia have been working on wedding plans and heard back from his daughter Cassidy. They have their date. They're going to get married at the ranch and keep it pretty low key. Just family and a few close friends. I was hoping you could stick around for it. They're set for Wednesday night after Jewel's celebration next weekend."

"Sure, I can stretch my trip out a bit. Since I'm officially no longer needed at the office, I'm free and have no schedule to keep."

"Oh, that's good. I was afraid you already made a flight reservation."

"Nah, thought I'd play it by ear. I'm trying to be more spontaneous."

She chuckled as she added a bit more honey to her tea. "I haven't had much spontaneity in my life until this last year. Losing Lee, then the house, turned my very quiet life into chaos. Moving here, while a blessing, was the most impulsive decision I'd ever made. As it turns out, it was the best thing and while it definitely pushed me way out of my comfort zone, it was so worth it. Now, I have a family of sisters and new friends. The unexpected has proven rather fun."

"You're my inspiration, my dear. I'm going to embrace this new chapter of my life and live it fully."

She smiled at the lilt in his voice. His mood was more upbeat than it had been over the past couple of weeks. "You better get to sleep so you're fresh for the drive. Promise you'll text me along the way and check in."

"Cross my heart. See you soon, Georgia. Sweet dreams."

CHAPTER SEVENTEEN

Friday, the farm was swarming with customers, which made the day go by quickly and with only a few minutes to go before they closed, Chuck's bright-yellow Chevy came crawling up the driveway.

With each thump of the engine, Georgia's heart beat faster. Only a half hour earlier, she took a quick break and changed into fresh clothes, used a curling iron on her hair, and brightened up her lips, in anticipation of Dale's arrival and their dinner date.

Dale parked near the house and came from around the driver's side. Olivia came from the barn, behind the wheel of the UTV, and her mouth hung open. She parked near the retail tent to collect the totes and rushed over to the shiny truck.

Lydia tilted her head at Georgia. "You get over there, I can watch the till."

Georgia ran her hand over the new blouse she wore. She made it this week while she was at the fabric store. It was deep purple and had a soft ruffle of chiffon along the V-neckline.

She made her way toward him to admire the truck. Dale grinned at her. "You're a sight for sore eyes, Georgia. You look beautiful." He slipped an arm around her shoulder and squeezed her against him.

"The truck is beautiful." She reached out to touch the shiny chrome door handle. "I can't wait for Micki to see her logo. It's stunning against the bright yellow."

Olivia came from around the front of the truck. "I can't believe the transformation." Her smile widened. "Wait until you see the back of it. Such talent and detail."

Dale beamed as they circled the truck. Once Harry closed the gate, she and Micki joined them. "Wow. What a beauty," said Harry.

Micki fixated on the logo. The gorgeous lavender and purples with the soft greens and blues really popped on the side of the bright-yellow truck. The yellow reminded her of the cheerful sunflowers she loved.

Georgia found Olivia staring at the back of the truck, still grinning as she pointed at the three rescue dogs the painter had added. They looked like they were peeking over the tailgate, and the painter added in sprigs of lavender and a purple ribbon lettered with the Lavender Valley Farm Rescue & Sanctuary.

Georgia put her hand to her heart. "Oh, my, that's perfection."

Olivia rushed over to Dale and engulfed him in a hug. "Thank you so much for doing this. I wish Jewel were here to see it. She would love it."

Dale pointed up at the sky. "I think she's looking down on all of this and smiling." He pointed at the truck. "Giving the old girl a facelift has been my pleasure. Chip did a fantastic job on it. You should have seen all the happy honks and waves I got on the way down here. It's a wonderful tribute to Jewel and Chuck and a great advertisement for the experience you ladies have created here at the farm."

He glanced over at Lydia, who was busy cleaning up her space. He hurried over to help and sent her to join the others. "It's just perfect, isn't it?" She ran her hand over the flawless yellow paint and took in every detail.

Micki pulled her phone out of her pocket. "I think we need a photo of Jewel's girls with Chuck's truck." She looked across to the lavender field. "Let's move it to the field. That background is what we need."

Harry volunteered to drive it to the field, and the others followed, with Dale hurrying to join them after he parked the UTV with Georgia's totes in the barn. He offered to take photos with Micki's phone, and the ladies stood alongside the truck, making sure the logo was visible.

He had Olivia pose at the back with the dog rescue logo, then added the three goldens in the back of the truck and had Olivia hold Vera while he took a few more. He suggested Micki get behind the wheel and took several of her smiling.

Dale pointed at the back of it. "How about you all climb in, and I'll take a few that way." He helped them climb into the back and had them kneel along the side. They laughed as he took photo after photo.

After Dale helped them down from the bed of the truck, Micki collected her phone. "I think we need one of Dale and Georgia next to this gorgeous truck."

He slipped his arm around Georgia's shoulders, and she tucked hers around his waist. Micki had them laughing and smiling and captured several photos of them and even made

Georgia get behind the wheel for a few of them. She scrolled through her phone and smiled. "I think that does it. These are great. I can't wait to put them up on the website."

Dale held Georgia's hand as she stepped from the cab. "I need to shine her up and clean the windows for the car show tomorrow." He glanced at his watch. "I'll probably have to do that early tomorrow, since we need to get moving to make our dinner reservation."

Georgia pointed at her car. "We can take my car." While Dale retrieved his luggage from the cab of the truck, she waved to the others. "See you later."

He opened the driver's door for her, and she slid into her seat. As they set off for town, he turned to her and grinned. "I'm so glad to be here with you. I've really missed seeing you over these last weeks."

She took the turn for downtown. "I've missed you, too. The best part of my day is when I'm visiting with you on my walk or talking to you at the end of the day."

"Well, I'm thrilled to be here for the next ten days or so. I hope we can work in some day trips when you're not working at the fabric store."

Georgia pulled into Buck's driveway and parked. "I'd love that. I haven't had time to explore much and doing that with you would be such fun."

He squeezed her hand. "I've done a little research and picked out a few places to visit."

He opened his door and was able to get to hers before she could open it herself. He offered her his arm, and they strolled down the block and across Main Street, past the coffee shop to the end of the block to the Back Door Bistro.

The hostess led them through the crowded restaurant to a table and left them with menus and the promise of a server.

Within minutes, a basket of warm bread and dipping oil, along with glasses of water, were delivered to their table.

As they enjoyed their first bites of the soft bread, their server arrived and took their orders. She warned them they were busy, and the wait would be longer than usual, but to compensate, she could offer them an appetizer of potato skins.

Dale nodded with enthusiasm. She smiled and promised to be back with them in a few minutes. The flame from the candle in the middle of the table flickered between them. Dale winked at her. "I have a couple of rules I live by. One is never turn down free food."

She laughed and couldn't help but stare into his sparkling eyes. "I like that rule. I might have to adopt it."

It felt so good to laugh again. That was one of the things she missed most about Lee's absence. For years, they'd always enjoyed each other's company and could make each other laugh. The laughter didn't come as easily since he'd been gone.

Until now.

Dale had a charming and disarming way about him. He put her at ease and made her feel like she was the most important thing in the world. His attention never wavered, even when she was talking about quilts and fabrics.

Dinner took longer than expected, but Georgia's pasta with fresh tomatoes was divine, and Dale insisted on sharing a few bites of his steak with her. He also ordered a platter of rosemary truffle fries to share, and the combination of earthy and salty flavors was out of this world.

It was nine o'clock by the time they wandered outside. The town was still bustling, and the sidewalks were busy. They opted for a walk around the square. The trees along the streets were lit with white twinkling lights and along with the streetlights, gave all of downtown a warm and welcoming glow.

It was the perfect summer night, with a tinge of blue still left in the sky as the sun retired for the evening, and the first stars appeared above. They held hands as they wandered the blocks of shops and headed back to her car. Georgia tried to enjoy the evening and not worry about Dale leaving in less than two weeks.

If these last months had taught her anything, worrying did nothing but rob her of the present. She intended to enjoy every moment with her old friend.

Saturday, Georgia was up early. She and Dale were meeting at the property line gate to walk before they tackled polishing the truck. Her sisters had assigned her the task of spending Saturday at the car show where she and Dale were charged with using the truck to promote the farm.

Despite her concerns that they might need her help at the farm, they insisted and assured her they could handle things, especially since Clay and Heath were planning to pitch in for the big finale.

She laced up her walking shoes and hurried outside, where the soft-blue light of dawn was just breaching the horizon. Dale was already waiting at the gate when she arrived.

He handed her a tall travel mug, steam rising from the hole in the lid. "I brought us some coffees."

She took the cup and smiled. "You're so thoughtful." She took a sip and moaned. "That's good. With it being so early, I didn't have time for coffee."

They set out on the worn pathway as the sun appeared in the distance. "I'm going to join you at the car show," said Georgia. "The girls said they can handle the farm, and Clay and Heath are coming over to help."

"That's great news. I don't think it will take long to clean her up and get to town. We might even have time to grab breakfast after we get parked."

"Micki has a couple of shirts for us to wear. They have our logo on them, so we can advertise. She also gave me some postcards and flyers to have on hand for anyone who comes by to look at the truck."

"She's a smart cookie."

"Oh, and there's the barn dance tonight."

"Yeah, Clay and Heath told me about it last night. It's a must-do, apparently. It's actually at one of the wineries I thought we should visit, Harvest Moon."

"I guess we'll get a sneak peek tonight."

She took another sip of her coffee and stopped to take in the breathtaking view in front of her. The sun sat atop the tree line, and soft ribbons of golden light bathed the purple blooms of the lavender fields.

She handed Dale her coffee and pulled her phone from her pocket. Georgia wasn't sure the camera could capture the absolute splendor of the morning sunrise, but that didn't stop her from trying. "I think this is what photographers call the golden hour. The lighting is incredible, isn't it?"

"That it is. It's soft and glowing all at the same time."

They turned and made their way back toward the house. She finished her coffee and when they reached the gate, he offered to take her empty cup for her. "I'm just going to grab a shower, and I'll be over. Clay said I could borrow a couple of lawn chairs, so I'll bring those and a cooler with some cold drinks, and we should be set."

"It might take me longer to get ready, but I'll be as quick as I can and meet you at the truck." She hurried off with a quick wave and a full heart.

CHAPTER EIGHTEEN

The car show was in the park, adjacent to the farmer's market, with plenty of shade under the canopy of trees. After they parked Chuck's truck in a premiere spot on the end nearest the street, they walked over to the Grasshopper and had a delicious breakfast.

The cheerful yellow truck was one of the most popular vehicles of the day, and Georgia and Dale visited with dozens of people, with Georgia making sure they knew about the farm and received a postcard and Dale answering mechanical questions raised by all the car enthusiasts.

By the time the show ended at three o'clock, Georgia stifled a yawn, and Dale surprised her with a milkshake from the ice cream shop. He gave her first choice between chocolate or fresh marionberry. She frowned as she looked between the two of them. "Oh, that's a tough choice." She reached for the marionberry and raised her brows as she took her first sip from the straw. "Oh, delicious."

He took his seat next to her. "I thought after our long day, we deserved a little treat." He leaned against the back of his chair. "I also wouldn't say no to a nap."

She chuckled. "We got up too early."

He nodded as he sipped. "That sunrise was worth it, though." He sighed as he handed her the last quarter of his chocolate shake. She smiled and did the same with her marionberry.

He took his first sip of hers and raised his brows. "Oh my, that is good." He finished it off and sighed. "I don't know about you, but there's no way I'm going to make it through a barn dance unless I get a little shuteye."

After Georgia finished the rest of the chocolate shake, Dale piled their chairs in the back of the truck and held the door as Georgia climbed into the cab, holding their People's Choice trophy.

Dale maneuvered through the busy streets and turned onto the highway. It didn't take long to reach the farm, where he drove through the open gate and up to the house. Visitors were milling about, but with Dale's encouragement, Georgia went straight to her cottage, where she stretched out on her sofa and fell asleep.

After an hour, she woke, refreshed and with plenty of time to change clothes for the barn dance. She surveyed her closet, unsure of what to wear. It was a dance, but it was also a barn.

She settled on a light chambray skirt that came to just above her ankle and a white peasant blouse with subtle embroidery around the neckline. She'd made both of them years ago but couldn't remember the last time she wore either of them.

Shoes would be a problem. Her normal choice of sandals didn't seem right for a barn. Georgia rummaged in her closet and finally unearthed a pair of sneaker style slip on shoes covered in rhinestones. She bought them for some sort of dress-up day at school years ago. How they survived all the culling she did when she moved, she didn't know but was thankful for them.

She slipped them on and checked them out in the full-length mirror on the back of her bedroom door. She tilted her head back and forth. Despite her worries, they were cute and perfect for the outfit.

With one last adjustment to her hair, Georgia left the cottage and walked over to the main house, the trophy in her hand. She found Harry in jeans and cowboy boots, wearing a pretty wine-colored blouse, sipping coffee at the counter in the kitchen.

Georgia put the trophy on the counter and helped herself to a cup of coffee.

Harry smiled at her and pointed at the trophy. "Dale said you guys won a prize. How was it?"

As Georgia took a sip, she slipped into the chair next to Harry. "Busy. We had tons of people stop and check out the truck. I gave out all the postcards and flyers."

"Dale said you had a long day and needed a little rest before the dance."

"Yeah, we wanted to get a good parking spot, so we ended up getting up way too early, but it was a great day. Lots of nice people."

"Micki's thrilled. It was our best day yet. Tomorrow, it will be slim pickings for treats. Lydia's down to her last stash, and you don't have much left either."

"It's always good to leave them wanting more, right?"

Georgia smiled as she reached for her mug. "As great as this has been, I'm glad tomorrow is our last day. It's been a ton of work, and I can only imagine how Micki feels. She's done so much."

Harry nodded. "I agree. I think we all need a break." She lowered her voice. "Jade is putting up a fuss about going to the dance with us."

Georgia frowned. "Well, she can't stay here by herself. We made that clear when she arrived."

"Exactly. Heath is driving Lydia and Clay and will be here in a few minutes to pick me up. Duke is picking up Buck and was planning to take Olivia and Micki. Now, Micki is thinking about taking her SUV so she can drive Jade."

Georgia's brows arched. "Dale and I can take Jade in my car. She can get in it easily. Micki needs to go and enjoy herself." She rose from her chair. "I'll run out and suggest that we take her. Maybe that will calm things down."

Harry glanced out the window. "Here's Clay now. Thanks for doing that, Georgia. I just want to make sure Micki doesn't stay behind because of Jade."

"I won't let that happen." Georgia waved as she stepped into the mudroom and out the door.

The tense voices coming from the thin walls of the motorhome led Georgia to the pair. She didn't bother knocking and climbed the steps. Both of them were in the bedroom in the back. With an annoyed sigh and frustration etched in the furrows of her brow, Micki gave Georgia an exasperated look.

Jade sat on the edge of her bed, defiance oozing out of her.

Georgia touched the fabric of Micki's dress. "Micki, I love those boots with your dress. You look gorgeous in that bright yellow."

Georgia waited for a smile that softened Micki's face. "Harry needs you in the kitchen." With a slight nod, Georgia sent a reassuring message to her, and Micki scooted out the door.

She turned her attention back to Jade. "You better get changed. I was thinking that pretty green blouse we found for you, the one that matches your eyes, would be perfect for tonight. It looks great with jeans, but a little dressy."

Jade rolled her eyes. "It's not like I'm going to dance. It's just a waste of time. I'd rather stay home."

"You know that's not an option and by now, you must have learned you don't always get what you want. So, hop to it, get changed, and you can ride out with me and Dale. We're not going to stay long and can bring you home when we leave."

Jade crossed her arms.

"I'm sure you've seen how hard Micki has been working to make this festival a huge success. She deserves a night out to celebrate and enjoy herself. Now, you can be a part of that fun and help applaud her success and just maybe enjoy yourself at the same time, or you can go and be miserable and sulk in the corner. Either way, you're going."

Georgia had a hard time believing the woman sitting on the bed was only ten years her junior. It was like talking to a fifteen-year-old girl.

Jade glared at her. Georgia maintained steady eye contact.

"What's a cripple supposed to do at a dance?" Jade spat out the words laced with disgust.

"Everyone likes the music and company. I think you'll find lots of people attend dances without dancing. Not everyone enjoys it. And in case you still haven't figured it out, tonight is not about you. It's about celebrating our town, the festival, and all the work that's been put into it, especially that of Micki. One other note, you've got some injuries and will have to overcome them or learn to live with them, but I think a person in a wheelchair or missing a limb wouldn't appreciate you referring to yourself that way."

Georgia took a deep breath. "We all have challenges, insecurities, things we wish were different, but that doesn't give anyone a free pass. Whatever is wrong, you can still choose to be nice, be kind, be gracious, be helpful. Those are the things you need to work on more than anything else, Jade. Nobody judges you based on a brace on your arm or leg, but they do remember how you treated them or how you acted. That's what defines you, not your physical limitations."

She glanced at her watch. "You've got ten minutes. Meet me outside at my car." Without giving her time for a retort, Georgia went back to the house. Olivia and Micki were in the kitchen. Olivia was wearing the pretty sage-green blouse Georgia made for her.

Georgia made Olivia twirl in her long, black skirt. As she raised her leg in the air to showcase her cowboy boots, she grinned. "Courtesy of Duke. I've never owned a pair, but they're more comfortable than I thought."

"You look fabulous. I love seeing you with your hair down." She turned toward Micki. "Jade is going to come in my car. I'm picking Dale up from the ranch in a few minutes. So, don't give her another thought. We'll bring her home and probably won't stay too late."

Micki pressed her lips together and stepped closer to Georgia. She wrapped her arms around her. "Thank you," she whispered. "I've run out of patience today."

The three goldens were settled on the area rug, watching their humans, when they jumped up and hurried to the door. Olivia chuckled. "I think our ride is here."

She ushered the dogs back to their place and looped her arm through Micki's. "We'll see you there, Georgia."

Micki gave Georgia a wave and stepped onto the porch. While she waited, Georgia texted Dale to let him know she'd be there soon with Jade. She took a seat on the couch, and the dogs hurried over to surround her.

With every stroke across their soft fur, she relaxed. Georgia wasn't someone who thrived on conflict and didn't enjoy being part of it, but she was determined to insulate Micki from Jade's latest tantrum.

At the ten-minute mark, she gathered her purse, rewarded the dogs with a treat, and made her way outside to her car. She tossed her bag in the backseat and was about to march over to the motorhome when the sound of the door opening made her step back to the driver's door.

Jade came around the end of Gypsy and made her way to the passenger side of the car. Georgia settled into her seat, making sure her skirt was inside before closing her door. She waited while Jade climbed into her side of the car.

Georgia started the ignition and glanced over at her passenger. "One quick stop at the ranch, and then we'll be off to the barn." She'd said her piece to Jade and wasn't about to belabor her thoughts. Sometimes it worked to ignore a petulant teenager, and that was Georgia's plan for the evening.

Dale was waiting outside at the front of the sprawling house and climbed into the backseat as soon as Georgia stopped the car. The crisp scent of his citrus aftershave tickled her nose.

"Nice to see you, Jade," he said.

She mumbled a quick hello, and Georgia headed back to the highway. Harvest Moon was only about five miles out of downtown, just past Duke's veterinary clinic. Georgia was in a long line of cars making the same trip.

She took the turn and slowed as the cars crept down the long, tree-lined driveway that led to the vineyard. There was a sign with an arrow for drop off vehicles, and Georgia followed that fork in the road, which looped her to the side of the barn, only steps away from the entrance to it.

Dale hurried around the car to help Jade and then urged Georgia to wait with her while he took care of parking the car. With the way the world sometimes felt, Georgia wasn't sure true gentlemen still existed, but Dale was a testament to them.

She and Jade waited at the edge of the barn, watching for Dale. Georgia looked through the windows and spotted Harry and Olivia, who with their height, were easy to find in a crowd. She turned back to Jade. "Looks like they've got seats saved for us. I can wait for Dale if you want to go on inside."

Jade shrugged, then wandered over to the large opening and disappeared inside the barn.

Georgia surveyed the crowd as they passed by her, most of the men in jeans and cowboy hats, several of the young women in very short skirts or cut-offs, wearing cowboy boots. It was a look she could never pull off, but most of them looked right at home.

The touch of an arm around her shoulders made her flinch. She was so busy watching everyone, Dale was able to sneak up on her. He offered her his arm. "Shall we?"

As they walked through the tall sliding doors that were wide open, the strum of a guitar and the soft beat of drums greeted them. Beautiful chandeliers hung from the high wooden beams, and white twinkling lights were strung across the rafters and down the wooden posts that held the barn upright.

The huge space was filled with lots of hay bales positioned for seating, along with several chairs. From the midpoint of the barn, all the way to the other end, where a stage was set up and a band was playing soft music in the background, a huge wooden dance floor was installed over the wide strip of pavers that made up the middle of the barn. It extended past the edge of the pavers and over the dirt floor on each side.

Several barrels of wine rested in heavy racks along the outermost perimeter of the barn, while others were positioned as cocktail tables. Clay and Heath waved them over to one of the few large tables set up next to the wine racks.

"Wow," said Dale, eyeing the long charcuterie board. "That looks fantastic."

Duke smiled. "Courtesy of my sister May and her partner in crime Janet. They spent most of the day making these up for the dance." He pointed to a booth in the corner, next to the bar. "The festival is selling them to raise money for next year's event."

Clay pointed at two empty chairs next to Harry. "Those are for you. I was just on my way to help Heath with drinks. What can we get you?"

Georgia took her seat and glanced up at Dale. "If Dale is willing to drive, I'd love a glass of white. If not, iced tea works for me."

Dale rested his hand on her shoulder. "I'm happy to drive. I'll come with you, Clay, and check out their soft drinks."

Georgia kept her gaze straight ahead while she whispered to Harry out the side of her mouth. "How's it going with Jade?"

"I think she's pouting, hoping we'll fawn over her. We all decided the best path forward was to ignore her sulking and only engage when she's positive."

"After I told her what I thought before we came out here, I decided the same. Micki warned us she likes attention, and I think she's one of those who'll take it whether it's good or bad."

Harry nodded. "Exactly. We don't need to feed the monster."

Clay, Heath, and Dale returned with drinks for the table. Heath put Jade's ginger ale in front of her and handed Lydia a glass of red wine. Clay and Duke, along with Dale, were driving, so Dale placed Arnold Palmers at their seats, while the others were treated to adult beverages.

Buck raised his glass of wine and gazed over at Micki. "Before the night gets away from us, I wanted to toast Micki and all of you ladies. I know the long hours and hard work you all put into making Jewel's festival at the farm a success. She would be overjoyed to see all the visitors and your new ideas, Micki. Here's to all of you."

They all clinked their glasses together and took their first sips. Buck leaned over and kissed Micki, who smiled at him and murmured her thanks and appreciation to everyone.

Moments later, Harry's voice came from the speakers positioned throughout the barn, and Georgia turned her attention toward the stage. Harry welcomed everyone to the event and asked the festival committee to approach the stage. After introducing them, on behalf of Lavender Valley, Harry thanked them for their dedication and hard work at making this year's festival a success. She touted the record-breaking number of attendees and the positive feedback they'd received from businesses and visitors alike. She encouraged the audience to give them a round of applause.

Harry and Micki returned to the table, shaking hands and smiling at people along the way. The band played another song, and Dale leaned closer to Georgia. "May I have this dance?"

She happily accepted his hand, and they made their way to the dance floor. A young woman stepped to the microphone and sang the lyrics to the soft and slow notes of "Second Chance," and Georgia rested her head on Dale's shoulder as they swayed to the tune.

CHAPTER NINETEEN

Sunday morning, Georgia hurried from bed, brushed her teeth, and rushed out the door. Despite their early night at the barn dance, she and Dale stayed up late talking and sipping tea in her cottage.

It was close to midnight when the others came home, and Dale caught a ride back to the ranch with Clay. Six hours later, here she was, hurrying to meet Dale for their morning constitutional.

It had been just over a year since she lost Lee. So much had changed over the last twelve months. In those weeks that followed his death, Georgia would've never imagined she'd be in Lavender Valley, excited to get up early to take a walk with a man who, in a short time, held a special place in her heart.

She found him at the gate, where he handed her a travel mug. She took it and chuckled. "You know we're not teenagers anymore. Caffeine doesn't hold the magic it once did to make up for too few hours of sleep."

He led the way down their path and as they took their

first steps, they were treated to another stunning sunrise. As they walked, Georgia chattered on about how much fun she had at the dance. "Did you notice Jade was smiling and visited with the guy from the band who had a prosthetic leg?"

Dale nodded. "Yeah, I think she would have stayed longer, had we not been ready to call it a night. He seemed like a great guy. He's a veteran and doesn't try to hide his leg. I thought the design with the flag on it was really cool."

She stopped to take a drink. "Yes, it would be nice if Jade could find a few friends of her own. I think her neediness wears Micki out. I forgot to tell you, she's going to work at the soup kitchen at the church on Tuesdays and put in some hours at the senior center on Wednesday. I told her she could catch a ride to town with me, since I'm working those days."

"That will be good for her. It's easy to feel sorry for yourself until you meet a few people who are struggling. You soon realize your problems are pretty small compared to theirs."

She nodded. "It's the best way to find a sense of purpose and belonging. Something we both understand all too well."

They walked for several minutes in silence, holding hands while they enjoyed the quiet and beauty of the pristine morning. As they turned, Dale caught her eye. "I thought we could take a road trip tomorrow if you're up to it. From what it sounds like, today should be an early day. Harry said you're almost out of products to sell."

She grinned. "I think we're all tired and wouldn't mind a slow day. Micki mentioned the idea of closing the gate at noon and calling it done. It sounds like most of the visitors leave by then, and Lavender Valley goes back to the quiet town we remember."

"Well, I've got a list of ten wineries within a few miles

that look promising, plus Buck and Micki said we need to drive up to the Dragonfly Estate."

"We should be able to squeeze all that in before Lydia's wedding."

They arrived at the gate, and she handed him her empty cup. "I'll run home and get ready and pick you up. The pancake breakfast is the last activity of the festival, and I'd like to support it since it helps fund next year's events."

"You had me at pancakes," he said with a wink.

After bacon, eggs, and pancakes with fresh peaches and berries, all from local farms, Dale and Georgia took a walk around downtown. He wanted to see her winning quilts, and she took him by the fabric store where they stopped to take in the display in the window.

He gazed at them and then turned to her. "I admit I know nothing about making quilts or sewing, but I can tell quality workmanship when I see it. You're quite talented, Georgia."

She blushed. "I just enjoy doing it. It's relaxing." She sighed as she looked back at the store. "I'm done with the quilting class, but I have plans to make a new dress for Lydia's wedding this week. Hopefully, I'll be able to get that done without staying late."

His eyes widened. "I'm not sure if you gave me a few months, I could make a dress."

"I bet if I had a light switch that wasn't working, you could fix that in a matter of minutes, though."

He grinned as they wandered back to her car. "Yeah, if it has wires and involves electricity, I'm your man." He chuckled. "These past weeks while I was home, I tackled lots of little chores I'd been neglecting. I thought that would keep me busy, but they're all done. Everything is in tip-top shape." He shrugged as he opened her door for her. "I'm so used to working and being busy, it's hard to slow down."

"You'll have to ask Harry if there's anything that needs fixing around the farm. She's our organizer, and I'm sure she would love the help."

"I'll be sure to ask her. Clay and Heath are taking me on a horseback ride to tour the ranch on Tuesday, while you're at work."

"Oh, you'll have a grand time with those two. Like you, they're true gentlemen and so good for Harry and Lydia." As she drove them back to the farm, she smiled at the wild sunflowers that bloomed along the sides of the highway.

When they got home, Dale helped retrieve the few totes left in the barn and pitched in to help Lydia carry hers from the house to the tent. True to his word, he asked Harry for some tasks that she needed done around the house, and he happily set out to find some tools in the barn. From Georgia's spot at her table, she had a perfect view of the tall sunflowers against the barn. She associated them with the end of summer and their happy faces were the perfect way to end one season and usher in fall.

Most of the visitors that came through the gate only stayed for a short time, intent on a few last photos with the cheerful sunflowers or the elegant dahlias, or by the yellow truck in the lavender fields. By noon, Lydia had sold all her packaged baked goods, and Georgia was down to one apron and one table runner.

While she worked on balancing the cash drawer, Dale transported the empty totes to the cottage with all their supplies. He carried the two Lydia used to the kitchen to be washed before they were stored for the season.

Harry closed the gate to the property, and they officially

declared an end to this year's festival. Tyler and one of the other ranch hands from the Nolan Ranch were ready and took down the tents while everyone else wandered toward the house.

As Georgia climbed the steps to the porch, Dale offered her a hand. "I don't think we've taken any photos together in the field, except with the truck. Are you game?"

"Oh, yes, let's do that and get the others, too. I'd love to have these memories of this first festival together."

Dale and Georgia led the way, with the others following. Dale served as the photographer with Jade assisting. He took dozens of shots of the five sisters of the heart, without their official aprons, just as themselves, laughing and smiling, their arms around each other. They squeezed together on the white sofa, sat on the bench, and held the large photo frames in front of them. Dale had them in hysterics when he asked them to get in a line and kick out their legs.

Georgia suggested Jade join them for a few photos and then had Dale capture some of Micki and Jade together. It took some joking and prodding to get the two of them to relax and smile, but Dale managed to get a few decent shots of the two of them.

Micki offered to take some of Georgia and Dale together. With Dale's arm around her as they sat on the velvet couch, Georgia smiled. She never thought she'd be this happy again but sitting here with the lovely fragrance of lavender all around her, surrounded by the sisters she never knew she needed, her heart was full. Sitting next to a wonderful and kind man, one she wished would never leave, was even better.

Micki handed Dale the phone, and he scrolled through all of the photos. Georgia gasped when he came to one of them. Micki captured the sheer joy on their faces when Dale pretended to be pushing the back of the bike, with Georgia atop the seat, laughing. "Oh, this is one of the best. It might be my favorite."

Everyone wandered back toward the house, with Georgia and Dale taking their time, lingering in the fields. They wandered to the dahlias, and Dale insisted on taking a few photos of Georgia among the blooms.

She pointed at one, a gorgeous pink with petals galore. "Have you ever seen anything so beautiful?"

"Only the woman next to it," he said, smiling as he took a photo of her.

She waved away his compliment. "You're a charmer."

He took her arm in his. "It's the truth. I don't know if you ever knew, but I had a crush on you."

Her eyes went wide in disbelief.

He grinned. "Just a tiny one, but there was something about you. You were so kind to me and made me feel good just being around you. I thought you were the most beautiful girl I'd ever seen."

She shook her head and laughed. "Oh, yes, the auburn braids were a real magnet, I'm sure."

He chuckled and put his hands on her shoulders, meeting her eyes. "It wasn't the braids. It was your heart. In my experience, most truly beautiful women, like you and Sarah, never think they're beautiful. It's the glow that comes from here." He put his hand on his chest. "Your kind and true soul that shines from the inside. That's what makes you irresistible."

He embraced her in a tight hug, and tears spilled from her eyes. The sweet boy she remembered with fondness was here, with his arms wrapped around her, saying the most romantic thing she ever heard. For the first time since Lee's death, she felt safe and steady.

As they made their way back to the house, they walked by the shelter, and Olivia was coming out the door with a few furry friends. In a flash, a black dog made a beeline for Dale, rushing to his side and thwacking her tail against his legs.

He bent down and rubbed the top of her head. "Hey there, sweet girl."

Olivia, with leashes in her hand and two small terrier mixes attached to them, hurried to Dale's side. "I'm so sorry. This is Suki, and she's so shy, I can't believe she bolted like that." She looked down at the dog, who was fixated on Dale, her dark-brown eyes unwavering.

He continuing petting her. "She's a sweetheart. Look at those eyes."

Olivia chuckled. "In my experience, a dog often picks a person. I think Suki has her sights set on you, Dale." She wiggled her brows at him. "If you're thinking about a dog, she's a great one."

He laughed and bent down to Suki. He ran his hands along the side of her face, and she closed her eyes, leaning into him. "She's hard to resist."

Georgia joined him and scratched Suki's chin. "Look how her black coat shines in the sun. She's gorgeous."

Olivia caught Dale's eye. "I haven't posted her on the website yet or done any outreach. You give it some thought. I've never seen her that excited to meet anyone. Just sayin'." She smiled and picked up Suki's leash. "You two could give her a test drive tomorrow morning on your walk."

She left with a wave, and the three goldens followed her and her charges. Dale stood and watched them for a few minutes. Georgia noticed Suki look back at him. "I think she's smitten."

He laughed, and they continued to the house. "I have been thinking it would be nice to have a dog again."

"It's been wonderful to have Hope and Willow and Chief here, along with little Vera and Olivia's rescues. They're such great company and have a way of lifting your spirits without even trying."

"I'll see if Olivia is willing to hold onto her for a few weeks. I want to give it some thought."

She tugged on his arm. "Let's get inside. I promised I'd cook dinner tonight, and I could use a sous chef."

CHAPTER TWENTY

M onday, Georgia collected Suki from the shelter building, and the two of them took off to meet up with Dale at the gate. She proved to be a good walker and didn't pull on the leash or get distracted.

She matched Georgia's pace and when Georgia stopped, Suki stopped and sat at her feet. "What a good girl you are. Did Olivia teach you or did you already know how to do all these things?"

Suki's jaw relaxed and mouth opened, the tip of her pink tongue visible, and Georgia laughed at what could only be construed as a smile on the dog's face. "Aww, you like being praised, don't you? Well, I guess we all do."

They made their way down the path and found Dale waiting at their spot. He handed Georgia her travel mug and put his on the fence post while he bent down to greet Suki. While he was rubbing her face and ears, he slipped her a dog cookie, and she gobbled it down.

He took hold of her leash and collected his cup before

they set off on their route. Georgia pointed at the dog. "She's really smart and a total lovebug."

"Yeah, I have a feeling I won't be able to say no." He glanced down at the sleek dog and smiled.

Georgia nodded. "I think something new in your life that brings you happiness and joy can never be wrong."

He touched his shoulder to hers in a playful manner. "I like how you think, Georgia."

At the halfway point, Georgia pulled a bottle of water from her jacket pocket. "How about a little drink, Suki?" She bent and carefully poured the water in a skinny stream, aiming for the dog's mouth.

She lapped it up and drank about half the bottle before they set out to finish the walk. "So," said Georgia, "what's on our agenda today?"

"Heath recommended Red River Winery and a place for lunch in Applegate."

"That sounds good. That's where he proposed to Lydia."

"He told me about that. Quite the romantic gesture from a crusty old cowboy."

"They're a sweet couple. I'm so happy Lydia found her soulmate."

As they made their way back to the gate, Dale took a long sip from his cup. "Do you think it's possible to have more than one soulmate?"

"Hmm. Years ago, I probably would have said no, but a bit of life experience has changed my mind. I do think you can have more than one if you're lucky."

"Yeah, I think I feel the same way. I used to think you got one shot. Now, I'm not so sure."

"When we're young, it's easier to view the world in absolutes. Black and white. You're not focused on thirty years in the future; you're focused on the right now. As you get older and experience the peaks and valleys life throws at you, it's easier to see the gray areas. When I met Lee, I knew he was the one. We had an immediate and strong connection. I think if you only had one shot, the world would be without hope. I felt that way initially, but now, over these last months, I've found hope and so much more."

They arrived at the gate, and Dale bent down and gave Suki a good scratching behind her ears. "You, my sweet girl, are in the company of a very wise woman." He stood upright and collected Georgia's empty mug. "I'll be waiting for you when you're ready. They don't open until eleven, so no rush."

"I'll come early, and we can take the scenic route."

"Sounds perfect." He stood and watched as the two of them set out for the farmhouse.

As they walked, Georgia whispered to the dog, "Don't you worry, Suki. You've got him wrapped around your paw."

Georgia pulled up to the ranch a few minutes after nine o'clock and settled herself in the passenger seat of her car, content to let Dale drive so she could gawk at the countryside. They set out toward Applegate, but instead of taking the main highway, Dale turned onto a small county road.

They meandered through sprawling acreage and a couple of wineries that weren't open on Mondays. As they approached the Applegate River, Georgia spotted a sign for a farm and bakery. She pointed at it. "That looks interesting. Shall we stop?"

He patted his stomach. "I didn't have breakfast today, so a bakery sounds good." He turned into the driveway and parked in front of a tall planter filled with sunflowers. Past the planter stood an old barn with its iconic gambrel roof. A wooden sign advertised a country bakery, and another one in the shape of an ice cream cone was attached to the exterior wall. An addition with a shed roof boasted a sign welcoming visitors to the farm market.

The rustic deck in front of the barn was littered with patio chairs and umbrellas. Dale took Georgia's hand as they walked toward the door of the market. A cheerful woman with red-framed glasses and graying hair greeted them with a smile, while the delightful smell of baked sugar made Georgia's stomach rumble.

"Welcome to Barlow Farms. Can I help you find anything?"

Dale pointed at the bakery case at the other end of the room. "We saw your bakery sign and couldn't resist."

She finished putting jars of jam on a shelf. "I'll meet you down there. I just took some fresh cinnamon rolls out of the oven a few minutes ago, and we've got raspberry danish and marionberry scones this morning."

Dale glanced over at Georgia and winked. "We might have to take some back with us."

The woman met them and along with the items in the bakery case, she pointed at the sheets with baked goodies stashed on the counter behind her. Georgia admired her pleasant demeanor. She was one of those people who even when she wasn't smiling, had a happy look about her. It probably came from being surrounded by baked goods and the beautiful scenery. "I haven't had time to put these in the case yet."

"Ooh," said Georgia. "Everything looks so good. I think I'll go for one of those cinnamon rolls, but we're going to need a box to take a few things with us."

She added one of the rolls to a huge plate and set it on the counter. She arched her brows at Dale.

"I'd like a raspberry danish, please."

She set it next to the cinnamon roll and asked, "Would you like coffee, tea, lattes, with those?"

He glanced over at Georgia, who nodded. "Yes, two lattes would be wonderful."

"Have a seat, and I'll bring them to you. We've got some tables out the side door that are nice and shady." She pointed at the door across from the counter.

He carried their plates and led the way outside to a table with a red umbrella and a view of a huge plot of berry plants and the hills beyond. As they enjoyed the tranquil setting, the woman returned with two frothy lattes in ceramic mugs. "By the way, we're just putting out baskets of fresh berries, if you're interested."

Dale laughed. "We're interested. We'll be in to do more shopping when we're done with these beauties." He cut off a chunk of his danish and slipped it onto Georgia's plate.

She smiled and did the same with her cinnamon roll. As soon as she took her first bite, she groaned. "Oh, my, that is delicious. I daresay, it might be as good as Sugar Shack's."

Dale took a bite of the flaky goodness with raspberry oozing from every corner. "I've met very few pastries I wouldn't eat, but this is one of the best. This is quite the little hidden gem out here in the middle of nowhere."

As they sipped their lattes and savored every bite of their breakfast treats, Georgia realized how much she would miss her time with Dale when he left for home next week. Truth be told, she would have never ventured off the main path, not knowing where she was going, and she would have missed this wonderful spot and this time.

Lee had been a little like Dale. He was much more

adventurous than she. That was some of what she missed being on her own and not in any position to take a risk. So many things were easier with a partner. Some things weren't quite the same without that special someone to share them.

By the time they finished breakfast and shopped for things, they toted two bakery boxes, a flat of fresh raspberries and marionberries, and a box of homemade jams to the back of Georgia's car. After making sure everything was stowed and couldn't slide around, Dale slid behind the wheel. "If we do nothing else today, I'd call it a success. What a great spot."

He drove back to the road and continued over the river to the highway. The winery wasn't far and within a few minutes, they turned into the driveway. Like the farm they visited, the winery was quiet today. They were one of the few open on Monday, and Dale took advantage of the almost-empty parking lot and chose the spot nearest the door.

They strolled up the walkway to the wooden building with the metal roof. A young man behind the counter welcomed them and explained the wines they made, all of a Spanish variety.

He asked if they'd like a tasting, and Dale held up his hand. "I'm driving today, so not for me, but I think Georgia would like one."

She smiled. "I don't need a whole flight. I'd just love to sample that signature red one you mentioned."

He retrieved a glass and poured a splash of the gorgeous ruby-colored wine in it. Then, he handed Dale a bottle of water. "There you go. Feel free to wander the grounds. We've got an open tasting area in our barrel barn and lots of tables down by the river, as well as on the patio."

"Thank you," said Georgia, swirling the wine in her glass. They wandered outside, taking in the pretty stone fireplace on the patio and meandering over to the barrel barn. It was made from huge wooden logs and outfitted with tables and chairs. Dale pointed across the grassy area. "That's the river right there. How about we find a spot near it?"

She followed, and they found a table positioned at the edge of it, where they could hear the water splashing over the rocks. "What a gorgeous setting," said Georgia, taking a sip from her glass.

"Yeah, Heath made a good choice for his proposal. It would be impossible for Lydia to say no against this backdrop." He chuckled and gazed at the river. "How's the wine?"

"It's good. I'm not a real wine critic, so I couldn't tell you much about it, but it's nice. Izzy, now, she's the one who could analyze it for us. She and the others were such fun to meet."

He grinned and took a sip from his water. "Speaking of Izzy, I've been tossing an idea around." He paused and added, "I'd like to take a little trip to the San Juan Islands and visit them. Would you go with me, Georgia?"

Her eyes widened, and she swallowed the sip of wine in her mouth, willing herself not to choke on it.

"I've been wanting to ask you and waiting for the right time. I don't want you to feel obligated, and I'm not suggesting any funny business. I don't want this to be awkward. I emailed Izzy and the others and told them I was hoping to plan a trip over in the coming weeks. I mentioned you might accompany me, and they all offered their houses. Jess lives down the street from Izzy but doesn't have much room. Izzy has two guestrooms, and Sam has a huge house with lots of guestrooms. Izzy is on the golf course, and Sam is on the water. Kate has a smaller house in town, so only one of us could stay there. If you're interested, you get first choice on accommodations."

Her heart thudded in her chest. For once in her life, Georgia didn't think about it and mull it around her mind. Instead, she grinned and said, "Yes, I'd love to go with you."

His blue eyes held hers and twinkled as his smile reached all the way to the corners of them and magnified the tiny creases at their edges. He reached for her hand and held it to his lips, kissing the top of her knuckles. "You've made my day, Georgia. I was nervous to ask you but am so pleased you said yes. I think you'll love it there."

He sighed and added, "It'll be an adventure."

She smiled and put her other hand atop his. "I've decided I need more adventures in my life."

CHAPTER TWENTY-ONE

After more meandering along the country roads, while they discussed the logistics related to their spontaneous trip to the San Juan Islands, Georgia and Dale did some window shopping in Applegate and the small towns surrounding it. They opted to have dinner at a golf course Dale spied from the road.

It had an elegant restaurant overlooking the lush green grounds with the river snaking through it. Georgia was worried they were dressed too casually, but the hostess assured her they weren't. They sat on the terrace and enjoyed the view. Dale had a steak, and she had salmon with wild mushroom risotto. It wasn't quite as good as Lydia's but still tasty.

By the time they got back to the farm, it was almost dark, but Duke's truck was in the yard, and Georgia urged Dale to come in for a cup of tea before he went back to the ranch.

He helped her carry in the bakery treats and after the dogs greeted them, they found Olivia and Duke in the kitchen. "Oh, what did you two find?" asked Olivia, eyeing their loot.

"The best little farm with a bakery."

Duke smiled. "Barlow Farms, I bet. They have the best jam in the world."

Dale set the boxes on the counter. "Not to mention their pastries. We brought some back to share."

Duke talked Olivia into sharing a cinnamon roll with him, and all four of them sat at the dining table with steaming mugs of tea. The dogs were stretched out on the area rug, settled in for the evening.

Georgia took her seat. "Where is everybody?"

Olivia added a bit of honey to her tea. "Buck took Micki out for a nice dinner to celebrate the end of the festival, and Clay and Harry went to look at a horse and have dinner in Medford. Lydia and Heath are at the ranch, of course. Jade is in the motorhome."

Duke tilted his head toward the window. "We volunteered to keep an eye on Jade and let Micki have an evening to herself. I brought some takeout from Roosters, and Jade ate with us but was tired and went to bed early. We've just been talking." He smiled at Olivia.

Olivia set her mug on the table and glanced over at Georgia. "I'm glad you're both here. We have a huge favor to ask, but we don't want you to feel obligated." She sighed and shifted her eyes to Duke who nodded.

"Now that the festival is over, we'd like to take a little getaway. We thought we'd leave Sunday morning, after Jewel's celebration and be back on Wednesday in time for the wedding. Just a few days away, but I need someone to take care of the dogs in the shelter. I thought maybe you and Dale might be willing."

Before Georgia could say anything, Dale said, "Sure thing.

I'm going to stick around for the wedding and need something to do. I'm happy to help and can stay here when Georgia's working in town."

Georgia grinned at Dale. "What he said. We'll just need a lesson, but I'm happy to do it."

Olivia raised her brows at Dale. "And you'll get to spend more time with Suki."

He chuckled. "A bonus. She's a great dog."

Duke reached over and put his hand on Olivia's. "May can take care of Dad those days, too. We're going to head over to the coast. First, to Bandon and drive up to Depoe Bay."

Olivia smiled at Duke and then turned to Georgia. "I really appreciate it. I hate to ask, but we're trying to squeeze it in before the end of the month and while I thought about asking Jade to give her more responsibility, I'm not sure she can handle it yet, and she's busy with her therapy and community service."

Dale took a quick sip from his cup. "Over the years, I worked with lots of guys who needed a second chance and had sketchy pasts. I'm willing to try to engage with Jade and see if I can get her to help me with the chores while you're away."

"That would be great. She's already shown an interest in the dogs and seems more relaxed around them. I'm not going to take in any new dogs until I get back from the trip. They can be hard to transition, and I don't want to leave you with a problem. I have a couple interested in the two terriers, so they may be gone to a forever home by then."

Dale shrugged. "Don't stress about them. I can handle it, I'm sure."

Georgia stirred her spoon in her mug and cleared her throat. "Speaking of getaways. Dale asked me to visit the San

Juan Islands with him. We'd go after the wedding, and I'd be gone for about twelve days." She gritted her teeth. "I'm going to ask Edith for a couple of days off and make it up to her when I get back. With the festival over, I don't have anything pressing."

Olivia's smile widened. "I think that's fabulous. You'll have a wonderful time."

Dale glanced between Olivia and Duke. "The ladies who visited and stayed at the ranch offered us a place to stay, which is great, since it's always busy during the summer, and lodging is hard to find."

"Oh, that's even better. They were all so nice." Olivia turned to Duke. "That would be a fun trip to plan. Maybe later in the year?"

"Kyle is set to stay through October, but I've asked him if he'd like to move here and work at the practice permanently. If he doesn't, I'm going to search for another vet to add to the practice, and it will make it easier to have an extended vacation."

Dale put a hand on his shoulder. "Take it from someone who didn't always make time for vacations, make it a top priority to find another vet. We let our business run our lives and only in the last few years started to make living life a bigger priority than work. You think you'll have time, but time is sneaky. It has a way of slipping through your fingers when you're not even paying attention."

Georgia noticed the sadness in Dale's eyes. She put a hand on his arm. "We were talking about that on our ride today. Neither of us expected this next chapter in our lives, to be on our own, but we decided we're going to live it to the fullest, embrace every chance for an adventure, and create all the new memories we can."

Olivia and Duke exchanged a sweet smile. She met

Georgia's eyes. "Duke and I are thinking along those same lines. Coming here, after everything I went through, finding a family and finding Duke… it's taught me that change doesn't have to be bad and can lead to new and wonderful opportunities."

Duke leaned closer to her and kissed her cheek. "Couldn't have said it better."

Saturday, with all the work for Jewel's celebration, Georgia and Dale opted to skip their morning walk. They'd be getting plenty of exercise toting things back and forth.

The week had flown by with Georgia busy at the fabric store and sewing a new dress. She had to stay late on Wednesday to get it finished, but it was ready and one of her best efforts.

Dale spent much of the week with Olivia, helping in the shelter and getting the dogs used to him. Last night, while they were enjoying a moonlit walk, Suki came with them. It was easy to see the bond that had formed between the two of them in just a week. Georgia suspected Suki would soon be living in Lake Stevens, with the man who held her heart, too.

The celebration for Jewel was on the casual side, but they had requested all the attendees wear purple or lavender to honor her. Along with making her new dress for the wedding, Georgia sewed a blouse in a gorgeous deep-purple fabric she found at In Stitches. She fell in love with a pattern for a crossover hem blouse with ruffle sleeves and couldn't resist making it for the special occasion.

It hung in her closet, but she slipped on an old shirt, ready to help with the setup of the celebration. She found Micki on the porch, working on making flower arrangements for the tables. She was adding dahlias to a vase.

Georgia took the empty chair at the small table and made another vase. As they worked, Clay's truck pulled into the yard. Behind it, a trailer held a huge grill. He waved as he continued by them and toward the fields. Harry was already out in the field, supervising the setup.

Soon, another truck arrived loaded with tables and chairs and another with a large white tent and portable restrooms. Yesterday, Tyler mowed the field closest to the lavender and dahlias, so they could set up the tent.

As Georgia finished the last vase, this one filled with sunflowers, Heath and Lydia pulled up to the house. They unloaded several stainless-steel serving pans from the back of his truck and climbed the steps to the porch.

"Morning," said Lydia as she gazed at the flowers. "Those look gorgeous."

"Thanks," Micki said as she glanced over at the motorhome. "I'm going to roust Jade and have her help me get started on the tables."

Georgia stood and held the door for Heath and Lydia. "I'm on kitchen duty with you, Lydia."

Heath left his trays on the counter, and Georgia noticed they were filled with produce. He left Lydia with a kiss and hurried to help Clay with the grill.

Georgia and Lydia slipped aprons over their heads and chopped veggies and fruit for all the salads on the menu. Micki had left a huge basket of fresh tomatoes from the garden on the counter, and Georgia tackled those first.

As Lydia ran a knife through a pineapple, she gestured to the stainless trays. "Heath and Clay are going to set up a big trough with ice, and then we can put these trays in it for serving the cold items."

"What a smart idea." Georgia couldn't resist popping a few pieces of fresh tomato in her mouth. "These are so good. There's something about tomatoes fresh from the vine. These are even still warm from the morning sun."

"They definitely spoil you and make it almost impossible to eat one from the store."

"How are things going for the wedding?"

Lydia grinned. "Well, as much as I wanted to do the food and make my own cake, Heath finally convinced me to have Darcy do the cake, and Cheryl and Cyrus are doing the food for us. It's a small event, so it won't be overwhelming. That eliminated all my stress."

"Oh, I'm glad you relented. That's way too much work for a bride. How about your dress? Did they get the alterations done?"

She nodded. "It's gorgeous and yes, we picked it up yesterday in Medford. Suzy is doing my bouquet, and Micki is putting together the other flowers using the dahlias for decorations. We're trying to keep things simple."

"Well, I couldn't help myself and splurged to make a new dress." Georgia scrunched up her nose and smiled.

"I'm not surprised at that. Harry told me she even bought a new dress. I can't believe she's going to wear a dress."

"That just shows you how special you are to her." Georgia slid the diced tomatoes into a bowl and reached for more. She gasped. "I wonder if Jade has a dress. We didn't buy anything when we took her shopping."

Lydia cut into a watermelon. "Micki said they're going shopping tomorrow. She's taking Jade to Medford to treat her to a dress and shoes for the wedding."

"Oh, that's good news. It seems like this week especially things have improved between the two of them."

Lydia added the cubes of red melon to the stainless tray.

"Yeah, Micki seems less stressed, and I think Jade is trying a bit harder."

"She's been working with Dale in the shelter, and he said the same thing. I think helping the dogs and also her service at the soup kitchen and senior center are having an impact." With the mountain of tomatoes done, Georgia reached for the bunch of fresh basil, also from Micki's garden.

Lydia split open a second watermelon. "It's always easy to feel sorry for yourself until you meet someone who is worse off than you; helping someone else always makes you feel better. I think that's what cooking has always done for me. It's been a way I can make someone happy or brighten their day. Even when I was at my worst, I could do that, and it helped me focus less on my own worries."

As Georgia added the chopped basil to the tomatoes, she nodded. "We all need a sense of purpose. It sounds old fashioned, but people tend to rise to your level of expectation. I've seen it countless times when working with students. Teachers who expressed doubt and expected little from a student, got exactly that. On the other hand, students who had teachers with high expectations and who conveyed their belief that their students could succeed, performed at higher levels, often surprising themselves. It boosted their confidence and often changed their trajectory."

"Olivia is so good with Jade. Like those teachers you mentioned, I think she's helping encourage Jade and reassure her that she can do something. The dogs are so accepting and don't judge, so it's a great fit for Jade."

Using the tip of her knife, Georgia pointed at the red onions. "I want to do those last. They always make my eyes water."

Lydia grinned and pointed at the bag of potatoes. "You

can start on those, and we'll get them boiling. I can tackle the onions."

Georgia moved to the sink to rinse the potatoes. "I agree about Olivia. She has such a kind heart. She's probably the most like Jewel of all of us."

With a glance around the kitchen, Lydia smiled. "It's hard not to feel Jewel here today. I think she'd be so happy to see all of us together."

"She would love that you found your soulmate in Heath."

As she slid more cubes of melon into the tray, Lydia beamed. "From the looks of things, I'd say you and Dale might have a story to tell. She would adore the thought of you two reconnecting."

Letting Lydia's words sink in and imagining the smile on Jewel's face, Georgia floated on air as she reached for the first of many potatoes to peel.

CHAPTER TWENTY-TWO

W ith all the food prepared and Heath and Clay manning the grill and watching over Jade, who was tasked with filling the trough with cold drinks, the five women dressed in purple and lavender shirts with their jeans, took the urns from the bedroom closet and used Chuck's old truck to make the trek down to the lake.

Harry parked near the tree that was so special to Chuck and Jewel. She and Olivia helped Micki and Lydia from the back of the truck. First, they stopped at the double headstone between the tree and the lake.

Along with their names and dates of birth and death, the stonemason had carved sprigs of lavender across the headstone. He'd done a fabulous job and added REAL LOVE STORIES NEVER HAVE ENDINGS along the bottom of the stone. Holes had been dug and prepped for the urns in front of the stone.

As Georgia reached out and put her hand on the cool stone, tears fell from her eyes. Despite knowing Jewel was gone, seeing her name etched on the stone intensified the finality of her passing. Like the others, Georgia often felt Jewel's presence around the farm. A scent, the feel of the stitches on one of her old quilts, or seeing Jewel's handwriting would trigger a memory and take Georgia back to those days when she first arrived and the months and years that followed where she found the love of a family.

Staring at the headstone, running her fingers in the grooves of the letters of Jewel's name, erased the illusion that Jewel might walk through the door, her signature smile bright, and her arms open to welcome Georgia with one of her epic hugs. As much as she understood Jewel was gone, a tiny part of her pretended she wasn't. It was a defense mechanism and with everything that had happened over the last year, it served her well.

They all stood in front of the headstone, and Olivia looked out at the lake and pointed. "Chuck and Jewel will have the view they always treasured forever. They loved coming here to sit under the stars. It's a fitting place for them to be remembered, but I believe they're up above looking down on us, like their beloved stars."

Harry handed Georgia one of the three urns. "This is the one that has their ashes comingled. With you being the eldest and the first young girl they fostered, we think you should do the honors and scatter them."

Georgia pulled a tissue from her pocket and wiped her eyes. She took the urn and walked nearer to the lake. She unscrewed the top and shook out the cremains. The subtle breeze carried them and deposited some in the clear water and others along the shore and in the grassy field. Through her tears, she noticed the glittery effect they had on the top of the water and smiled. "Goodbye, Jewel. I'll always love you."

She replaced the top on the urn and glanced back at the

others, all with tears in their eyes. "Farewell, Jewel and Chuck," said Micki.

Lydia sniffed and dabbed at her eyes. "I like that they'll be part of the lake and land forever."

Harry took Chuck's urn, engraved with a horse, and handed Lydia Jewel's, decorated with sprigs of lavender. "We can place these in the ground. Clay said he'd cover them as soon as we were done."

Georgia, Olivia, and Micki gathered the flowers from the back of the truck and placed them along the base of the stone. Colorful dahlias, cheerful sunflowers, and Jewel's beloved lavender brightened the deep-gray stone.

The five of them linked arms and walked back to the truck in silence.

There wasn't a dry eye in the field when Harry finished her speech honoring Jewel. Instead of each of the women speaking about Jewel, they told their stories to Harry, and she wove everything together for her tribute.

The guests ate the food Jewel would have loved and complimented Lydia, along with Heath and Clay, on their delicious fare. As dessert was served, Harry let everyone know they were welcome to walk or ride down to the lake and pay their respects at the headstone.

Several people elected to walk, while Clay and Heath, along with Buck, shuttled others through the field and to the lake. At the urging of the others, Duke and Olivia left to get on the road to the coast.

After hours of visiting, the guests left, and the field was cleared of the tent and tables and chairs. Micki made sure

Jade was settled in the motorhome, and Lydia checked on the dogs.

With the farm quiet, the four couples drove down to the lake where Heath and Clay set up a fire ring, and they spent the rest of the evening telling stories and enjoying the happy memories of Jewel and Chuck. As Georgia sat in a camp chair, watching the flicker of the orange flames rise into the dark sky, littered with twinkling stars, she too was sure Jewel and Chuck were watching over them from above.

The fabric store was quiet on Tuesday and Wednesday, and Georgia was able to make two more blouses to take on her upcoming trip to the San Juan Islands. With her new job and ability to sew for hours each week, she was putting a dent in her stack of fabric she brought to the cottage.

Along with giving her permission to close the store early on Wednesday for the wedding, Edith was happy to give Georgia the next week off and take her up on covering some extra shifts to make up for her impromptu vacation. As much as Georgia was looking forward to their trip, once it was over and Dale went home, she would need the distraction.

Not wanting the gloom of that idea invading her happy mood, Georgia pushed the thought aside and filled out the meager deposit sheet for the day before locking the door at four o'clock.

The wedding was at six, but she wanted time to change and go over to help Lydia with the others. She hung her new blouses on the hook in the backseat and hurried to the farm.

Once inside her cottage, she touched up her hair, added a little color to her lips and cheeks, and then slipped into her dress. She smoothed the fabric of the skirt and admired the copper and burgundy flowers that adorned the white fabric of the lower part of the skirt and the neckline of the bodice. She'd been drawn to it because the colors matched her hair so well. She added the sheer coppery colored metallic long jacket she made to go over it and smiled. After slipping into the sparkly sandals she reserved for only the most special occasions, she hurried to the main house.

Olivia was in the kitchen, adding a bowtie to Chief. Hope and Willow were already outfitted with sunflower wreaths around their necks. Georgia stared at Olivia, taking in her shiny hair, curled and draped around her shoulders. Her dress was stunning—a steely blue with a subtle floral pattern just a shade darker than the dress. It reminded Georgia of watercolors. It had a sheer long jacket that reached to just above the hemline.

Georgia waited until the bowtie was secure. "That dress is stunning on you, Olivia."

She turned away from the dogs and smiled. "May and I went shopping a few weeks ago. It was on a huge sale."

As her eyes drifted toward the dogs, Georgia grinned. "They look so cute and fluffy. How was your trip?"

Olivia glanced up at her, and joy radiated from her smile. "It was perfect. We had the best time. So relaxing, and the scenery was gorgeous. I took a ton of pictures." She sighed and adjusted Chief's tie. "We got home about noon today, and Jade and I gave them all a bath, so they'd be nice and clean. I need to grab a photo of them before anything happens to their accessories." She reached behind her on the counter. After she took a few of them, posed together, Georgia took the phone and offered to take some with Olivia in the midst.

As they finished the photoshoot, Harry came from her

bedroom. Olivia and Georgia stood, their mouths gaping, as she walked into the kitchen. Her deep-burgundy dress hit just below her knee, with a barely there lettuce edge hemline. A short, sheer jacket in the same color covered the sleeveless V-neck bodice. Olivia brought her hand to her mouth. "You look gorgeous, Harry."

Georgia nodded and went to feel the soft chiffon-like fabric. "This is lovely."

"I found it on one of our rides to Medford. While Clay was talking horses, I ran into town and found a little boutique. The sales lady was so patient and helped me find this one."

Micki came downstairs wearing a deep-purple, knee-length column dress with a draped front. Jade came from the mudroom, wearing a maxi dress, in a green and black floral print.

"You both look beautiful," said Georgia. She pointed at the dogs. "Look how cute the dogs look with their flowers and Chief in a bowtie." At the mention of the dogs, Georgia noticed the unease disappear from Jade's eyes.

She hurried to them and petted their heads, talking to them, as they posed.

Micki reached and moved the skirt of Georgia's dress. "And you made this?" She shook her head. "It's beautiful. I love the fabric, and it looks like it came from one of those fancy shops."

Harry smiled at Georgia. "You're so talented. If I had to make a dress, it would look like a square with holes for the arms." Harry looked at the clock. "We better get going." She held up her keys. "I'll drive."

Micki nodded. "Jade and the dogs can ride with me. We don't need to get squished into one car."

They made their way to the ranch, parking in the front by

the statue. Harry opened the front door without knocking and led the way to Clay's wing of the house. "Lydia's staying in Clay's guest room, and the boys are in Heath's side of the house."

The dogs took off in the direction of the kitchen, on the hunt for Ace and Maverick. As the women followed Harry down the hallway, their heels clicked across the floor. Harry tapped on the door of the guestroom. "It's just us, Lydia."

"Come in," she said, from behind the door.

The women gasped when they saw Lydia standing in front of the mirror. She turned and smiled. "I can't stop staring at this dress. I love it."

Georgia stepped forward and examined the intricate lace bodice of the ivory gown before running her fingers over the skirt with the glittery tulle underlay. "It's perfect on you, Lydia. You look like a princess."

Olivia stood to the side of the bride. "That high neckline is so elegant."

Lydia turned and gazed at all of them. "You're the ones who look gorgeous." Her mouth hung open when Harry stepped forward. "I don't think I've ever seen your legs. You look fabulous."

That made them all laugh. Lydia wasn't wearing a veil, so she didn't need much help, except to button what looked to be dozens of fabric-covered buttons on the back of the dress, where the lace bodice continued. Georgia and Olivia got to work on that task.

Jade was studying Lydia's blond hair, sans her normal ponytail and styled in a pretty up-do with a few tendrils of hair framing her face. "I love your hair that way."

"Thanks, Jade," she said, turning to check it. "I would wear it down but thought it might bug me. I'm so used to having it up and out of my face."

Georgia tapped the ends of the gorgeous diamond and pearl earrings hanging from Lydia's ears. "And we couldn't see these beauties if your hair was covering them. They're perfect with the dress."

Lydia blushed. "Heath gave them to me as a wedding gift."

Georgia fastened the last button as someone knocked on the door. Micki was nearest it and opened it a crack. "Hi, Skip." She opened the door wider. "Your photographer is here, Lydia."

He stepped inside the room and greeted everyone. "What a beautiful bride. I thought we could take a few of you getting ready and some candid shots. I've got several of Heath with Clay and Cassidy."

The women gathered around Lydia, and Skip snapped photo after photo. When he finished, it was time for the ceremony. Skip hurried outside to capture the procession.

The ladies walked with Lydia as far as the great room, where the doors were already opened to the patio and beyond. After many hugs, the four sisters and Jade made their way outside.

Near the pond, with the beautiful backdrop of lush green fields and the tree line in the distance, white chairs were set up for the guests. A burlap aisle runner, with white rose petals sprinkled along the sides, stretched from the steps of the patio to the flower-covered archway. With so few guests, they all had a front row seat, and Georgia spotted Dale and slipped into the chair next to his.

She noticed Heath, handsome as ever in his black tuxedo, grinning while he waited for his bride. Despite Heath and Clay knowing every living soul in Lavender Valley, they succeeded in keeping the ceremony small, with only Heath's daughter Cassidy joining Lydia's newfound sisters and their significant others.

Between the two brothers, they could have had hundreds of guests, but it touched Georgia's heart that Heath wanted to make today all about Lydia and what she wanted. Micki, seated next to her, reached over and gripped Georgia's arm and whispered, "The guy marrying them is Judge Hastings. The judge who sentenced Jade."

Jade sat on the other side of Dale and hadn't noticed yet. Georgia hoped she wouldn't make a scene. It was too late to worry about. Notes from the string quartet seated to the right of the archway, drifted through the air, and everyone stood to await Lydia.

She was nothing short of gorgeous as she came from the patio and across the grass. Her gown sparkled in the evening sunlight, and the beautiful stems she held of white peonies, roses, and ranunculus with just a few springs of lavender were perfect.

She made her way up the aisle and reached for Heath's hand. As Judge Hastings began, Georgia noticed Jade flinch, and her cheeks reddened with embarrassment. She focused on her lap, and Georgia turned her attention back to the main event.

After lovely words from the judge about knowing the groom and his family and Jewel forever, he was honored to be uniting Heath and Lydia in marriage. It was a quick ceremony with Cassidy stepping forward to take Lydia's bouquet when it came time for the ring exchange. After an affectionate kiss as a married couple and a few clicks from Skip's camera to capture the magic of that moment, the guests clapped and whistled.

Judge Hastings let everyone know they had dinner set up on the patio, and the bride and groom would be taking a few photos before joining them.

Olivia and Duke walked next to Dale and Georgia as they

made their way across the thick grass to the patio. Olivia pointed at the couple wearing black aprons, standing near the dinner table. "That's Cyrus and Cheryl, the owners of the Ranch House, where Lydia worked."

Georgia glanced over at them. "Oh, I haven't eaten there yet but have heard great things. That's nice that they're doing the food. Lydia and Heath are both such wonderful cooks and foodies, I'm sure they kept them on their toes."

They were all sipping drinks and enjoying the assortment of appetizers, when Heath and Lydia, along with Harry and Clay, came from the house. Heath with his hand linked in Lydia's raised them. "It's official, the marriage certificate is signed and witnessed." He glanced over at Harry and Clay.

Everyone cheered and raised their glasses, while Clay toasted the couple. "I couldn't be happier for my brother who found the love of his life and for adding a wonderful woman and sister to our family. Congratulations to Heath and Lydia."

After glasses were clinked and more champagne poured, everyone gathered around the table, decorated with dozens of votive candles flickering and vases of dahlias, sunflowers, and lavender. Heath pulled out a chair for his bride and took the one next to her. "Judge Hastings sends his regards but couldn't stay for dinner." He glanced over at Skip, who took a few candid photos. "Pull up a chair, buddy. Take a break."

He laughed and slipped into the open chair next to Duke.

After an exquisite meal of a fresh salad, filet mignon, Lydia's famous mushroom risotto, roasted veggies, and fresh garlic rolls, Skip took photos of the cake table, with a beautiful rustic tiered cake, wrapped with a lavender ribbon.

He suggested a few more photos of the group on the lawn by the pond before the cake was served. Along with the group photos and those with the five sisters, he took each couple's photo.

Georgia beamed when Skip showed her the preview of her photo with Dale. They looked so happy and with him in his suit and the burgundy tie that matched her dress perfectly, they made a smart couple.

She couldn't wait to get a copy and frame it to keep in her cottage. She wanted to hold the memory of this night and all its happiness forever.

CHAPTER TWENTY-THREE

Thursday morning, Georgia was up early, with her suitcases packed and ready. Harry had a meeting in Medford and offered to drop her and Dale at the airport for their flight to Seattle. She was already taking Cassidy to the airport to catch her flight to California.

Heath and Lydia had left at the crack of dawn for their honeymoon. They were making the trek to Glacier National Park and would be gone for two weeks. After a quick goodbye to Micki, Jade, and Olivia, Harry helped load Georgia's suitcases in the back of her SUV, and they headed next door to pick up the others.

Cassidy and Dale were waiting under the portico, and he loaded the luggage before joining Georgia in the backseat. He chuckled as he fastened his seatbelt. "Harry, if the mayor thing doesn't work out, you could always start an airport shuttle service."

She smiled at him in the rearview mirror and sped toward the highway. "It wouldn't be a bad gig. No traffic out here."

As she drove, the others chatted. Cassidy was on her phone, tapping in replies to emails and texts, but when Georgia asked when she might come back for another visit, her smile widened. "Heath and Lydia invited me to come for Christmas, so I'll be here for the holidays."

"Oh, that's wonderful and will be special for all of you."

Harry pulled into the parking lot and drop-off area of the airport. Dale hurried out to unload the bags. Cassidy hugged each of them before hurrying to the door to check in for her flight.

Dale took charge of their bags, while Georgia collected her purse from the SUV. "Thanks for the ride, Harry. I'll be in touch and will let you know if my flight changes."

Harry smiled and accepted Georgia's embrace. "We'll miss you, but we all want you and Dale to have the best time and say hi to everyone for us. Clay and I are seriously talking about a trip to visit them before the end of the year."

Georgia hugged her again. "You should do it. You two deserve a nice getaway."

Harry waved and hollered. "Be sure to check in and let us know how you're doing. See you soon."

Dale waved and handed Georgia the handle of her suitcase. The airport was small and friendly, and it didn't take them long to get checked in and find their gate. Dale settled into a seat. "It's a short flight. Only about ninety minutes."

Georgia checked her watch. "Not much longer now."

Dale reached for her hand. "We'll get a car from the airport and should be at my place by one o'clock or so. Then, we'll go have some lunch, and I can give you a tour."

Her entire body hummed with excitement. She hadn't been on a vacation in years and despite not a huge fan of flying, she was looking forward to their adventure. "You said we need to leave early tomorrow to catch the ferry."

"Yeah, I want to take the one at nine o'clock, so we miss the Friday rush, if possible. It will take us over an hour to get to Anacortes, so I'd like to leave before seven, so we have plenty of time. Traffic can be a bear."

"I can't remember the last time I was on a ferry."

"It's a beautiful trip. You'll love the scenery."

The woman at the desk called for boarding and in a matter of minutes, they were buckled into their seats, and the small plane inched toward the runway.

Georgia gripped Dale's hand as the plane gathered speed and lifted into the air. He squeezed it and leaned closer to her. "We're up and away, just sit back and relax."

After leaning her head back and taking a deep breath, Georgia closed her eyes. After a few minutes, the flight attendant took their drink order and returned with two ginger ales and pretzels for each of them.

Georgia sipped on the drink and relaxed. When the flight attendant returned, she had to gulp the remaining ginger ale down and dispose of her cup. They were already preparing to land.

As they descended, she held onto Dale's hand, but before she knew it, they were on the ground with barely a bump as they landed. It seemed to take longer to get to the gate than it did to fly, but they finally exited the plane, and Dale led her to the baggage claim.

He was on the phone and by the time they collected their bags, their car was only a few minutes away from the parking garage rideshare pickup area. They hurried from the terminal and arrived seconds before their car.

Dale loaded the bags in the trunk and helped Georgia into the backseat before hurrying around to his side of the car. The driver, a young man who explained he drove to make extra money while attending UW, was pleasant and knew the layout of the airport.

Georgia enjoyed the view as the car sped north, slowing down for traffic around Renton, and then it was smooth sailing all the way up to Lake Stevens. When the car pulled to an elegant gate across a long, paved driveway, Georgia gasped. "Oh, my, this is gorgeous, Dale." She caught a glimpse of the expansive roofline behind the trees planted in the circle of grass where the driveway looped.

He smiled and got out of the car to punch in the code. The gate swung open, and he hurried through it to meet the car as their driver moved forward. Dale pointed at the driveway. "Just loop around and drop us at the front door. The gate will open automatically when you leave."

The car stopped at the covered entry, and Dale unloaded their bags. Georgia gawked at the sprawling Craftsman-style home. It and the surrounding grounds were immaculate. Their car drove away, and Dale tapped her arm and led the way to the leaded glass entry doors. She wheeled her suitcase while he took charge of her other one and his. He unlocked the door and gestured for her to go first.

She stepped onto the thick rug over the shiny wooden floors and stared at the huge floor-to-ceiling windows across from her. They offered a wide view of Puget Sound in the distance. It was beyond stunning.

Dale took hold of both of her suitcases. "Come on in, and I'll show you the guest room."

Georgia took a few steps forward into the large living space and studied the formal dining room to the right of the entry. It was sleek and elegant, done in dark wood and muted neutrals. She walked further into the living space and noticed the patio she recognized from Dale's texts. It was situated off the living area through huge sliding glass doors. An L-shaped leather couch stood in front of a brick fireplace with a flatscreen television mounted above it. To the right, she noticed the kitchen and a small eating area, all open to the great room.

As she took it all in, she couldn't get over the windows at the rear of the house and how they all offered a stunning view of the lush grounds and the water beyond. The kitchen, which rivaled Heath and Clay's, used the same dark wood, whites, and neutrals to create a welcoming but stylish space. She pointed at the telescope in the corner of the breakfast nook.

"Oh, I love to gaze out at the water and look for boats." He pointed across the living area to the staircase. "You have your choice of three guest rooms, but I'll show you my favorite first."

He trudged up the stairs with her two bags and led her down the hallway. He stopped and gestured to the open door. She stepped into the room, her feet sinking into the thick, beige carpet. "This one has a television and a view of the water. The other two are on the front of the house with a view of the yard."

She took in the muted beige and grays of the décor. "I love it. This is perfect."

He placed her bags on a low bench near the closet. "The bathroom is right across the hallway and should have everything you need. Lots of spare towels and toiletries in the bathroom closet if you need them."

He glanced over at Georgia, who was staring out the window. "I'll let you get settled. Just come on down when you're ready, and we'll go grab some lunch."

"Wonderful, thank you. I won't be long." She opened her

suitcase and took out the blouses she didn't want to leave to wrinkle but left everything else.

After a quick stop in the bathroom with its heated tile floor and copper and glass accents that looked more like a hotel bathroom than one in a home, she went downstairs. She saw Dale sitting on the patio and stepped through the doors to join him.

He rose from his chair and smiled at her. "Are you ready?"

She walked to the edge of where he was sitting, and her eyes widened. The patio extended past the living area and all along the side of the house. There was another door off the kitchen that led to the outdoor kitchen with a grill. "If I lived here, I'd never want to leave. Your view, the whole house, is breathtaking."

He nodded and joined her near the edge of the concrete. "I've become accustomed to it, but you're making me remember the first time I saw it all done and ready to move into, and I felt the same way. How about I run and grab some takeout and get something to grill for dinner. You stay here, relax, and enjoy the view."

"If that's not too much trouble, I love that idea. I'd like nothing more than to stare at that water for the rest of the day."

He pointed back at the house. "Help yourself to anything you want. There are some cold drinks in the fridge. I'll be back in a few."

He left her with a wave and at the sound of the door to the garage closing, she retrieved a bottle of water from the fridge and settled into a lounge chair to gaze at the water.

By the time he returned, she was so relaxed, she had a hard time keeping her eyes open, but the scent of food roused her from her chair. She found him in the kitchen, storing things in the fridge. He pointed at the bag of takeout on the granite counter. "I stopped by one of my favorite places and got a variety to share for lunch. Then, the more I thought about cooking and cleaning up, I decided we could order something later for dinner unless we have enough leftovers, we don't need it. We're only here for a few hours."

"Works for me," said Georgia, peeking inside the bag. "It smells delicious."

He retrieved two plates. "Salad, tacos, and a burger. Their portions are huge, so we can easily split them."

There were enough steak and chicken tacos for both of them, so the burger went in the fridge for later. They took their plates outside to the table. Dale flicked a switch, and the firepit in the center of it came to life, with golden flames sprouting from the blue glass. "Oh, how pretty. I bet that's stunning when it's darker outside," said Georgia, taking the chair he offered.

"What would you like to drink? I picked up some white wine that was already chilled, and we have water and iced tea, plus some other soft drinks."

"Water would be wonderful, and I'll reserve a glass of wine for later."

He dashed to the kitchen and returned with two tall glasses of iced water. He took his seat and speared a bite of salad. "This is so good with the strawberries and almonds."

She nodded. "Yes, it's quite good." She bit into a chicken taco. "Oh, I can see why this is a favorite. Delicious. Even better than Rooster's, but don't tell him."

He chuckled as he dug into his tacos. "Sam said to stop by her coffee shop when we get off the ferry tomorrow, and Jeff will take us out to their house. They've organized a barbecue at their house Sunday to welcome us and invited the other ladies and their significant others, plus a few more people."

"That sounds terrific and so nice of her. I had a tough

time choosing which house, but the idea of being able to sit outside and gaze at the ocean on vacation is my idea of heaven."

"Izzy wants to host a lunch for the ladies while I join the guys for a game of golf, so we'll get to visit with her at her place, too. She's right on the golf course, and Jess is just down the street from her."

"It's going to be hard to sleep tonight. I'm so excited to see the islands and them."

He gathered their empty plates and took them into the kitchen. When he returned, he held out his hand to her. "How about a quick tour of the rest of the house, and then you can enjoy that glass of wine and wait for the sunset?"

She slipped her hand in his and relished the warmth and affection. "Sounds heavenly."

He guided her to the opposite end of the main floor, away from the kitchen. "This is where my office is and the master bed and bath."

First, he stopped at the double glass doors to his office. Two desk chairs sat atop the gleaming wood floor, and the space held built-in bookcases and granite counters that matched those in the kitchen. The huge desk space with computer monitors stretched across the room and offered those seated a gorgeous view out to the water.

"What a wonderful workspace. Is it hard to concentrate with that view?"

He smiled. "It makes working here very enjoyable. Nowadays, I don't do much actual work, but it served me well."

He led the way down the hall to the master suite. In a word, it was enormous. Another wall of windows provided an exceptional view from the back of the property. Along with a huge bed, there was a velvet fainting couch, two chairs, and a table with a bookcase, a flatscreen television, and nightstands.

The master closet held built-in dressers and drawers, hanging rods, shoe storage, and even had a small couch. Georgia had never seen anything like it. She noticed one whole wall was empty except for hangers.

Next, he led her into the master bathroom, which was bigger than her entire cottage. It held a huge soaking tub, a walk-in shower, and a long counter with double sinks. The toilet was in a separate space with its own door. The same neutral cabinets and colors from the kitchen carried through to the space. She felt the floor made from huge square tiles and smiled at the warmth.

It could have been in an architectural magazine. "It's stunning, Dale. Just gorgeous. I love the subtle colors and décor."

"Aww, that's all Sarah's doing. She had a keen eye and didn't like fussy."

"Well, it's beyond beautiful."

"Let's go upstairs, and I'll show you the game room. That's always been a favorite gathering place when the grandkids are here." He held her hand as they climbed the stairs. She poked her head into the other two guest rooms and another bathroom, then he smiled and held out his hand at the entry to the bonus room.

It held a pool table, some exercise equipment, a huge television, several couches and chairs, and was decorated with some sports memorabilia. At one end, there was a small kitchen, with a snack bar for eating. "Wow, you've got everything you need to live in this room."

"It's been a great place for the kids. Anymore, I barely come upstairs. Everything I need is on the main floor. That's how we designed it. We didn't want to have to trek up the stairs in our old age."

Sadness filled his eyes but disappeared as quickly as it arrived, and he smiled at her. "How about we catch the sunset?"

She followed him down the stairs to the kitchen, where he poured her a glass of wine and grabbed a beer for himself. They settled back into their chairs at the firepit and as they sipped, were treated to a show only nature could deliver. Ribbons of purple, lavender, pink, and magenta rose from the water as the sun dipped into the sea for the evening.

It was stunning but made all the more beautiful because of the man whose hand she held as she enjoyed it.

CHAPTER TWENTY-FOUR

F riday morning, they were on the road in Dale's SUV before seven o'clock and had an easy ride to Anacortes. He took the turn for the ferry landing and pulled in front of a restaurant.

"We've got time, and they make great pastries." He hurried around the front of the SUV and opened the door for her.

After a cup of coffee and a fresh berry turnover, they made their way to the ferry lanes and waited to board. Georgia took in the beauty of the space, overlooking the water and before she knew it, they were driving over the apron and parking on the vehicle deck.

She smiled and took his hand as he guided her up the stairs. "We can grab a table with a window."

They found an empty one and settled into one side of the booth-style table, facing forward so they could take in the sights as the ferry moved toward the San Juan Islands.

More and more passengers arrived, and almost every table was full by the time the horn sounded and the ferry pulled away from the dock. Georgia's worries about getting seasick disappeared at the slow and gentle motion of the ferry. She settled back to enjoy the ride.

As they pulled further away from Anacortes, she pointed at the window. "I can't believe how many little islands there are."

He laughed. "I love seeing how excited you are. Wait until we get closer to Friday Harbor."

Georgia was enjoying her journey when he squeezed her hand. "Let's go out on the deck. I want you to see the harbor as we pull into it."

He led the way to the outside deck, lined with benches. She spied a woman with a golden retriever sitting on the bench. "Aww, Olivia would be all over that sweet dog. She looks a bit like Hope, doesn't she?"

They couldn't resist and wandered a bit closer and asked if they could pet her dog. She smiled and said, "Of course. Mabel loves the attention." They both petted the sweet girl and then walked over to the railing.

He pointed in the distance. "Just a few minutes, and you'll get your first glimpse of Friday Harbor."

She gasped when the ferry turned, and it came into view. The colorful buildings that surrounded the cove area were so inviting. The ferry maneuvered between the tree-covered islands, and Georgia couldn't resist taking a few photos of the quaint harbor.

The captain's voice alerted the passengers to make their way to their vehicles and prepare to disembark. Dale took her hand and led her downstairs. He maneuvered through the hallway and stairs, navigating the ferry like an expert and in no time, they were back at his SUV.

"Whew," she said, climbing into her seat. "I would have never found the car."

"I've made this trip countless times, so it's like old hat to me."

He waited to start the engine until cars in front of theirs moved and then followed them, and their wheels thumped over the metal apron, where he drove onto Front Street. "Sam's coffee shop is just up here."

The streets were busy, and people filled the sidewalk. "Finding a parking place might be tricky." He drove by the shop and pointed at it. "Harbor Coffee and Books, that's it."

He drove down the street and turned into the parking lot of the hardware store. "Sam said her husband owns this, and we could park in the back if we couldn't find anything." He drove around the building and parked next to a pickup truck.

Hand in hand, they walked across the street and to the coffee shop. When it was their turn at the counter, Sam looked up and grinned. "Oh, hooray. I'm so glad you're here."

Dale pointed out the window. "I parked at the hardware store like you suggested."

"Perfect," she said. "Jeff knows, so don't worry. He'll be over soon and can take you out to the house so you can get settled in. In the meantime, how about something to drink? I've got a yummy peach iced tea."

"That sounds perfect to me," said Georgia.

Dale nodded. "Make it two." He took out his wallet, and Sam shook her head.

"I've got an umbrella table reserved out there with your name on it. You two have a seat, and I'll bring your drinks. My treat. Welcome to the island."

After thanking her, the two of them found the table on the deck, with a nice view for people watching. Dale spotted a black lab walking by and pointed. "That dog reminds me of

Suki." He sighed and added, "I've been thinking about her and would really like to adopt her. What do you think?"

"She's a great dog and has really taken to you. I think it's a perfect match. Dogs make you smile each day and force you outside to exercise. They're really spectacular in every way. Not having had one for so long, I forgot how much joy they bring."

He nodded. "That's what I think, too. They're wonderful companions, and Suki needs a good home."

"Your yard is all fenced, so she should be safe there."

He nodded. "Yeah, the main part is fenced, so she could have the run of the backyard without getting in trouble."

She winked at him. "Something tells me she'll be sprawled out on your couch most of the time."

He chuckled and took a drink from his cup. "You're probably right about that. I'm a soft touch."

A few minutes later, Sam arrived with their tea and a plate of warm brownies. "Just popped these out of the oven. It should tide you over until lunch. I'm going to take off at noon and pick up lunch, and we can eat at the house. Downtown is a madhouse on the weekends."

"Oh, these look so good. Thank you, Sam. You're really quite the hostess," said Georgia, taking a brownie.

"We love having company. It will be such fun." She hurried off to wait on more customers.

As they enjoyed the brownie and the gorgeous view of the harbor, a man wearing a Cooper Hardware ballcap came up to their table. He greeted them with a cheerful grin and extended his hand. "Hey there, I'm Jeff, Sam's husband."

Dale stood and shook his hand. "I'm Dale Campbell, and this is my longtime friend Georgia Moore."

Jeff shook Georgia's hand and as he took his chair, Sam

came up behind him with a large glass of iced tea. She tilted his cap back and kissed his forehead. "Hey, you."

He took the tea and held her hand. "Hey, sweetie. How's it going?"

"Busy," she said. "I've got to get back in there, but I'm still planning to be home no later than one o'clock, and I'll bring lunch."

"Sounds good. We'll head out soon."

She rested her hands on his shoulders. "You're in good hands with Jeff and don't let Zoe and Bailey maul you. They love visitors."

Georgia smiled up at her. "No need to worry. We're dog people. In fact, Dale and I were just discussing a black Labrador named Suki. She's in Olivia's shelter, but Dale has his eye on her."

Sam patted Jeff's shoulder. "Bailey is Jeff's dog, a chocolate Labrador. She's a love and although I'm partial to golden retrievers and my sweet Zoe, Labs are a very close second to the best dog in the world."

Dale smiled. "I can't wait to meet both of them."

Sam turned at the sound of her name. "Gotta run, but I'll see you all soon."

Jeff finished off the rest of his brownie and drank his tea. He set the empty glass on the table and adjusted his cap. "Shall we take off?"

Dale and Georgia both nodded and before she could gather their empty glasses, Jeff had them in his hands, along with the plate, and deposited them at the station at the end of the deck.

Dale pointed across the street. "We parked behind your hardware store. Sam told us we might not be able to find a place and she was right."

"Yeah, this time of year, the island is bustling. You can just follow me. We're out on Hidden Cove Lane. It's about a twenty-minute drive depending on how fast I go. If we get separated, I'll pull over, so don't worry. Sam gave me your cell numbers, too."

He led the way across the street. "I'm going to run in and collect the dogs, and I'll see you out back in a few." He hurried inside, and they made their way to Dale's SUV.

At the sight of the two dogs leaping into the backseat of Jeff's truck, Georgia pointed at them. "Aww, they're adorable."

Jeff backed out and led the way out of town, with Dale sticking close to him. They made their way along the main road that traversed the middle of the island. As they drove by the resort Jeff's family owned, Dale pointed it out. "It's a beautiful spot with a nice little bay."

Georgia soaked in the lush countryside and the glimpse of the water she caught when they went past the turnoff for the resort. Jeff turned off the main road, and they followed along a winding driveway. As they approached the garage, Jeff stuck his hand out the window and pointed at the driveway near the front door. Dale followed his directions and pulled up to the gorgeous home.

As Georgia climbed from her seat, she sucked in her breath. "Wow, what a house and look at that view."

"I'm glad you're not disappointed you chose the waterfront location," Dale joked as he unloaded the back of the SUV.

Jeff came over to help them. "I put Zoe and Bailey in the backyard until we get you settled. We don't need them tripping you as you go upstairs." He grabbed the heaviest suitcases and lugged them inside, urging them to follow him.

Jeff set the bags on the large landing and pointed down the short hallway. "Sam's got all the bedrooms ready, so your choice. The bathroom is stocked with everything you need, and there are more towels in the linen closet, plus extra blankets if you need them. Just make yourself at home. I'll be out in the yard, exercising the dogs, so just come down when you're settled."

He left them with a smile and hurried down the stairs. Georgia peeked inside the doorway of the first bedroom, drawn to the soft coastal-blue colors of the comforter and accent pieces. It didn't hurt that it had a view of the water. "I'll take this one," she said, smiling at Dale.

He placed her suitcase at the edge of the bed. "I should have known with that glimpse of the ocean out your window. I'll take the one across the hallway." He left her to unpack and moved his suitcase to the room done in beige and gray.

By the time Georgia got done hanging her clothes and unpacking the rest of her things, along with making a stop in the powder room, Dale had left his room. She made her way downstairs, marveling at the huge stone fireplace that was the centerpiece of the great room.

She made her way to the kitchen and stepped out onto the deck. Down below, she spotted Jeff and Dale playing ball with two dogs, running after the toys. She looked out at the ocean and took a deep breath. Something about the vastness and the sound of the water slapping the shore made her relax.

She hadn't spent much time near water, but this view, like that from Dale's house overlooking Puget Sound, was calming, and she felt her heart rate slow and her worries diminish.

While she was lost in thoughts and the peaceful view, Sam came from the house carrying a tray of drinks. "I can't believe Jeff didn't even get you two something cold to drink."

"Oh, he helped us carry our stuff upstairs; he and Dale have been entertaining the dogs. We're fine, really."

"I've got deli sandwiches and salads from Dotty's. We can eat outside if you're up for it. The view is lovely out here."

"That would be perfect. I was just standing here soaking it in." Georgia went inside to help Sam gather the food and by the time they returned, Dale and Jeff were seated at the table, sipping their iced teas, with the dogs resting at their feet.

Jeff introduced both of them to Georgia, who gave them lots of chin scratches and ear rubs. "They're both such cuties. We've got three resident goldens on the farm, and they're such wonderful friends to all of us."

Sam rested her hand on top of Zoe's golden head. "She's definitely my bestie, and she loves Bailey. They took to each other the moment they met."

Jeff planted a kiss on Sam's cheek. "Sort of like us, huh?"

She smiled and urged everyone to load their plates with lunch. As they ate, Jeff let Dale know they had a tee time reserved at the golf course for Saturday morning, followed by lunch at the clubhouse. "We've got kayaks available, too, if you'd like to go out on the water here, or I could make a call and get you a spot at the resort."

Sam refilled their iced teas. "Dale, you've probably visited the alpaca ranch and the lavender farm, but those are always fun spots to explore."

He glanced over at Georgia. "It's been years, but yes, Georgia should definitely see those spots."

"The girls would love me to check out the lavender farm. Micki mentioned that to me before I left."

Jeff scooped out more pasta salad on his plate. "Usually, visitors don't run out of things to see and do, they run out of time to do it all. I'm sure Izzy will take you to the vineyard, and there are endless hikes you can take."

"Sitting here on the deck and gazing at the water is top of my to-do list," said Georgia, with a chuckle. "We've all been working so hard over the last month, it's wonderful to relax."

Sam nodded. "I definitely understand that. You just come and go as you please. Jeff has a spare key he can give you and just make yourself at home. We've got about eight acres here you can wander and quite a bit of shoreline that's always fun to walk along. The dogs love doing that each day."

Dale turned to Georgia. "This trip is all about Georgia, so she's our tour guide. I'll leave it up to her."

"A walk along the shoreline sounds perfect to me."

Sam finished the last bite of her sandwich. "Jeff has the firepit ready, so we thought tonight, it would be nice to let you both relax on your first day here. We can grill something for dinner and then sit by the water and enjoy the evening. It's one of our favorite summertime activities."

Dale reached for Georgia's hand and squeezed it. "That sounds wonderful."

Georgia savored the warmth of Dale's hand in hers. With him by her side and the view in front of her, she wasn't sure life could get any better.

CHAPTER TWENTY-FIVE

Saturday, after Sam treated them to a yummy breakfast casserole and scones Jeff picked up at the bakery, he and Dale took off to meet up with some other golfers, including Sam's best friend from childhood, Max.

As Sam wiped the counter, she explained that Max moved to the island not long after she did. "Kate and I thought we'd take you downtown for a little window shopping. We have a great store I think you'll love called Knitwits."

"I love the sound of it already."

"Annie owns it, and she's a sweetheart. I can't sew a stitch but can't resist stopping to check out her gorgeous yarn, and she'll make things for those of us who aren't good with a needle."

"I'm dangerous in yarn and fabric stores. I hope my credit card holds up." Georgia added another plate to the dishwasher.

"After shopping, we're going to meet up at Izzy's for lunch and then tomorrow, we're hosting a barbecue here with everyone you met at the Lavender Festival and a few other friends. Outside of that, we didn't make any plans, so you and Dale can explore the island and have lots of free time."

"That sounds marvelous to me. I'm so grateful for your hospitality. Your home is lovely."

Sam waved away her compliment. "You all saved us when we were stranded in Lavender Valley. It's the least we can do. We hope Clay and Heath will come to visit soon. Maybe you can twist their arms."

"I don't think it will take much when I share my photos. Everyone is itching for a little getaway, so I imagine you'll have company over the next few months."

She drained the last of the tea from her cup. "We love having you and thank you for your kind words. I designed the house years ago when my ex-husband and I vacationed here and wanted a place. Long story, but he's the reason I'm here now. After our divorce, I was in a very dark place and decided I need a change of scenery and came here. As they say, the rest is history."

"Well, you did an outstanding job with it. We had the best time visiting with you around the firepit last night. I could get used to falling to sleep to the sound of the waves. I slept like a baby."

"And you managed to get a walk along the water in this morning."

Georgia grinned. "Yes, we did. We were both up early, and I'm in the habit of walking. Dale and I often chat on the phone and walk together in the mornings, but since he's been at the farm these last weeks, we've been walking the property. I thought nothing could improve on my view, but your shoreline takes the cake."

"It's so calming and beautiful. I sometimes forget how

lucky we are to live in this gorgeous spot. It's a very healing place for me." Sam touched her hair. "I need to finish getting ready, then we can head downtown."

Georgia brewed another cup of tea, and she and the two dogs sat on the deck. She didn't want to miss one minute of immersing herself in the panoramic view.

Sam parked behind her coffee shop, and she and Georgia found Kate, Izzy, and Jess already there at a table, waiting for them. Sam stopped to chat with her barista and after hugging the other ladies, Georgia took a seat with them.

"It's wonderful to see all of you. Everyone says hello. I think they're jealous and will be planning trips of their own soon."

Kate grinned and took a sip from her cup. "We'd love to see them, so send them over."

Sam stepped over to their table and brought two steaming cups with her. "Chai tea latte," she said, raising her brows at Georgia.

"Oh, wonderful. Thank you."

Sam took her seat and tilted her head toward Jess. "Did Dean make the golf party?"

"Oh, yes. He was all too happy to get the invite. Spence picked him up this morning. I think they were going to breakfast first."

Kate nodded. "Yes, Spence was excited about the prospect of an outing, especially with this perfect weather."

Izzy took a swallow from her cup. "Colin, who manages the golf course and is my beau, was looking forward to the day. I think they've got eight guys, so two foursomes. I'm not a golfer, but I guess it's frowned on to have more than four golfers at once. Anyway, Jack, he's a local realtor and Dean's boss, is joining them, along with his son Nate."

Kate smiled as she set her cup on the table. "That should make for a fun day for them. I know Spence doesn't get to golf as much as he would like to, so it's wonderful for him."

Jess glanced over at Georgia, "I'm still talking about our trip to the lavender farm and our adventures in staying at the ranch. I'm fascinated by the idea of all of you foster sisters never having met. It's such a wonderful story, and you all seem to get along so well."

"I'm so thankful for all of them. I always wanted a family, and I couldn't be happier to have four new sisters. It's made me feel so much less alone, and we all get along and work together well. The festival was a busy time, and we managed to get through it without any major problems."

Izzy rolled her eyes. "Part of the reason I came to live on the island, along with having my brother here, was an escape from part of my family. I have a fractured and strained relationship with my daughter, and I also have one sister who is beyond difficult. I wanted a little space and living here has been wonderful."

Sam nodded. "I'm another transplant who came here for a new start. Like I told you, my divorce almost destroyed me, so this was a second chance, and it turned out to be the best decision I've ever made."

Kate smiled at the others. "I also came here to get away from some traumatic memories. I had a store in Seattle and decided to downsize and open a smaller shop here and live the island life. Now, I can't imagine living anywhere else."

Jess shrugged. "That leaves me, I guess. I'm relatively new to the island. I'm newly retired and was a teacher for decades. I also lost my mother right before I retired and have had a difficult relationship with my son since my divorce years ago. I met Dean on a cruise to Alaska. He was moving here, and I decided to come, too. Like the others, I fell in love with the island and more importantly, with this lovely group of friends. I was missing that in my life."

Sam put her hand on Georgia's arm. "You'll meet a few of our other friends tomorrow at our house. I'm an only child, and all of these ladies feel more like sisters than friends."

Georgia took a sip of the creamy latte. "Sounds like you might also be sisters of the heart."

The five women spent the rest of the morning strolling the sidewalks, window shopping, and stepping into the unique shops around the harbor. Mixed in with the tourist-centered shops were some lovely boutiques, a jewelry store, and Kate showcased her gorgeous art and antique store.

It was filled with beautiful furniture and inviting displays in all types of décor. Georgia admired a thick wooden dining room table decorated with green and purple dishes, glass baubles that looked like grapes, beautiful cloth napkins, and a gorgeous arrangement of silk flowers.

In another niche, was an antique desk with a leather chair and accents of deep green in the paintings and prints on the wall and the wooden ducks on the credenza. It immediately brought to mind a man's study.

"You've got such a keen eye for design and décor, Kate. Your store is enchanting." Georgia fingered an antique mirror.

Izzy put her hand on Kate's shoulder. "She's a magician. She decorated my house for me."

Jess nodded. "Same for mine. She found the exact furniture I needed and has such great ideas."

Kate blushed and smiled at her friends. "It's not as difficult as they make it sound. I love helping people personalize their homes. I've done it for so long, it's second nature to me."

Sam smiled at Georgia. "I saved the best for last. Shall we take a walk to Knitwits?"

Georgia could have spent hours in the store, touching the soft yarns and exploring all the colorful skeins. She was drawn to the alpaca blends, and Annie, the owner, told her it comes from fiber from the local alpaca farm.

She couldn't resist buying a few balls of it and a washable Merino cashmere blend. Georgia loved the blue-gray color and could picture Dale wearing it as a scarf. It would accentuate his charming eyes.

Along with all her yarn, bolts of fabric were displayed across the open floor area of the shop. Thinking about Dale's desire to adopt Suki, she searched through some colorful prints that were on sale and selected several of them to make Suki some bandanas.

While Annie was cutting Georgia's fabric, Izzy suggested Kate and Jess join her to pick up the things she ordered for lunch, and they'd get things ready at the house. "We're not in a hurry, so take your time," said Izzy, as they waved goodbye.

After a bit more browsing and adding some beautiful fat quarters in coastal colors to her stack of purchases, Georgia, with her bag from Annie's on her arm, let Sam lead the way back to the coffee shop and her SUV. She drove out of town and turned at the sign for the golf course.

Georgia took in the manicured grounds of the neighborhood and the beautiful homes they drove past. Minutes later, Sam pulled into a driveway in front of a gray house with white trim. "Here we are. This is Izzy's place, and Jess' is just down the street."

Izzy opened the door before Sam could ring the bell. "Come in, welcome." She led them into the kitchen where the huge island counter was covered with food. "I've got it set up buffet style, and we can eat in the dining room or on the patio."

"Wow," said Georgia, eyeing the bowls of salad and huge charcuterie board. "This looks fabulous."

"I ordered most of it from the clubhouse restaurant, but I did make some lemon chicken soup, and it's in the slow cooker there on the end." She turned to the counter near the sink. "I've got iced tea, lemonade, water, and of course, wine."

Sam said, "I'll take iced tea."

Jess grinned and stepped closer to examine the wine. "I can walk home from here, so count me in for wine."

Georgia chuckled. "I'm not driving either, so I'll join you."

Kate put her arm around Georgia. "Make it three for wine."

Izzy laughed as she filled four wine glasses and a tall glass of iced tea for Sam. "Georgia, you're our guest of honor; please go first and fill up a plate."

Soon, the others joined her in the dining room, with a view of the green golf course off the patio. Everything was beyond delicious and the more she experienced charcuterie boards, the more Georgia thought they were a genius way of entertaining.

She nibbled on another bite of cheese and was just about to pop another one in her mouth when Kate turned to her. "Dale is such a sweet man. When we were at the ranch, I remember him saying he knew you long ago."

Georgia took a swallow of her wine and cleared her throat. "Yes, Dale was actually a foster child at the farm when I lived there. He was there just a short time and then was adopted. He was such a nice boy. He showed up at the Lavender Festival, and I recognized him. Those eyes."

Izzy whistled. "Yes, his eyes are dreamy, and he is beyond nice."

Georgia laughed. "He lost his wife a few months ago and was on a road trip with his grandson. They were spending the summer together, and Dale wanted to show him where he lived. I couldn't believe it when he walked up to the table."

Jess put her hand to her chest. "I love that. How wonderful that you were reunited."

Georgia nodded. "It truly has been. I never dreamed I'd see him again and being with him, talking with him, it's effortless. He has a way of making me feel better, just being near me. It's like we were never apart all these years."

Sam smiled from across the table. "That sounds like a second chance to me."

Kate put her hand on Georgia's arm. "Don't let it slip away."

CHAPTER TWENTY-SIX

In the late afternoon, as the ladies wound down their leisurely lunch, the doorbell rang. Izzy returned from answering it and ushered Jeff and Dale into the dining room. "Ladies," said Dale. "So nice to see all of you again."

After exchanging pleasantries, he reached for Georgia's hand. "I have something I want to show you. Can I steal you away for a few minutes?"

Georgia's eyes widened. "Sure, we were just getting ready to leave anyway."

She thanked them all with hugs and collected her purse and shopping bag from Knitwits before following Dale outside. He pointed at his SUV. "It's just a short drive. Jeff said he can catch a ride home with Sam."

He opened the passenger door for her and climbed behind the wheel. She glanced over as he pulled away from the curb. "Did you have a good day golfing?"

"Phenomenal. It was a fantastic day. Jeff introduced me to the other guys, and they're a great group. Colin runs the place, and we had a terrific lunch at the clubhouse. One of the best days I've had in a long time."

He drove further down the street and took a turn. "Jack, he's Dean's boss and a long-time realtor. Anyway, we were talking about the real estate market and housing on the island. He mentioned a house here on the golf course that's for sale. He said the contract fell through on it this morning, and the owners are anxious to get it sold."

Her forehead creased. "Are you looking to buy a home here?"

He grinned and shrugged. "I wasn't planning on it, but I wouldn't mind having a place that I could visit year-round. The resort is great, but more of a summer place."

She nodded, and he pulled into a driveaway. A home, in the same style as Izzy's, but a bit lighter gray color, with a wraparound deck, stood before them. He helped her from the car and led the way to the front door, a shade of blue that reminded her of the yarn she bought.

He unlocked it with a key and let Georgia step inside first. She moved from the small entry area into the open living area. She took in the wooden floors with their hand-scraped finish and the natural light that flooded the space from the large windows facing the backyard, with the greenbelt from the golf course bordering it.

A thick area rug in muted coastal blues and ivories sat atop the wooden floor and designated a space with a couch and several chairs and decorative tables. A fireplace opposite the seating area was done in a neutral brick.

The kitchen was black and white, with touches of gray and included a solarium with a breakfast table that looked out onto the backyard. Dale pointed down the hallway. "It's only two bedrooms, but it's got a small bonus room that could be an office or den."

"Does all the furniture come with it?"

He nodded. "Yeah, it was a vacation home that they didn't use much. Sounds like they're in financial trouble and don't have the means or time to empty it. At the price, they're basically giving all the furnishings away."

"Wow," said Georgia, running her hand over the cool granite counter. "This sunroom is nice and lets so much light in." The muted blues, lavenders, grays, and beiges in the prints on the wall, the pillows and fabrics used in the furniture, and the rugs and towels, were calming and reminded her of the ocean.

"Come see the bedrooms." He led her down the hallway.

The master had a sliding door off the deck in the backyard and was done in beige and gray, with the master bathroom sporting a huge walk-in shower and double sinks.

The guest bedroom was smaller and had access to a bathroom in the hallway, done in the same colors, but on a small scale. The office had a small desk and chair in it and looked out on the backyard.

A laundry room off the two-car garage rounded out the space. Georgia stepped from it and noticed Dale smiling at her. "So, what do you think?"

"It's charming and has a lovely view from the backyard. I love the deck and the patio area outside. I noticed it had a firepit, too."

"Oh, yeah, plus a nice little garden area that's fenced." He wandered back to the living area. "No formal dining room, but I never use the one I have."

She laughed and pointed toward the kitchen. "They've got a small table in that solarium space. You could find a different-sized one and make it work."

He nodded. "It's a good deal, and the beauty of the golf course is that all the yard maintenance is included in the monthly fee. So, I wouldn't have to worry about any of that."

Georgia opened the stainless-steel fridge. "Nice appliances, too. Izzy mentioned she liked the idea of not having to worry about the yard. She said she looked at a place on the water, but the upkeep was too much for her and living here is so much cheaper."

He nodded. "Yeah, you pay dearly for a water view."

"It's in a great location. Close to town, but yet you feel like you're in the country."

He pointed toward the backyard. "And you have access to all the walking paths around the golf course."

"Oh, that's nice. Do you think your kids or grandkids would be disappointed not to go back to the resort?"

He shook his head. "Nah, this was really the last summer I suspect we'd be there. Once Chet goes to college, it'll be like the others. They transition into their own lives, have things to do, and hanging out with their grandparents isn't always top of the list. Mark and Sally haven't come for years."

"Are you sure you still want to vacation here? Not too many memories?"

He reached for her hand. "All the memories here are happy, and it's a special place for me. I love coming here and now that I've gotten to know the others, it holds even more appeal. I can imagine spending a few months at a time here."

"Wouldn't that be lovely. I told you I couldn't imagine ever leaving your house in Lake Stevens, but there is something special about this place. It's a bit like Lavender Valley and stepping back in time. Things seem slower and simpler here, plus you're so close to the water. I love that."

"So, it has your seal of approval?" He raised his brows at her.

"Oh, yes. It's charming, laid out well, and the setting is

lovely. Not to mention, I love the coastal colors. They're so soothing."

He squeezed her hand. "I'll sleep on it and do a little more research, but I like it, too. I can see myself here."

Monday, Georgia was up early and sipped a cup of tea while she waited for Dale to join her for their morning jaunt along the water. The house was quiet, with Sam going in early to bake and Jeff leaving with the dogs for an early day at the hardware store.

Last night had been a wonderful evening, filled with delicious food and never-ending conversations. She enjoyed meeting Izzy's brother Blake and his wife Ellie. They made them promise to visit the winery while they were on the island.

Max and Linda were so kind and welcoming, giving them ideas for places to visit and eat. Nate and his wife Regi were warm and friendly, and Georgia loved meeting Rebel, Dean's service dog, most of all. He was a beautiful golden, and she took his photo and sent it to Olivia, knowing how much she'd enjoy seeing him.

Despite having only known the group of friends for a few hours, Georgia could tell they were special and enjoyed being with them. They reminded her of being with her sisters at the farm. It was wonderful to laugh and feel so alive.

As the night progressed, they gathered around the fire pit, and she and Dale were drawn to Spence and Kate. They were closest in age and so very interesting. Kate spoke a bit about losing her daughter, and it broke Georgia's heart to see the grief in her eyes when she spoke of her. Spence regaled them with stories from his days working as a police detective in Seattle.

Harry would love him, and they would have so much in common. She made a mental note to encourage Clay and Harry to plan a visit.

Part of her worried Dale was making too quick of a decision to buy the house he'd shown her, but the other part of her hoped he'd invite her to visit on one of his trips. She would never tire of the view or watching the gentle waves lap the shore.

She added more tea to her cup, took a blanket from the stack Sam had set out for them, and went out on the deck. She settled into the lounge chair, under the warm blanket and gazed at the ocean.

This was all she needed to be happy. They had plans to stop by the winery, lavender farm, and see the alpacas this week, but even if all she did was sit here all day, it would be a good day.

Kate had a gift card for a mini-spa treatment and suggested Georgia join her on Friday. Georgia couldn't remember the last time she'd had a pedicure or manicure, but the thought of both sounded heavenly.

Dale told her not to make any plans for Friday night because he had reservations for dinner, just the two of them. They were set to leave on the Saturday morning ferry, and he wanted to treat her to a special dinner on their last night.

Her fairytale vacation would be coming to an end much too soon. Not that she wasn't happy to be living on the farm with the others, but her heart already ached at the thought of leaving Dale. She might have to get over her aversion to flying and plan a trip this fall.

As she contemplated, Dale came from the house. "Good morning. Sorry, I slept later than usual."

He stepped closer to her and offered her a hand. "Ready for our walk along the beach?"

"Always," she said, as she gripped his hand. This is what she would miss when she went back to the farm. She hated the idea of not being able to see his grin or feel his hand in hers.

CHAPTER TWENTY-SEVEN

F riday, with freshly painted toenails, the softest heels she ever remembered having, and a pale-pink polish on her fingernails, Georgia came downstairs to find Dale waiting in Sam's kitchen. Jeff and Sam were over at Linda's house for dinner and had taken the dogs, so the house was quiet.

Dale was tapping something on his phone, and she caught a glimpse of him before he saw her. Her breath caught at the sight of him in his smart jacket and blue button-down shirt that matched his eyes. She wore one of the new blouses she'd made in a beautiful emerald green and paired it with her dressiest black pants. He wouldn't divulge where they were going, just that it was special, and she worried she didn't have the right outfit.

He looked up and slipped the phone in his pocket. "You look stunning, Georgia. Just beautiful." He reached for her hand. "Ready to go?"

"Ready as I'll ever be. This is all quite mysterious."

He laughed. "I just thought it would be fun to splurge on our last night."

They made the trip to town, and he pulled into the parking lot behind the hardware store. "Jeff told me just to park here. We just have to walk a short way."

He linked her arm in his, and they set out toward the harbor. He pointed at a restaurant perched above the harbor, its roofline and the trees along the stairs decorated with white twinkling lights. "Max told me this place is fabulous. It just opened a few months ago, and he pulled some strings to get us in tonight."

He held her hand as they climbed the stairs to the entrance of The Bluff. A hostess welcomed them, and Dale gave his name. She took two menus and led them to a table outside on the deck overlooking the water with a view of the marina, the ferry landing, and the open water beyond.

There were several decks at different levels, and they had a great spot next to a long planter that was a firepit with flames dancing in it. The hostess sat them next to each other and left them with their menus and the flicker of a candle on the table. Georgia sighed as she took in the view. "This is fabulous, Dale. Thank you."

"Thank Max, he's the one who put me onto it."

They read their menus and at the same time, they said, "Salmon."

Dale laughed and said, "How about we start with some crab cakes? We'll see how they compare to Lou's from the other night."

"Sounds delicious."

The server came, took their order, and left them with fresh bread and dipping oil. He pointed toward the water. "It looks like we're going to get treated to another gorgeous sunset."

She sucked in her breath at the sight of the pinks and orange reflected in the glassy waters. "It's so beautiful, it makes it hard to leave."

The server delivered their crabcakes and refilled their waters, promising their entrées would be out soon.

They nibbled on the crabcakes, both agreeing Lou's were just as delicious and less than half the price. As she reached for her water, Georgia met Dale's eyes. "I've had a wonderful time and can't thank you enough for inviting me to join you here. It's been the highlight of my year."

He grinned at her. "I feel the same way. I've had a week I won't soon forget. I like this whole idea of making new memories. Especially, with you." He reached for her hand and kissed the top of her knuckles. "Thank you for coming."

The server arrived with their plates of salmon, and they dug into the tender fish, with a brown sugar glaze. As they ate, the sun sank lower, and golden ribbons of light shimmered atop the dark water.

After their plates were cleared, the server brought out a piece of triple chocolate mousse cake and two forks. "Enjoy," she said.

"Oh, my goodness. That looks so yummy. I really shouldn't, but I don't think I can resist it." She smiled at him, and he reached for her hand.

He met her eyes. "I've had so much fun with you this week here and over the last weeks in Lavender Valley. I was convinced I was destined to live a life without love, without a partner. I figured I had my one shot and with Sarah gone, my life would be diminished and lonely. That is, until I walked up to a table at a lavender farm and saw you. You showed me, my heart could love again. It wasn't destined to be broken forever or shrivel away. It could grow and expand and make room for a new love."

Tears filled Georgia's eyes as she listened to the thoughtful words of the man she'd grown to love.

He chuckled and added, "Like I told you, I had a crush on you all those years ago and now, meeting you again, at this stage of our lives, both of us alone, I think we were meant to find each other again."

He took a deep breath and reached into his jacket pocket. "What I'm trying to say, my dear Georgia, in a very clumsy way, is I'd be honored if you'd agree to be my wife. I love you. I think a part of me has always loved you and no matter what you say tonight, will always love you." He opened the blue velvet box, and the diamond ring glittered in the light from the flames next to their table.

She tried to focus on what he was saying but was riveted by the gorgeous ring.

He plucked it from the box. "I know this is fast, but if I've learned anything this past year, it's that time is indeed a fickle and cruel mistress. I'm not willing to waste a second of it. I've talked to Mark and Sally, and you'll be glad to know Chet vouched for you." He grinned at her as he placed the ring on her finger.

Georgia laughed as tears leaked from her eyes. "I knew I liked that boy."

"They want me to be happy, and they know I'm not happy alone. They understand we've known each other long ago and think it's a wonderful idea."

She sighed and looked into the blue eyes she'd never forgotten. "I love you, Dale. I'm not sure I had those same feelings for you when we were kids, but I knew you were good and kind and special. Finding you again, as you say, now, is most definitely the work of someone up there," she glanced at the heavens above, "who thinks we need each other. My biggest concern is what your family thinks, so I'm glad you talked to them. I was already feeling sorry for myself and trying to figure out how I could come visit you next month."

He smiled and leaned closer. "So, is that yes?"

She laughed. "Yes. Yes, I'll marry you, Dale. You've made me the happiest woman on the island."

As the sun kissed the water, their lips met. Like Dale, Georgia thought her one chance at love ended with Lee's passing, but the jolt of electricity that traveled from her lips to her toes reminded her she still had some life left in her.

After their long kiss, she leaned her forehead against his. This was perhaps the best night of her life.

He leaned back and reached inside his jacket. "I have one more little surprise for you." He unfolded a sheath of papers. "I bought that house I showed you and put it in your name only. I don't want you to ever feel insecure or worry about having a place to live. I know the stress that created for you and with me having children, it makes a second marriage a wee bit more complicated. Izzy helped me this week, and I've set up a trust for you that's independent of the business and property that will be passed down to my children. I've also taken out a life insurance policy with you as the beneficiary. If something happens to me, you can live in the house in Lake Stevens for as long as you like, but if you pass away or decide to move, it goes to the kids. The house here is yours forever and only yours. I don't want you to worry about your future."

She brought her hand to her throat. "Oh, Dale. That's the most thoughtful thing I could imagine you doing. I can't tell you what that means to me. As happy as I am tonight, there was a little nag of worry about what would I do in the future, if anything did happen."

He grinned and kissed her cheek. "No more worrying.

From here on out, it's only fun and happy times. We're making new memories. Together."

She took a deep breath and gazed at her hand. The sparkle of the ring was nothing compared to what she felt deep in her heart.

CHAPTER TWENTY-EIGHT

After a wonderful breakfast with Jeff and Sam, where she and Dale shared their news and Georgia showed off her ring, they made their hosts promise to keep their news a secret. Georgia was committed to the farm until October and would let her sisters know then, when they all decided what to do with Jewel's property. She and Dale hugged them goodbye, promised to let them know the moment they could share the news, and that they'd be back soon.

After the two of them had eaten the chocolate mousse cake last night and cherished the twilight view of the harbor for as long as they dared, they took a long walk along the harbor. As they strolled hand in hand, they went over options for the wedding and decided to get married on the island and wanted to get the new house organized so they could spend the holidays there together.

Dale wanted to start new traditions together and was eager to spend the holidays somewhere other than the house in Lake Stevens. Georgia's new home on the golf course was the perfect place and they were both excited about the prospect.

Georgia wanted to keep their plans a secret from her sisters. She didn't want to take anything away from Lydia and Heath and their recent wedding and wanted to fulfill her promise to stay at the farm through October. They'd already made an exception with her late arrival, and she wasn't about to renege on her commitment.

It would also give her more time to figure out how to break it to them gently. She had imagined spending the rest of her life in Lavender Valley on Jewel's farm. She didn't want them to think she was abandoning them. As much as she loved the farm and them, the chance at a life with Dale was a dream come true. She'd loved being married and missed that special companionship and was anxious to start a new chapter with Dale by her side.

As they boarded the ferry, she turned to Dale. "What would you think if we went back to Lavender Valley each summer to help with the festival?"

"I think that's a wonderful idea, and I'd love it. Count me in."

"Provided, of course, that one or more of them decides to stay on and run the farm. There's no way I can commit to doing it, not at my age. Maybe the three of them will stay and run it. I don't see any of them eager to leave."

He gripped her hand in his. "It will all work out, and everything will be okay. Try not to worry about it, or they'll know something's up."

She laughed. "Yeah, I'm not the best at faking or fibbing. I need to practice my poker face."

He squeezed her hand tighter. "Do you think you can handle one more surprise?"

Her eyes widened and her brows arched. "A good one or a scary one?"

"Good, I think."

She took a deep breath. "Okay, lay it on me."

"While Izzy was working on the legal framework for our marriage, I asked her about trying to find your sister Amelia."

Georgia's heart pounded in her chest. "She found her?"

He nodded and smiled. "Yes. Her name is Amelia Lancaster now. She was adopted by a Canadian couple and lived in White Rock. She recently divorced and moved to a little town called Driftwood Bay on the coast of Washington, near Port Angeles. She's opening a bookstore."

Georgia gasped. "I can't believe she's been this close all this time." She glanced out the window. "I wonder if she remembers me."

"I've got her contact information and thought you might want to reach out to her. If she's open to a visit, Driftwood Bay is only about a three-hour drive from my house or shorter if we take the ferry at Edmonds."

Georgia shook her head in disbelief. "Wow, I'd given up on ever finding her. Now, I'm worried she might not want to see me."

"Remember, no more worrying. Send her an email and see what she says. If she doesn't want to see you, you've lost nothing, but think what you could have if she says yes."

Georgia leaned her head on his shoulder. She wasn't sure she could love him any more than she did right this minute.

The day after they returned to Lake Stevens, they set out in Dale's SUV, bound for Lavender Valley. The back of his SUV was loaded down with a dog bed and toys. He called Olivia while they were on the island and let her know he wanted to adopt Suki and would pick her up when he brought Georgia back to the farm.

The hours of driving flew by with the two of them chattering about the new house on the island and Georgia making a list of things they needed to get for it. Dale was excited to set up video chats with his son and daughter, so they could meet Georgia. They also talked about Amelia.

"I've been composing drafts of emails in my notebook," said Georgia, gazing out the window as they drove south. "With her being newly divorced, just moved, and opening a new store, I don't want to overwhelm her, and I also don't want to make another trip and leave the farm again so soon. I need to honor my promise to stay there and to work at Edith's shop. I'm going to wait until October and let Amelia know I could visit toward the end of the month or first part of November, on my way to your place."

"That makes sense. And we can always make a trip over from the island. Whatever works best for her, we can make work."

She sighed. "I'd really like you to come with me, so I love that idea."

He reached across the console for her hand. He brought it to his lips and kissed the top of it. "I'll always be by your side, my love. Our paths diverged, but destiny brought us back together. I truly can't imagine my life without you, and I can't wait to travel along our new journey with you. We've lived through heartache, but now, we have the chance to create something new, something beautiful."

As she held his hand, Georgia's heart fluttered. She felt their past and present merging and their hearts intertwined in a dance of rediscovery. As their souls united, love bloomed in Georgia's heart. She'd loved Lee, but this was different this time around. There was such a strong connection with Dale and finding him again all these years later was a reminder of the possibilities life could deliver and the hope and joy that she never imagined feeling again.

Even after a tragic loss, he reminded her love can bloom again.

Dale was her hope. Her joy. Her love.

She leaned closer to him and kissed his scruffy cheek. "I'll always love you, and I'll never leave your side, either."

He squeezed her hand and made the turn into Lavender Valley.

Georgia sighed as they passed through Main Street. This sweet little town, with some help from Jewel, had worked its magic once again.

EPILOGUE

Late October

Georgia admired the lunch Lydia had prepared for them. Buck was just coming through the door with his briefcase, and Harry ushered him into the dining room, where the beautiful table was set.

Lydia and Olivia delivered plates with turkey, cheese, and apple sandwiches, along with a bowl of butternut squash soup to each place setting. Lydia added a huge bowl of an apple and pear salad to the center of the table.

The five sisters gathered around the table with Buck. As they ate, Buck explained with the exception of Lydia, they'd all met the conditions of Jewel's will and could now decide about the state of the farm. The four women, or any number of them, could retain ownership and continue to run it, or they could sell it or even lease it.

Harry glanced around the table. "I wouldn't feel right

selling Jewel's farm, but I also need to tell you all a secret I've been keeping. Clay and I got married on our trip over Labor Day." She held out her hand and pointed at the sparkling diamond ring. "I'm not one for fancy weddings, and we didn't want to make a big deal about it. We visited Danny in Lake Oswego and married there at the courthouse, so he could attend."

Everyone stared at Harry as she delivered her news in her typical no-nonsense fashion. "That's so exciting," said Olivia, as she leaned to examine the ring.

Georgia slid out of her chair and went over to hug Harry. "I'm so happy for you, dear. You and Clay deserve every ounce of happiness."

Lydia grinned and shook her head. "Heath and I thought something was up. You two seemed a little different, almost giddy. I'm so happy for you and excited to have you not only as a sister, but now a sister-in-law."

Harry smiled at them. "All that to say, I have my retirement, and I don't need the money that would come from a sale, plus now I'm married. It sounds very selfish, but I'd hate to see the place sold to a stranger. Do any of you want to stay and live here and manage the farm? Clay and I would continue to help with it and of course with the festival, but he would really like me to move into the house at the ranch."

Buck chuckled. "That's understandable."

Georgia cleared her throat. "Since we're sharing secrets, I have one, too. Dale and I decided to get married." She took in the surprised faces staring back at her. "I know it might seem fast, but we've known each other for a very long time, and he's a good man. We love each other and know time is precious, and neither of us wants to waste it. It's a little complicated with him already having a home and children.

He asked Izzy to set up the legal framework. Anyway, he bought a house on the island, in the same golf community where Izzy and Jess live and put it in my name. That way, I'll always have a place of my own to live. I wasn't sure what would become of the farm, and he didn't want me to ever have to feel insecure again."

She sighed and added, "He also had Izzy work on finding my sister Amelia. She lives in Driftwood Bay, on the coast of Washington, and I just got an email reply from her last night. She's excited for us to come to visit. We're going to stop there on the way to Dale's when we head out at the end of the week."

Everyone around the table showered her with congratulations and hugs. Georgia dabbed at her eyes with her napkin. "So, like Harry, I'd hate to see it sold to a stranger, but I'm also at the age where my abilities to contribute to running it are waning. If the farm stays in the family, Dale and I are committed to returning each summer and helping with the festival. We'll spend part of the year on the island and start our life together there. The other part of the year, we'll be at Dale's lovely home in Lake Stevens."

Buck looked between Micki and Olivia. "Well, I have a sense of what Micki has been thinking, but what about you, Olivia?"

She sighed. "I'm torn. I want to continue Jewel's dog rescue program and love working with the dogs. I adore the farm and living here." She put her hand on her heart. "It saved me again, but like Harry and Georgia, Duke and I have been contemplating marriage. I love him with all my heart and sometimes I have to pinch myself to realize this is all real. I never thought I'd find happiness again, and now my life is so full."

Georgia put an arm around Olivia's shoulders. "That's

terrific. Duke is such a kind man, and you make the perfect couple."

Olivia shrugged, "So, I don't know what that means for the farm. Like Harry, I would be in town and can help and of course be here for the festival, but it makes sense for me to move into Duke's house and if we sell the farm, I could still run the dog rescue and build a shelter at Duke's."

Buck turned toward Micki. "That leaves you." He grinned and held her hand in his.

Micki took a deep breath. "I've been giving this a lot of thought, talking to Buck, trying to figure out the best thing to do. I love the farm and want to stay in Lavender Valley. Buck and I have talked about getting married, but not right now. I would like to get Jade on stable footing, and I want to talk to Chad and Megan and especially give Chad the opportunity to meet Buck and get to know him. I'm not in a hurry, and neither is Buck. Things are good as they are."

He nodded and smiled at her.

"Realistically, I'm not sure Jade will ever be able to hold down an actual job. It will be at least a year before she works her way up the list for housing, so it makes sense to stay here and give her a place to heal. It's what Jewel did for all of us and so many others. Jade is doing better and making progress. Even her arm and leg are getting stronger, and she shines the most when she's working with the dogs and Olivia. I love the farm and enjoy the work with the flowers. I can continue to work as long as I want at the software company, so I don't have to rely on the farm to support myself. And looking at the figures, I think we can make it self-sustaining. I need to hire someone, like Tyler, to do the heavy lifting, though."

Harry reached for her glass of water. "Clay and Heath discussed Tyler and wanted me to pass on that as long as the farm stayed in the family, they were happy to let Tyler continue to stay here and work. They'll pick up the tab."

Micki turned and smiled at Buck. "That's so nice and great news. That will make it easy to stay in the black. The online store is getting more popular. I'm training Jade on how to fulfill orders, so that's another thing she can do."

From across the table, Georgia caught Micki's eye. "I know how hard it was for you to have Jade here and let her back in your life. I truly admire you for going above and beyond and helping her figure out how to chart her new reality. Jewel would be so very proud of you. I know she isn't easy, and opening your heart and showing her love and kindness makes me love you even more. You really are a special person."

Tears pooled in Micki's eyes and spilled onto her cheeks. "I couldn't have done it without all of you." She sighed. "Part of me hoped we could all stay here together forever, but I know that's not realistic. I'm just so glad you're all willing to come home each year and help with the festival, and that Harry and Lydia will be next door, and Olivia is only a few miles away."

After a long swallow of water, Olivia turned toward Micki. "It sounds like it would work to retain the rescue program here at the farm and after Duke and I are married, I could treat this more as my workplace." She gasped and added, "I forgot to say Kyle agreed to stay on at the practice and is moving here, so Duke will have a little more freedom. Our first trip is going to be over to the San Juan Islands. It will be nice to have Jade around to handle the shelter when I'm gone, and I won't leave her before she's ready."

Buck scribbled on his legal pad. "So, it sounds like the three of you are willing to relinquish your claim to the farm and give up your shares to Micki. She can take official ownership of the farm and property and will be responsible for it. We could put a clause in that if she or her heirs choose to sell it in the future, each of you would have the chance to buy it before it's sold to anyone else. It probably makes sense to give Harry that option, with the Nolan Ranch being next door. They would most likely want to buy the property before letting an unknown entity take it."

Harry nodded. "That makes sense, and I'm sure Clay and Heath would agree."

Buck poised his pen above his notepad. "I'll make that provision and include Lydia, since this is a new agreement and has nothing to do with her arriving in time for Jewel's original will."

Georgia raised her hand. "Put me as the last person with that option. I think we're talking decades into the future, and at my age now, I'd be the least likely to be able to handle the farm, so would be the last choice among us."

Buck nodded as he made a note. "Okay, I'll work on this paperwork and get everything transferred over to Micki."

They finished their last bites of lunch, and Lydia rewarded them with a plate of soft pumpkin cookies slathered with a cinnamon cream cheese frosting. Buck had to get back to the office, but she made him take a few to go. Georgia couldn't resist them.

As she bit into her second one, she smiled at the sisters she'd come to know and love. "Now that all the legal mumbo jumbo is done, and we've made our decisions, I want to invite all of you to Friday Harbor. Dale and I set a date and are going to get married there next weekend. You don't need to come for that. It's going to be a quick ceremony, but we'd love to have you come and visit when you can. Either all of you together, or whenever you can make it work. We're going to stay there through the holidays. His son won't be making the trip this year, and his daughter and grandchildren are taking a cruise for Christmas, so we'd be on our own. We decided it's easier to make new memories in a new place."

Olivia's eyes lit up with excitement. "You can count on us. Duke and I have been talking about it, but knowing you'll be there, we'll get a trip scheduled."

All the others chimed in with ideas on what might work for a visit. They were excited to see the island, connect with the ladies they'd gotten to know when they visited the farm, and see Georgia's new vacation house.

"You're always welcome at Dale's house in Lake Stevens. It's beyond gorgeous and huge. We'd have room for everyone there, and it's just an hour from the ferry terminal, so if you find a time that works next year, just let us know. We can always make the trip over with you."

That elicited more ideas and chatter as they polished off the cookies and another pot of tea.

As she looked around the table, Georgia's heart was full. She couldn't imagine a happier reunion than with all of her sisters of the heart. Knowing Jewel's beloved farm would be in Micki's capable hands, settled the angst Georgia felt about leaving. She would have all this to look forward to each summer when they'd all reunite for the Lavender Festival.

She couldn't wait to talk to Dale tonight and tell him the news about Harry and Clay and Olivia and Duke's plans to marry. Tomorrow, Dale was flying in so they could pack her things and drive to Washington. Then they'd be buttoning up his house, taking Suki and their clothes, and embarking on their new life together.

Her life was full and blessed. She had found everything she needed in Lavender Valley and as she made her way outside to her cottage, the autumn breeze carried the scent that would forever be Jewel's. Georgia stood and gazed across the fields, resting for the season. She took in the beautiful blue sky and the dark hills in the distance. She would never forget Lavender Valley. It and Jewel had saved her twice. Part of her heart would always be on the farm. This place was her refuge and home to those she held most precious—her memories of Jewel and her treasured sisters of the heart.

Reunion in Lavender Valley is the final book planned for this series. If you enjoyed this series and want to learn more about the women who live in Friday Harbor, you'll want to read the Hometown Harbor Series. Along with that series, the Glass Beach Cottage Series is another favorite and takes place in Driftwood Bay, mentioned in this book.

Don't miss a book in the SISTERS OF THE HEART SERIES.
Six women. Four decades. One long, unexpected reunion.
Book 1: Greetings from Lavender Valley
Book 2: Pathway to Lavender Valley
Book 3: Sanctuary at Lavender Valley
Book 4: Blossoms at Lavender Valley
Book 5: Comfort in Lavender Valley
Book 6: Reunion in Lavender Valley

ACKNOWLEDGMENTS

I loved writing Georgia's story and giving her a new chance at life and love. I enjoyed using the theme of reunion throughout the book in a variety of ways. The hope of a second chance for two people close to sixty, after such sad losses, makes me happy.

It was also great fun to bring the Lavender Festival to life and writing it made me feel like I was there with the sisters. I've already had readers asking if I'll write more in this series. I don't have any plans to write more in this series, but I've learned to never say never. I do enjoy the cross-over with the characters from Hometown Harbor, so I have a feeling you'll see more of these characters, but I'm not sure where or when yet. There's a chance we might meet Amelia in Driftwood Bay.

My thanks to my editor, Susan, for finding my mistakes and helping me polish *Reunion in Lavender Valley.* This gorgeous cover and all the covers in the series are the result of the talents of Elizabeth Mackey, who never disappoints. I'm beyond grateful to have such an incredible team helping me.

I so appreciate all the readers who have taken the time to tell their friends about my work and provide reviews of my books. These reviews are especially important in promoting future books, so if you enjoy my novels, please consider leaving a review and sharing it on social media. I also encourage you to follow me on Amazon, Goodreads, and BookBub, where leaving a review is even easier, and you'll be the first to know about new releases and deals.

Remember to visit my website at http://www.tammylgrace.com and join my mailing list for my exclusive group of readers. I also have a fun Book Buddies Facebook Group. That's the best place to find me and get a chance to participate in my giveaways. Join my Facebook group at https://www.facebook.com/groups/AuthorTammyL-GraceBookBuddies/

and keep in touch—I'd love to hear from you.

Thanks for spending time in Lavender Valley,

Tammy

MORE FROM TAMMY L. GRACE

COOPER HARRINGTON DETECTIVE NOVELS

Killer Music

Deadly Connection

Dead Wrong

Cold Killer

HOMETOWN HARBOR SERIES

Hometown Harbor: The Beginning (Prequel Novella)

Finding Home

Home Blooms

A Promise of Home

Pieces of Home

Finally Home

Forever Home

Follow Me Home

CHRISTMAS STORIES

A Season for Hope: Christmas in Silver Falls Book 1

The Magic of the Season: Christmas in Silver Falls Book 2

Christmas in Snow Valley: A Hometown Christmas Book 1

One Unforgettable Christmas: A Hometown Christmas Book 2

Christmas Wishes: Souls Sisters at Cedar Mountain Lodge

Christmas Surprises: Soul Sisters at Cedar Mountain Lodge

GLASS BEACH COTTAGE SERIES

Beach Haven

Moonlight Beach

Beach Dreams

WRITING AS CASEY WILSON

A Dog's Hope

A Dog's Chance

WISHING TREE SERIES

The Wishing Tree

Wish Again

Overdue Wishes

SISTERS OF THE HEART SERIES

Greetings from Lavender Valley

Pathway to Lavender Valley

Sanctuary at Lavender Valley

Blossoms at Lavender Valley

Comfort in Lavender Valley

Reunion in Lavender Valley

Remember to subscribe to Tammy's exclusive group of readers for your gift, only available to readers on her mailing list. **Sign up at www.tammylgrace.com. Follow this link to subscribe at https:// wp.me/P9umIy-e** and you'll receive the exclusive interview she did with all the canine characters in her Hometown Harbor Series.

Follow Tammy on Facebook by liking her page. You may also follow Tammy on book retailers or at BookBub by clicking on the follow button.

FROM THE AUTHOR

Thank you for reading REUNION IN LAVENDER VALLEY. I love all the characters in this new SISTERS OF THE HEART SERIES and am excited for readers to get to know each of them. I started this series with a prequel book that gives readers a peek into the lives of all the women in the series. It's a great way to try it and see if the story appeals to you. Then, each subsequent book features one of the foster sisters as the main character in her own story.

If you enjoy women's fiction and haven't yet read the entire HOMETOWN HARBOR SERIES, you can start the series with a free prequel that is in the form of excerpts from Sam's journal. She's the main character in the first book, FINDING HOME.

If you're a new reader and enjoy mysteries, I write a series that features a lovable private detective, Coop, and his faithful golden retriever, Gus. If you like whodunits that will keep you guessing until the end, you'll enjoy the COOPER HARRINGTON DETECTIVE NOVELS.

The two books I've written as Casey Wilson, A DOG'S

HOPE and A DOG'S CHANCE have received enthusiastic support from my readers, and if you're a dog lover, they are must reads.

If you enjoy holiday stories, be sure to check out my CHRISTMAS IN SILVER FALLS SERIES and HOMETOWN CHRISTMAS SERIES. They are smalltown Christmas stories of hope, friendship, and family. You won't want to miss any of the SOUL SISTERS AT CEDAR MOUNTAIN LODGE BOOKS, also featuring a foster sister theme. It's a connected Christmas series I wrote with four author friends. My contributions, CHRISTMAS WISHES, CHRISTMAS SURPRISES, CHRISTMAS SHELTER, and CHRISTMAS HEARTS. All heartwarming, smalltown holiday stories that I'm sure you'll enjoy. The series kicks off with a free prequel novella, CHRISTMAS SISTERS, where you'll get a chance to meet the characters during their first Christmas together.

You won't want to miss THE WISHING TREE SERIES, set in Vermont. This series centers on a famed tree in the middle of the quaint town that is thought to grant wishes to those who tie them on her branches. Readers love this series and always comment how they are full of hope, which we all need more of right now.

I'd love to send you my exclusive interview with the canine companions in my Hometown Harbor Series as a thank-you for joining my exclusive group of readers. You can sign up www.tammylgrace.com by clicking this link: https://wp.me/P9umIy-e.

ABOUT THE AUTHOR

Tammy L. Grace is the *USA Today* bestselling and award-winning author of the Cooper Harrington Detective Novels, the bestselling Hometown Harbor Series, and the Glass Beach Cottage Series, along with several sweet Christmas novellas. Tammy also writes under the pen name of Casey Wilson for Bookouture and Grand Central. You'll find Tammy online at www.tammylgrace.com where you can join her mailing list and be part of her exclusive group of readers. Connect with Tammy on Facebook at www.facebook.com/tammylgrace.books or Instagram at @authortammylgrace.

facebook.com/tammylgrace.books
twitter.com/TammyLGrace
instagram.com/authortammylgrace
bookbub.com/authors/tammy-l-grace
goodreads.com/tammylgrace
amazon.com/author/tammylgrace

Made in the USA
Middletown, DE
09 October 2023